The Untidy Witness

The Untidy Witness

A Nick Drake / Laura Wexler Paranormal Mystery

A novel by

Julie Hutslar & Ed Hunt

Luminous Epinoia Press

Luminous Epinoia Press
Sandpoint, ID 83864
www.luminousepinoia.com

ISBN: 978-0-9753000-1-5
Library of Congress Control Number: 2014943620

Cover graphic of the *eyes* from *Portrait of a Soldier* by Sohrab Esfehani.

This is a work of fiction. Names, characters, businesses, places, events and incidents are either the products of the authors' imaginations or used in a fictitious manner. Any resemblance to actual persons, living or dead, or actual events is purely coincidental.

However, the methods and examples the character, Laura, uses in this book are directly taken from the professional experiences of the author. For more information on spiritual/energy healing concepts, check out the author's professional web page.

www.jrhutslar.com

In Appreciation

Deep appreciation to each person who read and gave us their honest opinions as we wrote and rewrote *The Untidy Witness*.
Liz Adkinson, Craig Bivins, Luke Coward, Kurt Forget, Jan Hutslar, Paula Lewis, Diana Parker, Jody Pignolet, Gretchen Steen

With special thanks to Sohrab Esfehani for the cover graphic of the *eyes*, taken from his work, *Portrait of a Soldier*.

1

Can you ever go back and *unsee* something? Or would you be inexplicably drawn to it again and again no matter how many times you replayed it, especially if you knew it contained the power to completely change your life? Is that destiny? And can just *seeing* something enact a person's destiny?

In my case, it wasn't just seeing with the eyes, it was feeling what I saw, maybe that is *seeing within*. And could you stop that from happening? Would you try? Could you have taken another road? Yet, I knew this event was far from coincidence. Hadn't I just heard the quote recently: Sometimes you meet your destiny on the road you took to avoid it? No, it didn't matter what road I took, destiny had found me and there was no going back.

It was late fall, November 10th to be exact. All the leaves had fallen off the trees, but the snow had not come yet. We were already starting to lose our daylight. By 4:30 it would be completely dark. The seasons are extreme up here in this mountainous and remote area of North Idaho. I wouldn't say it is common for a woman to be living on her own in such a rugged place, yet it was days like this that everything felt so perfectly natural. That's why I was not prepared in any way for what happened.

There isn't a lot of traffic on the dirt road that ends about 8 miles up beyond my place. Occasionally a logging truck passes me when I'm hiking or I see guys in camouflage gear heading up the road to hunt. Not used to vehicles up here, when I hear the sound of a motor, I stop by the side of the road and make sure my dog, Hilde, is right beside me. She instinctively wants to heel the trucks, being a blue heeler, so I have trained her to stay on my side, off the road as vehicles pass. I did that same thing this one day while hiking up my road as a truck passed. Only as *this* truck passed, something different happened. I had stopped and was bending down to pet Hilde to encourage her to stay put. I could hear the truck nearing and slowing a little even though it had gathered some speed coming down from the mountain above me. Just as I turned to see the driver from my stooped position, my eyes caught his straight on. And in that one second, all I held secure and safe vanished.

I was not prepared for the emotions that came rushing up. I was raw and open, feeling so safe in these familiar mountains, that nothing blocked or dampened the offensive slaughter of my soul. In that one brief second of connection, I had received his condemnation. It overwhelmed me. The eyes seemed to be suspended in midair, unconnected to anything, simply boring a pathway of darkness into my being. I know I must have visibly stepped back, trying in vain to distance myself from this energetic demon loosed into me. That's what it felt like, a demon had jumped into my soul and was wrestling me from any peace I ever had, certainly from the safety of my forest home.

Then the truck was gone. Could I say what color it was, what model or make? Did I notice the license plate? No. I was only trying to cope. But could I recognize those dark eyes, that evil incarnate seeping through the pupils? Absolutely. It had been bored into my skull, and not by my choice, but by destiny's.

Half stooped and half trying to bring myself fully erect, I needed to get the breath back into my lungs. I had to find balance before I could walk another step. Hilde knew too. She was spinning in circles, which is what she does when she is upset and confused. She looked at me, hoping I would pet her and calm her. I could not. I braced myself on a lone tree branch sticking out towards the road. What just happened? I was in that one moment completely unsettled, wracked with pain, torture and … what? Death? Why was I saying this? Yes. I could feel it. I smelled it. Death. Not peaceful, old-age death, but torturous, wicked, twisted death. I cringed.

Without knowing how I got there, completely unpresent to the road or having turned around to come back, I found myself at home. I knew a virus of negativity had penetrated my system. Something evil and abhorrent was beginning to spread within my being.

I went into the bathroom to splash water on my face. Looking back at me were my own brown eyes, not black like the ones that had bored a hole in my soul, but not with the usual olive green sparkle to them either. Just seeing my own eyes dulled and dark offered an elemental clue to my present situation. I knew something had compromised my inner me.

Usually I was the one assisting others locate the source of lackluster in their souls. But this day, I knew *I* was the one needing assistance. Without hesitation I began the process of breathing and centering, then following an energy trail into my core essence. It was not difficult to follow since the feelings that identified it were still fresh and the trail contained such intense darkness.

What I found did not surprise me, in fact, it validated the magnitude of the emotions I felt up the road earlier. This energy is the manifestation of perfect evil, taking shape as my greatest fear, pointed directly at my heart like a poison arrow. It seems it had inadvertently been unleashed into me. But then as I pondered this, did I really believe something this toxic could have been by *coincidence*? I hoped so, but my gut refused to believe that. I moved it through my system. I sat and felt the calmness return. But not entirely. Something in me knew that my life would never be the same again.

That night sleep did not come effortlessly like it usually does. Not consciously thinking about the eyes and the evil they contained, just as I closed my own eyes, there they were again, clear as if I were gazing into them that first time. I opened my eyes and looked out into the starry black sky to make the image disappear. I watched the flickering of the stars from my bed. Slowly, I tried to breathe out the negative energy as if it were just a germ I could dispel. I felt some calm, but there was still something in there. It felt like a black seed or something. I imagined it to be like a GPS tracking device and cringed thinking about *who* was observing me.

It was then what I was afraid of began to manifest. My overactive imagination engaged gears. I imagined all sorts of cruel and unusual things that the guy with the eyes had been up to. And then I felt a vulnerability I had never felt before living alone up here in this high mountain house, not visible from the road, the last house before many miles of uninhabited terrain. My neighbors were about half a mile away and they all kept to themselves. My dog, as wonderful as she is, is not a great watchdog. As I lay there, I knew that if uncontrolled, my mind would run me through all the possible scenarios of him coming in the house and trying to kill me in erotic and twisted ways while Hilde ran around in circles.

At some point, I must have drifted off to sleep because I remember being awakened by a disturbing dream. Normally, I don't remember my dreams so to wake up to a nightmare is very rare. I did not see the eyes, but I felt a ring of fire threaten me around my property. It wasn't really fire, as dreams are like that, but I knew it had the power to burn down my world. It was poised and watchful. It gave me the chills.

The entire night was restless. I was glad for early dawn, which is when I choose to get up to prepare for my clients. I realized it was Saturday however. And although I occasionally do have clients on the weekend, I didn't today. Something in me made a mental note. It was Saturday. That means yesterday was Friday. I glanced at the calendar on the kitchen wall, expecting to see Friday the 13th. No, only the 10th. Something in me wrote that date in indelible ink on my soul.

2

You can be going along just fine, smooth sailing, no bumps. Then in an instant the fine is gone. Like driving along a smooth, smooth road, then hitting the pothole from hell.

It was like that. I was OK. Maybe not every day, or maybe not every minute of any day, but OK, all in all.

Then I saw the email from the colonel. Took me about a minute or so to remember the last time I heard from him. Three, maybe four years. Not long enough for sure. Don't know how he got my email. Wouldn't have minded if our history together stayed back in history. I never liked him. Always wondered why he had been in my life. Still wonder why he was my teacher. Really just one of my teachers, but to be honest, he was my teacher.

Damn mouse wouldn't click delete. Damn finger wouldn't click delete. Damn eyes had to read the email. When the colonel says come, you come. Don't you love coincidence? Saw a great bumper sticker today. American flag in the rear window of an old pickup, VFW sticker in the window, infantry sticker in the window. Infantry, humph, who the hell would go infantry? Anyway, sticker said, "Sniper" then said, "you can run, but you'll just die tired." Damn infantry, damn snipers. Goddamn colonel. I hate coincidences.

Had to cancel three flight lessons and one IPC. That's not like me, I don't cancel and I don't stand people up, and when a guy needs an Instrument Proficiency Check because he's about to lose his currency, I'm there when I say I'll be there, and we fly. I doubt anyone I've trained ever said it was fun. Lots of them sweat a bit, to be nice about it. But my pilots don't make stupid decisions from lack of reality training. I'm not the kind of flight instructor who's using dual instruction time as a way to pad my logbook on the way to the airlines, just passing time in that right seat. Actually kind of funny thinking of me in the front office of a flying bus with a few hundred cattle in the back on the way to Disney World, or some anniversary cruise out of Miami. I've done my time in the front office, but there were no tourists in coach class. Goddamn colonel. What would he want from me that he hasn't already had?

November in St. George, Utah is a nice time. It's a nice place. The skies are clear, the air is like glass, and the desert is magical. Red rock, spires, canyons. Thousand miles of nothing bordered by a thousand miles of nothing. Nothing like some other places a man can be. November in Minot, North Dakota is not. Not any of those things. Minot. Can you believe anyone would live in Minot and not be stationed there? Goddamn colonel.

So, weather depiction chart looks like crap. Weather prognosis charts—crap. Winds aloft—don't get me started on the wind direction. Pilot reports for icing—yes, and yes some more. This would take me about a millisecond to make the *go, no-go* decision. Take Delta and let some other fool and a couple hundred thousand pounds of aluminum deposit my safe ass at the airport. *No-go*. No decision there. Goddamn colonel. "Fly yourself and bring summer clothes. Something that we can go far enough south to play some golf in." Damn that man. My Cessna 182 is too slow, can't take known icing. I'd be illegal and we'd both be dead. Jerk.

I'm not beyond giving out favors, and I believe in the quid pro quo. I'm not past asking for favors either. At least I didn't take too much flack when I asked for the A36 Bonanza. Buddy of mine has modified the heck out of it. Certified to fly into known icing conditions, turbo normalized, fast, flies high enough to get over the top of the weather—I hope. Fast enough to get the old man to the nearest tee box. Golf. The colonel and golf, all in the same sentence. I guess that's where they got the term, *insult to injury*. If I didn't know myself, I'd promise myself that this would be the last time I'd jump when he called. But it wouldn't be true, and he's never called before, so I guess he's got some credit up on me. Still a jerk, though.

Took off from St. George about nine in the morning. Smooth enough, that's for sure. I like the flight levels up around 20,000 feet, or so. Way faster, usually smoother, and today, at least above the weather. Pushing the ceiling in this old gal, but not getting any complaints. Still no icing, so maybe this won't be too bad. Not really looking forward to spending a few hours with him in lack of conversation. Not at all looking forward to hearing what he has to say that he couldn't have said on the phone.

So, I'm a little shy of Rock Springs, Wyoming, thinking that this isn't so bad. I've got 190 knots true airspeed and the gods have turned the winds in my favor. It does not get any better than this. Then Salt Lake center comes on and I swear on mom's grave they tell me this. "November 992 foxtrot echo immediate left turn to heading of 326, intercept victor 328, descend and maintain 18 thousand. Cleared as filed to Sandpoint, Kilo Sierra Zulu Tango." OK, that's only 500 miles out of the way, and not requested or filed, or anything else. That's also not how things are done, and that's certainly not what happens when you're on a filed instrument flight plan ... to Minot, North Dakota. I come back with a request that they repeat the previous instruction, and they do. Then I ask for verification that it is me they're talking to, and they confirm. Then I, as politely as I can, ask what the hell this is about, and they pass on the name and rank (that's long time ago retired and therefore no longer meaningful rank) of the goddamn colonel.

Well, my mind's image is full of him back in the day. That's the day when he was a far cry from being no longer meaningful. I'm glad I've been on autopilot because I don't know how long he was inside my head polluting the hell out of my mind and taking me away from the simple task at hand—that's flying the airplane, when center came on and, in that voice that they have perfected, so sarcastically asked me if I copied last transmission. You really can impart a lot of feeling in a voice. I said affirmative (puppets usually do, don't they?) then made my turn, reprogrammed the GPS, got the weather from flight watch and remembered Sandpoint. Never been there, but it's on the FAA chart for the instrument pilot written exam. That was a long time ago, but I guess that airport, that chart, and that lake, were burned into my mind when I was a young hopeful. Hoping to pass that test, at least.

Spent a few minutes deciding that I could still make it with IFR fuel reserves (love those wingtip tanks, and love this Bonanza) and not be in any violation of the FAA, but sure could be in violation of my own free will. I guess I could ask the colonel about free will when I see him. Goddamn the man, the old retired, not really a colonel anymore, old man. Spent a few more hours reprogramming the GPS back to St. George then back to Sandpoint, then back to St. George. Landed at Sandpoint and wondered what I got myself into, and why was my past catching up after all this time. Tried to lie to myself that the books were all in balance, back in the day.

Nice little airport at Sandpoint. Not fancy, that's for sure. Not a place for the jet crowd, but at least some kid came out and tied her down and fueled her up and offered to put her in a heated hanger. Colder than hell, that's for sure. What a stupid saying. Colder than hell. Sure accurate when you step out of a warm airplane with the whole world free and ahead of you only to be slapped by a cold wind and the hardest, damnedest, and … saddest face you've ever seen. I was ready to man up and take him down a few notches for messing with me with the Minot thing, and the south to golf thing, and the how the hell did you get air traffic control to redirect me thing. I already had a few hours to rerun that speech in my head a few thousand times, when I saw his face. Everyone who knows the man knows the hardness, and the coldness. We all knew the jerkness, and even the meanness. Most of us were there to be part of those wrinkles and that squint, the glare, the turned up corner of the mouth and the scowl that made you think you just stepped in something. But nobody I ever knew ever saw any sadness. Sadness trying to crawl out of coldness and hardness. Took me about a millisecond to see how hard he was trying to control the sadness and the hurt. There was anger there. It was hot enough to freeze out the cold. Can't explain what that means, you had to see it. You really wouldn't have wanted to see it, not if you knew the man back in the day.

He didn't shake my hand, just turned on his heels and walked toward a local police car. I don't know if it was my history I heard, but I could have swore he muttered something about what took me so long. I was in the air two hours after I read that email. I trued out over 190 knots, and I borrowed an A36 half million dollar Bonanza. I'm just not the man to tell him off. I followed into the police car, trying to pull up my collar. The kid behind gestured, *what the*? So I just waved over towards the hanger and hoped he got the message to put the plane to bed in the warmth.

Local cop, officer something or the other (not good with remembering names the second someone tells me) shook my hand then got into the car. The colonel got in beside him and I in the back. Took about two minutes to get to the station and we all went in. Our driver introduced me to the chief, Chief Longfellow (any other time I would have had to hold down a laugh inside, but not now). Followed him into what must be the meeting room. Couple cups of coffee came out of nowhere and we sat down, all at a big table in the middle of the room. The chief pushed over a file and some photos, then got up and left the room. Took me about a second to scan the photos, then the colonel's face, then the photos, then his eyes, then I told him that I'm not going to kill anyone for him and I don't care who. Then he told me about what happened to Becky. And I swear to God in heaven that I'm the only man in this life who has ever seen tears in his eyes.

3

I guess it really didn't surprise me to get a knock on the door, someone asking about Friday. Could I say I consciously knew? Probably not. I thought I put those evil eyes out of my world, but I guess I was wrong. If only I had looked away and not straight into his eyes.

It was a police officer asking around to see if anyone saw anything unusual on Friday afternoon. Of course, I needed to know why, even though part of me already knew. As the officer gave me the details of a murdered woman whose body was found up the road behind my house, it began to occur to me that in that exchange, the eyes and I shared information now. I *already* knew something fatal and ugly had happened with him involved. It didn't occur to me until much later what he might know about *me*.

How do you explain what you *felt* when all they want to know is what you *saw*? I saw so very little, but didn't need to. I saw a million year's worth of a soul's evolution. I saw full possession of a human by the deepest of darkness. I saw this man had done something heinous, villainous even and felt no regret. Did this officer have questions that would allow me to share that? Could he have understood anyway? He was a kind and patient man, but he was looking for facts, not feelings. He thanked me, took my number and left.

I went to lie down, trying not to let my imagination fill in the gory details of the brutal murder. Why do humans find such fascination with evil, with cruelty, with even death? I had a theory. I used to speak on it, about how human monsters play an important role in our society. They take the position that someone must play in what Shakespeare called the stage of life—and therefore prevent the rest of us from having to live it out. We all have the propensity to be that cruel monster, each one of us, whether we believe it or not. Inside is the wiring for *any* potentiality—even that. So the evil ones in society provide an opportunity for judgment, blame, shame or forgiveness. I tried to remember this as I refocused on those demonic eyes. I had already judged him. I categorized him and labeled him, yet there is always more than we know. I tried to soften my heart to his story, to what might have led to this fatal decision. Quietly, I sent a blessing his way, knowing it may not reach him for a very long time, then drifted off to sleep.

As I began to wake up, I could see in my mind's eye some details I had not initially remembered. The truck was black. Yes, I am sure. It was black and it was a foreign make, not the big square American type. And there was a silver rack of some kind fastened to the pickup bed. It was not a rack for a boat, or lifting ATVs, it was custom made. It was also not a shiny silver, it was brushed nickel or something like that. Why didn't I remember that earlier? I knew. That was obvious. I felt so threatened at the very core of me, that all I could register was what I needed to keep me safe. His eyes held the information of death and my being went into response mode, rejecting all other stimuli other than escape. Now days later, I was safe. I knew someone in authority was on it and my subconscious could pass it up to me now.

I called the officer to tell him what I remembered. He wrote it down and thanked me again. I could tell he thought I was probably making it up, but if he had nothing else to go on he might be forced to investigate that further. For now, however, it was just a useless bit of information, and not terribly reliable.

Monday is my prep day and I get into a quiet space to allow myself to connect with my clients' unspoken needs and assess how I can help them. If I stayed in this space, I could get the entire week's preparation done in a few hours, rather than come back down into daily routine, rise up, come down and so on. But this Monday, I was not going anywhere. I could not get any altitude. Something was weighing me down to this plane of existence. I felt somehow I needed to assist the spirit of the murdered woman.

That Friday she had been living in a body, breathing and laughing, then crying and begging perhaps, then she was gone from the material world. So young, she was not prepared, I am sure. I stopped trying to engage in my prep work and turned my attention to this woman tied to me through the same eyes which must have been the last thing she saw before she violently exited her body.

Letting myself tune in, I *felt* her. Picking up the energy of the woman the police officer had told me about, I could get a sense of her. She was coming through clearly. She was panicking. She was afraid, alone. This meant she had not crossed over to the spirit realm. Out of her physical body, certainly, but not *gone on*. Remaining in this plane simply puts her journey on hold, and unfortunately for those who have passed in suffering, and I know this first hand, they stay in the same despair or anxiety that propelled their physical release. In her case, she felt like she was not part of the story. She was in someone else's horror movie. Yet it was her story. How could it have been otherwise? Even if we don't like it, we wrote it.

My mind drifted back some twenty or so years. We used to disagree about this detail often. He believed in the *X* Factor, the randomness of nature, essentially in victimhood. And I knew why. How else could you explain *his* story? Who would have chosen that consciously? Yet as many times as I suggested that you don't choose it *consciously*, we never got any closer to agreeing than our first discussion about it. It was definitely what you would call a bone of contention between us. Me, believing he could shift his story, him, believing he could not. Bringing myself back from memories I knew were nothing more than distractions, I returned to the spirit of this woman.

I spoke to her in my mind, metaphysically. She felt relief and disbelief at the same time when she heard my voice. Someone could hear her, someone was speaking to her. She was so worried something horrid had happened. I explained to her that she had left her body. I told her I was there to help. She cried out in shock and resistance. "NO! It cannot be. I was just getting my life together. I was ..." Then her mind must have locked on to the violence and the eyes. I could feel her shiver. I knew what she was seeing. I had seen it too. Yet the only violence I felt was spiritual. Not to compare a person's pain, but I knew hers was something horribly violent and something no person should ever have to endure. I allowed my mind to go to her parents. Did the officer tell them the details? I had hoped not. I knew they would want to know for the same gory reasons we all do, self-punishment.

I knew I had work to do. This was not an easy case of sending someone on *to the light* as they say. Much understanding needed to happen before she would find any light. Allowing myself to connect with her, I tried to focus on the fact that she was free, that she had been involved in a story that

I did not know the purpose of, but that had come to an end. Perhaps she had finished something she needed to do? How could I know why this had happened to this particular woman? Yet here I was, doing spiritual healing work on the Eye's victim. Was I further entwining us?

Years ago, I remember a woman calling me crying, saying that the son of her friend had just been found dead on the ski resort the next mountain over from where I live. He was only 16 years old and had skied into a tree. There he died alone and cold, only two weeks before Christmas. My heart went out to his parents, but I knew I had work to do. Sure enough, when I connected with his spirit, his first question was, *where is everyone?* And after I explained what had happened and that he was in fact out of his body—I never say dead, because no one dies, they just change form—he so innocently wanted to know what would happen to his Christmas presents.

Hopefully, now that the murdered woman's spirit had passed into the other realm, her loved ones would feel her in a state of peace, which they could not while she wandered in the material world without form. I didn't know who was grieving this woman whose body was dumped only a few miles up the mountain from my house. I was only looking to help *her.* If someone else felt her release, they would certainly have to be saint-like. How could they not feel the anger and revenge propelled by such a vicious crime? And forgiveness cannot enter where there is anger and blame. Yes, she was my focus right now. I knew we were destined for this moment. That meant she wrote me into her story the same as I had written her into mine.

The only other time I had to do so much work to help a lost soul was when I worked with a man from Richland. He found me through someone who knew someone. As I began to assess his energy system, I became aware of a very sad and heavy energy. Silently, I followed it to its source and uncovered a person, or spirit, filled with much despair. I asked my client to wait while I took care of it, thinking it would just be a minute. He asked if the person could be someone he knew. I said I doubted it, "Unless of course you asked that someone to be with you." He said, "I did. My son killed himself at 18. Rode his motorcycle off a cliff three years ago." My heart constricted. I knew he was feeling his son's suffering and pain stuck at the moment of his demise. It probably had not subsided one bit since that day either. And then I found Rory. What ensued was an entire karmic healing session for Rory to bring understanding so that he could let go of his unfinished life. After we finished, I heard Rory's voice in my head say to me with humble gratitude that if I ever needed anything on his side, to just let him know. He said he would help me any way he could. I smiled. I had never had that offer before, but promised I would take him up on it.

The next morning, Rory's father called me from somewhere on his way back home to tell me that this was the first morning in three years that he had awoken to feel his son in peace. He sent me a photograph of the sunrise that morning, it was so inspiring for him. It held the promise of a new start for both him and his son. So this woman is with Rory somewhere, smiling together, making sense of their bizarre stories. At least, I could imagine that.

4

There are things that you can think about, maybe see in a movie, hear about that happen to other people. Be grateful when you're not the one in the story.

I met Becky a few times when she was just a little kid, heard about her on and off from the colonel when something happened. Graduation, got married, divorced, wrong guy, another school, moving around. Didn't seem to ever measure up to his standards, but nobody ever did, either, so that wasn't much of a surprise. After his wife died, he never seemed to have much beyond his work. At least that's the way I heard it. You could tell that Becky was important to him, but in a distant kind of way. Then or now, he was never the kind of man to let on much about himself.

For an instant, I couldn't say what hit me harder, the photos of her body, or the look on his face. Honestly, I think it was seeing him that hit me so hard. I've seen some ugly things and I think your emotions get glazed over after enough exposure to death and pain. I was probably born jaded. I don't have a positive view of the human race, and when they do what they do so well, it doesn't come as much of a surprise to me. That's not at all to say that I wasn't affected. Not at all true. But my connection was with him and what I saw was so far out of character, there was no way I could have prepared for that. Like waking up to see the sun green or something. Your mind searches for a place to put things. His strength was always there. Unwavering and certain and that's sometimes all you've got to go on. There are times when you're so scared that someone else's strength is all you've got. If it varies, you're lost because you don't have anything inside yourself to hold onto. If it's there, you keep on going. He was that guy and it was his strength that got the job done, even if only second hand.

Didn't last that long, though. A man like that can't let it down for long, and he didn't. I think maybe the runaround about a plane that could get to Minot, then south for golf was just him doing what he does. He set me up with the right tool to do the job he wanted done and the whole time had me looking one way while he was working on the other side. I think he wanted my raw reaction. Put him on top and me on task. He could have told me the truth from the git-go, though. Doesn't really matter one way or the other. He knew I'd soon be back at the flight levels and headed south just like he wanted me to.

Doubt I'll ever know how he does what he does and gets things done like he does. I ran into Longfellow in the parking lot on the way back out of the station. No doubt it wasn't accidental. There was no reason for the chief of police to be standing outside in his own parking lot.

"What's that man about?" He asked with a bit of hesitation. Like a man who is compelled to look into places he really doesn't want to go.

"About? ..."

"Yea, about. You know. How does he come in here from nowhere and how is he in control in my town in my station and how did I get to be his little bitchboy already?"

That's quite a question and I'm enough of a poker player to keep my feelings off my face. No reason to play with the man and no reason to lead him on either. I'd most likely be needing his help on this and no reason for me to have any more enemies than I probably have out there, anyway.

"Chief, I can tell you right now you're nobody's bitchboy. Not here, not with him. The way he is has nothing to do with you or me or anyone else he comes into contact with. Since you know we're together on this, let me apologize in advance for the way he is. Really, don't take it personally." That threw him off balance for a second. You could tell that he was expecting some kind of above-your-pay-grade kind of crap. Sometimes pure honesty is more unsettling than power plays.

"And," he paused, "he's still in my station while I'm out here in the parking lot. You. I don't know you from Adam and neither one of you has made any move to show me any identification and you're not standing there trying to explain why not."

"Chief," and in the next second's pause I think I must have stepped out of whatever time we were standing there in because when I said chief I was watching a patrol car drive through the parking lot behind him, but when I said the next word, the car was just passing on his other side. What, maybe one second? But what I experienced was way more than you can put in a second. Not like a flicker of memory, more like living through it again. Like living through an experience like I was there again. I've thought about that second a few more times and can't get a handle on it. Almost like I stepped up and out of the time that we were in and stepped into a mission that was thought out, planned, executed, and debriefed a long time ago. Long time ago. "The colonel was involved in some very high level operations in his career. He served continuously behind the scenes of several administrations and had his hands in some things that went down, and because of what he's done in his career, probably makes it possible we're having this conversation now."

You could see some disbelief in that expression of his.

"I'm not trying to blow the guy out of proportion, chief. There're just some things you've got to accept. I don't mean that just you have to accept, but that have to be accepted. You're old enough to understand, I hope. We're not all created equal, at least we're not all equal in how we live, that's for sure. You, me, those kids across the street, mostly every one you've ever met, we're the little guys, know what I mean? There are things that happen at higher levels, that we don't know about. We think we do because we see it on the news, or wherever we learn things that we think are important. It's just the story we're getting, and not even the best part of the story, just little pieces that keep our attention. I accepted that a long time ago, and …" I could see that face glazing over. What I wanted to tell him, what I thought he may grasp, being a seasoned policeman and all, was not what would fit in his head. My fault, my bad judgment.

"Anyway chief, he worked in really high places and he has friends who have friends who pull the strings of guys like us. Know what I mean? He'll be here 'till he's done. He'll get what he needs to get done and *his will be done* if you follow me." With that line, I think I must have plugged into the right socket in his head. He smiled and nodded like he knew exactly what I was saying.

"I been there, son." Now he was on top and back where he belonged, at least relative to me. "Like when the Feds come in and all we can do is wipe some asses and say yes sir!"

"Something like that, chief, but a little higher up the food chain. Look, I'm going to follow orders and get this put to bed ASAP. When I need your help, I'll ask for it, and if I can answer any questions, I will. I'll be gone and this SOB will be behind your bars, in your jail and you'll be the man to turn the key. Damn, if I could help you pull the lever and fry him, I would, but that's not my place. I'm somewhere in the world of *yes sir; no sir; sir, may I ask a question; sir, may I make a statement; and, no excuse, sir.* Those are the options they gave us back when I was just a pup at the Air Force Academy, and those are my options here, today. I've been there before and I'm OK with that. The mission is primary, then I'm going back home. Are we right on with each other here, chief?"

He paused long enough to put me back in my place and to pretend that he was the one I was saying *sir* to, and that was OK with me. I don't have an ego when it comes to the mission. "Sure are, son." And we shook hands and he even opened the door to a patrol car so I could go back to the airport.

To me, life is about choosing which wars to fight and which battles to run from. I needed this man on my side, since my side wasn't anywhere near official, maybe. Certainly not legal. Not technically, anyway.

5

Just when I thought everything was getting back to normal, Hilde brought it to my attention that it was not. She has this miraculous way of communicating with me, without words, but speaking volumes, even though she has very little change in her facial expression. Actually it often looks like she's had botox injections, it varies so little. Yet when she wants to communicate something, it's rare that I don't pick up what she is suggesting. A glance at the right time, a heavy sigh when I say something she doesn't want to hear or this funny way she has of touching my leg with her nose to tell me she is here. She used to break my heart the way she would rest her head on the lap of my husband in suffering. So much compassion for a dog, I often think of her as an evolved master choosing the body of a dog this time.

I went into the garage to switch the laundry to the dryer and there she was, standing there with longing in her eyes sniffing my hiking boots on the shelf of outdoor shoes. I could feel her words, *how long before we hike again? We need this!* In fact, we hadn't been up the road since last Friday. Or up the trail behind our house or anywhere else since last Friday. We were used to getting out every single day. Had I been avoiding going out? Obviously I was. Why? Was I afraid? Afraid of what? Was I quietly waiting for the perpetrator to be caught before I go back out? Is that like me?

My mind returned to my childhood for support. When I was young, my grandparents lived on a lake during the summer. One year the man across the street from them ice picked his wife and sister-in-law to death and hid them under some rugs in the garage. My aunt, still in high school at the time, was supposed to spend the night with them that night since the sister was visiting, but something came up and she could not. The next day, my aunt went over to see them and when no one answered, she went around to the windows to look inside. Finally when she got to the garage, she saw blood on the walls. I don't remember what happened after that, but it did seem like she had police protection until the man was later apprehended in Florida. Is that what I wanted?

That wasn't going to happen, nor did I want that. I needed to face my fear. The Eyes were not still up there, I told myself, so allow yourself to pass by that exact spot fearlessly and reclaim your peaceful mountain. So after pressing the button for the dryer to start, I went to the very shoes Hilde picked out with her nose and put them on and got my water bottle. As I started strapping on my fanny pack, the botox look was long gone, replaced by a magical grin from ear to ear, whole bottom end waging with her tail. I could tell she knew she had won and that she was doing what was best for us both. Like petting her when you feel emotional, it is good for *you*, she only sacrifices herself for the better good!

It felt good to be working my muscles again, not just my energetic ones. The trees were still there, the air was colder than the last time I was out. In fact, I could feel the witch of November was not playing with us anymore. She was here to stay. My ears were warm and cozy inside the new black hat that I got at a thrift store a month or so ago. I had been eager to wear it because it reminded me of a very favorite hat I lost years ago. And this one was just like it. It seems like we always keep an eye peeled for something we lost that we loved.

Hilde had run ahead, glad to be outside and she knew the route. The air cleared my head, allowing me to put everything into perspective. It all felt so perfect, that my heart warmed my body as I hiked up the road. I thought of every person I had recently dealt with and brought them into that warm heart space. I could actually feel their presence. I smiled with the wholeness of it. Nothing bothered me. All was as it should be.

Occupied with the smells and feel of being present, I had temporarily forgotten about the Eyes. They had fallen into the category where dreams live. Then I turned onto Fern Creek road. It is even rarer to see anyone on this out-of-the-way dirt road than the logging road. It dead ends up ahead just a few miles and is rarely traveled in the winter. It is not plowed and unless someone is snowshoeing or is on a snowmobile, they could not even access this road. Many winters the only tracks I see are my own except for large and small moose tracks traveling side by side, grazing on sticks and brush creating a zigzag trail along the road.

Up ahead I saw a truck stopped in the middle of the road. Two men stood by it. One locked on to me as through a rifle sight. My initial reaction was panic. I felt the warmth in my heart grow instantly cold, everyone out, shut the door, close up shop, with that one assessment. I must have hesitated. Perhaps it looked like I just stumbled on a rock. I could not risk turning around, would they come after me? *Hey, who are you, Laura? Is this how you want to live?* I heard my inner voice ask. I attempted a confident stride and returned the gaze with a faint smile. No one seemed to be moving around the truck. My mind was racing looking for clues as to what they were doing there. Had they broken down? Were they waiting for me? Were they cutting wood, and if so, where was the chain saw, why were they just standing there? It was much too cold to have a picnic.

Use your tools. Do not live in fear. I heard myself gently share with me. Yes, it was true. I had many energetic tools, why was I acting like a novice? Yet the experience with the Eyes had made me shy and had colored this potentially ordinary situation.

So I closed my eyes as I walked straight ahead. I opened my heart back up and greeted the two strangers in my mind's eye. Even if one of them happened to be the Eyes, this was my only asset. I invited them sweetly into my heart space. No fear, only openness and love. Even if I were walking into a death trap, I knew better. This was my story. I would go with an open heart.

But something strange happened as I invited them in. The first man came in warmly, smiling, and then a *woman* came in next. A woman? Why a woman? Was that a metaphor for something, I wondered? Was it someone who wished they were a woman, a homosexual, or me just getting an incorrect reading? It sent me off into wondering, until I got closer. My smile was now returned by the closest man. I could see they were cutting wood and had to change the chain on the saw. The one staring at me had nothing to do except wait. So staring at some hiker appearing in the middle of truly nowhere must have seemed the only thing to do. Then I got close enough to see their faces, their eyes and ..., a laughter bubbled up from inside me. It *was* a woman. Oh my gosh, it was a husband and wife out cutting firewood for the winter. She smiled so large, I knew it was she who had entered my heart. We greeted each other and they expressed interest as to where I had come from, making me realize I must have been odder to them than they were to me.

Once a few years ago when the snow was thicker than usual—in some areas above my property it was 15 feet—I could only get out and about with snowshoes. Hilde would jump from one snowshoe track I left to the other. Those were exhausting, yet exhilarating hikes. My nearest neighbor, Jimmy, had repaired an old 1970s snowmobile he had been working on and decided to try it out. He ventured as far as Fern Creek road and saw these massive round tracks. They were coming from *up* the mountain, not from civilization, as I had gone the reverse direction on my loop. Two days later when he saw me and my snowshoes you could see the visible relief. He admitted he thought it was Big Foot and had stayed close to home. Funny how our fears color our world.

The whole incident with the couple cutting wood put things into perspective for me. But what about the woman whose body was left to decay only a few short miles up the road from here? What if those hunters had not seen the black birds circling and investigated it, thinking it was an animal kill? No doubt, a few weeks or even days later, the snow would have covered all evidence of evil and the cold would erase any human warmth that had ever existed there. I shook it off, noticing my heart had grown a few degrees cooler and smaller.

Still I had to laugh about how much more we instinctively trust women than men alone on a mountain trail. Does that mean women are not as capable of committing cruel and violent crimes? Was I sure the Eyes belonged to a man's body? Now I began to wonder. What made me think it was a man? If I could have so mistaken a woman for a man just now, could I have done that then as well? I tried to recreate the scene from last Friday once more. I saw a cap on his head, like a tight knit cap that is more popular with young men. I saw his posture, upright and proud, and confident. It was definitely a man. I could feel the testosterone. Or was I just perceiving the power of the Dark One that inhabited the man? There I go again, making an energetic connection with this dark power. Why did I have to do that? Did I think I had something to learn, to prove, by touching into it, thinking I was strong enough to battle it? I knew better. I switched channels in my mind. I recalled one of my favorite hiking tunes. Even though their roots were going down to a distant and secluded underworld for many months, I believe the trees and rocks loved this song. I hoped they could still feel my presence. That thought made me feel a little more alone, knowing my beloved trees could not help me.

The next day my neighbor Jimmy came up to tell me he was leaving for the winter. It is a courtesy, an unspoken rule of living so far away from civilization, that you keep an eye out for anything suspicious happening on the property of someone you know is gone. Jimmy goes to Hawaii for several months each winter. He said he would not be back until March 6th. Don't look for him until things are thawing, I thought. He said not to call him unless there was a serious emergency. I hoped that did not happen. A little girl voice inside reminded me of the timing of his leaving, and the murderer on the loose who she had seen.

Why did I think the Eyes were the culprit? As soon as I asked myself, I knew the answer. Even if I were an accountant and not an energy healer, I would have to have been absent in every feeling way not to comprehend the severity of the evil locked in those eyes.

6

This was a hard one. I didn't choose this war, nor would I given any other circumstances. It is definitely a righteous war, though. Definitely. When the crime is so great, the size of the enemy is of no concern. When we went into Vietnam, we chose what we thought was a small enemy, which seemed OK given the fact that it wasn't a righteous war. Lies compounded by lies, told by Whitehouse liars. Money and drugs, power? Who knows? But I do know that guys like me can't know. Maybe WWII was a righteous war. When your homeland is attacked, you don't run and you don't lie down. You come back with full force. When your friends are attacked, you come back at their side. I've had a few Brits as friends and they were our friends back then, so my dad was one of the first in. He got his draft letter the day *after* he joined up. We didn't run from that war even though it wasn't a given how big the enemy was. We got our asses kicked back a few times, but we didn't lie down.

I never had any love for the gulf wars. Think they were about big oil money. Don't really care, weren't my wars and I'm sorry for the guys who bought it over there. I do respect the concept of shock and awe, though. I don't care how little the bad guy is, you come down with overwhelming force. You shock the skin right off him, then take him down. Overwhelming force not proportional to the enemy.

I don't know. Again I'm happy for autopilot. What, at least a thousand air miles running every war and battle in history through my mind. And my mind was a thousand miles from where it should be. And where it should be was answering a few questions. Not the least being, *how the hell did I end up in a battle in a war with overwhelming odds?* And how the hell did I get to be the guy who's going to get his ass shocked and awed all to hell? And mostly, why god, wherever the hell you are, did I get put on the scent of the goddamn piece of crap son of General Jack JB DeWitt, the goddamn chairman of the joint chiefs of staff of the goddamn United States of America? The man who sits in the seat that I've spent a lifetime believing is the most powerful goddamn seat in the world.

When your masters send you, you go. That's how it is. When your monsters come into your head, you put them out. If you've got to puke, puke in your mouth and swallow it back down, don't puke in my cockpit. I've heard it and I've said, but I've never wanted to do it until now.

At least I can give myself some credit. For the last 1150 nautical miles at flight level 190, I haven't reached over to reprogram the damn GPS back to St. George. Even that. What's this airplane rent for? $375 an hour with a three-hour minimum per day. Sure as heck more than I can afford. Here I am at max power not paying any attention to best fuel burn or the cost of avgas for the first time in my civilian career in a plane that I only get to left seat during transition training for too rich and too little flight time doctors. How come I'm still in it? Who's writing the checks? Can't imagine it's the colonel. Here I sit high as heaven being pulled, or pushed—I don't know, towards some landing in a place doesn't even speak English. I'm afraid to re-calculate how long it's been since I got the email that totally ruined my peaceful life. Maybe afraid to recalculate that for the hundredth time in the last hour.

I'll drop into Cedar City for a fuel load. It would be no problem making the next 50 miles to St. George, but there would be no way that I'd come back up after that. I'd get out and walk away, *again*. Sometimes you just walk away and try not to look back. Makes me feel stupid for feeling so good about the GPS since I'll be going right over the top of St. George anyway. Maybe that's really why I haven't reprogrammed the damn thing.

Smooth landing into Cedar. The kind the passengers ask, "are we down yet?" Guy in the fuel truck is moving before I shut down the engine. I know Brenda, who owns the FBO and have borrowed the Hummer for trips into town for dinner on the rare occasion I need to impress a date. Rare indeed. She's not in, but the girl at the counter asks if I'd like the ride for anything. I guess I could go into Walmart and buy the same stuff I could just get at my own place in another 20 minutes of flying. Nah, no Walmart, no walking away, and no going home again. Back in the plane with a cold chicken sandwich, couple of candy bars, and a few gallons of water.

Rotate at 74, best rate of climb at 100. Pegged to perfection, but I know I'll come out of this bloody. Never met the general, but he didn't get to the top by being a pussy. Man's been in war, led men in war, killed men in war, and done it all on a much bigger stage than I have. Shock and awe, all right. What will he do to protect his son? Or maybe he'd be the first one to put a bullet in the boy's head. Never heard one single word of impropriety about General DeWitt. Other guys cover up things on the way to the top, maybe affairs, favors given, secrets held. Maybe this guy is the same, but that's not the word you hear.

His kid got an automatic slot at West Point from the old man's Medal of Honor. Never got a handle on those guys. Rest of us got one kind of nomination or the other, most believed they worked for it and deserved it. Get the Medal, your kid gets a go-free card, their choice—West Point, Annapolis, or the Air Force Academy. Anyway, little shit was bad news. Never knew him, but heard a little. Just BS talking, mostly. Heard that female cadets at the service academies never set well with him. Kid's just a puke anyway. What, 26 years old? Class of ..., maybe that would have been 2008. So here's this little punk who wasn't even born when the first woman graduated from the Point still acting like he had anything to say at all. Story is that he should have been expelled for some problems with a female upperclassman, but that his dad got it fixed up so he could pretend like he resigned. Better for the family name and better for the Point. Always about covering up the dirty things and setting out the best dishes for the world to see. It's stuff like that that leads to stuff like this. I don't care how the entitled class gets to be entitled, you've got to earn it. Like the general did. Like the colonel did. Sure as hell like I did.

Something about this sure feels familiar. I think the colonel could have given me a fuller brief. And I've got no official anything. And I've got to get the kid, quietly, and bring him back safe. And I've got to find him. And I've got nothing to go on. I must still be one sick mutha because I'm starting to feel better than I've felt in a long time.

There is no feeling like being at the controls of your own aircraft, above everything, with the world anyway you turn. The engine is running smooth as only the big Continentals can. Exhaust gas temp, cylinder head temp, oil pressure perfect. Trimmed out, no turbulence here and not even thinking of turbulence ahead.

Now it's just plan and execute. The big man is out of my head. I find the kid, get him back and drop him off, then off I go. Lots of flight time. One more coin in the payback bank for the colonel. If I let that honesty monster sneak in, at least I had something do that was worth a damn for a change.

I do love seeing some student pilot's face when I step out of the plane for the first time and tell him not to crash it. You just stand there and watch him taxi away on his first solo flight. Hope he comes back alive. Then see that same face when he puts it down and steps out. You get that once in a life and it changes you. Happened to me when my instructor said "pull over" right after we landed. He got out and said, "don't crash my plane," and I soloed at eight hours total flight time when I was 17 years old. I still think to this day that he wanted to kill me because he liked my girlfriend.

But that's not the same. When you do certain things when you're young, then as you get older you stop doing them, you *feel* old. Your life becomes memories. You try to let the past live in the past and you try to tell yourself it's a young man's world, and let them have it, but you still miss it all. Here once again the colonel, damn him to hell, reached out and gave me some life. I don't doubt he'd like to kill me too.

Unlike the airlines, there's no FAA law that tells me to land and sleep before I kill myself. There sure is a law of nature, though. That sick in the stomach sputter you get when you run out of gas is enough to wake up even the dead. I guess I forgot to switch tanks and ran out the left wing tank. Lucky days. Switched tanks, had fuel in the right side, dropped into Nogales, Mexico, cleared customs, even that went way smoother than it should have—does he have eyes and ears down here too? Put her to bed, got a cab, and was fast awake as soon as my head hit the pillow. I don't know what it is about pillows, but I'm the most awake as soon as I get in bed. Mexico is not known for its quietude, either. Flipping and flopping for a while, don't think I ever fell asleep, but know I must have.

Some coffee and breakfast and a beyond the call of duty email brief by someone without a return address put a little smile on my face. The man must still have tentacles everywhere. We all used to imagine what he did, but I'll bet the truth was more messed up than we could fantasize about. Rumor was that he laughed in Clinton's face when he was offered a star. Something about his place being in the bird colonel ranks. Pure balls, no politics. No ass kissing. No entitlement and he was owed more favors than he owed.

You hear a lot of crap out there. I like the one that is attributed to Einstein, "Only two things are infinite, the universe and human stupidity, and I'm not sure about the former."

Here's the rule; when you're on the run, never go to where you've ever been. Never call who you've ever called, never do what you've ever done. You should know all that if you've ever seen a movie or read a book or spent any time online. Certainly don't head off to the beach house you've rented before in Puerto Vallarta, and really don't call up some old girlfriend so she can come down to meet you. Maybe when you're entitled you feel free from the laws of nature and man. Reading that email brief made me feel like I just bit into one of those beautiful European pastries. You know the ones, beautiful to look at, but not much sugar. Unfulfilling to be sure.

I go through the huge task of flight planning for Puerto Vallarta. Well, that took about 2 minutes. Not much challenge, but I do love that city. Worlds apart from Nogales. Maybe life really is just mundane. Maybe it really does all come too easy. Maybe I had my time and all this was a way to get shaken out of a deep sleep so I could fall back asleep again. I'm guessing I'll drop the kid off tomorrow night, then back to St. George late afternoon the next day. Total loss, five or six lessons missed, maybe an IPC too. Oh well, hurry up and wait. Some things never change.

7

Living alone is most often the place I want to be, but sometimes, like this evening, I miss someone else's perspective. Have I allowed this idea of a dark seed planted inside me to create a life of its own? I decided to call up my friend Linda. She is one of the friends I have that isn't afraid of challenging me. That is what I needed right now. I needed someone to set me straight, to shake some sense into me. Or did I want someone to convince me I was making the whole thing up?

No one ever accused me of being masterful at small talk, so after I explained what was on my mind, I heard her engage gears. She knew she was needed and that I was asking for clarity from her. "Laura, you have always told me that the bigger the light you are, the bigger moths you are going to attract. Isn't that what you said? You put out the brightest light I know. What sort of dark thing do you think will be attracted to you?"

I listened, knowing she was trying to convince me I could handle anything that came my way. Had I made her believe this? Did she really have that much confidence in me? I confided in her that I felt something still concerned me about this experience. When she asked me to elaborate, I could not. Finally, we ended up talking about her son, one of my favorite 13 year old clients, and I let go of the immediate need to define my discomfort.

I pondered our conversation. Was there something personal about this experience as she had suggested? I don't believe in coincidences and yet, what could I have had to do with last Friday, those Eyes, the timing, the exact moment of connection, the total knowing of who it was? Put it like that, how could it have been anything except perfectly planned? Who else except someone who deals with this kind of dark energy would recognize it? Who else but someone who reads energy for a living would understand the depths of its potential? It was not fully making sense, but I could feel a thread that I was afraid to continue to pull on. It was as if my mind would not let me take the energetic thread to the next connection, the one that put it all together for me, the one that brings comprehension. It just stopped. I could not follow the trail any longer. I know it did not die. I knew I was not permitting entry.

Some obstacle still needed to be removed before I could go further. What was it?

8

You learn some things in the service. Mostly you learn to follow orders and learn to not ask too many questions. You sure learn not to ask questions to yourself. It's about focus. You focus on what is at hand. And acceptance. You know that you're never high enough up the food chain to see the whole picture. You start asking questions to yourself when you don't have the whole picture and you start to get answers that just don't fit. So you go back to your focus. And you always focus on the mission. It's always bigger than you and it's always primary.

It took too long to fly from Nogales to Puerto Vallarta. And it took too little time to get out to where the kid was hiding in Boca de Tomatlan, a little tourist cove just south of town. And it was too easy to find the kid who was hiding. In that time that was too long and in the time that was too short, I did too much thinking and asked myself too many questions. That's all for sure.

Kid was a deer in the headlights when I found him. All I got was surprise, anger, entitlement, spoiled little brat. No remorse, no guilt. No fight. He didn't even try to run. When nothing fits you go back to your focus and your training. Soon as we got back to the Puerto Vallarta airport I put him in the back and zip tied his hands to the seat. I don't care what I was feeling. I don't trust anybody sitting behind me, and I sure wasn't going to put him up front with the right side yoke within hands' reach.

I had a few thousand air miles ahead and no desire to talk so I didn't give him a headset either. I probably spent too much time with the soul searching questions that can poison you on the way north to the border. I don't like it when things don't fit together, and nothing fit here. I had arranged with an old buddy, ex DEA, for a quick border crossing that I hadn't used in longer than I'd like to remember, and certainly one that I never thought I'd use again. I'd drop the kid and some men who didn't exist would give him back to me once I cleared customs. Like I said before, I don't like asking favors, but I still believe in the quid pro quo when I need it. Maybe some day I'll make two columns and see if I'm in debt or if I have more credits. I get the feeling I'll never know how to account for this strange affair I'm in.

Kid still was in the headlights when they drove away in some piece of crap Chevy pickup that had seen it's better days, and seemed in shock when I got him back on our side. Nobody looked in anyone's eyes and I get the feeling no one was any more happy about the whole thing than I was.

Must have been somewhere above southern Idaho when I woke up to what I had ahead of me. I guess I was on autopilot as much as the plane was. Zoned out, for sure. The colonel still had some serious favors and pull, that call from center rerouting me to Sandpoint proved that beyond a shadow. And how the hell he got control over the locals put the icing on. But I started to see the shadow of the great General Jack coming up in my face. That thought, that face, came straight out of nowhere and I suddenly got that sick feeling deep down in the gut at the same time my mind started to think of CFIT for no particular reason. That means *controlled flight into terrain*, and that's not what a pilot should be thinking when he's got the controls in his hands. I had about a second to laugh to myself before I saw what I must have been *sensing*. It's that way. You *feel* it in your gut, then you *see* what you were thinking about. The trick is to listen to that first feeling and not to question it or blow it off. Lots of guys I've been with never trusted it, and lots of those guys didn't come home either. Well, I had my second to laugh before I saw what brought on that crap in the pants feeling. It sure wasn't General Jack's face floating around up there in the sky, but sure as hell was close. Maybe the second worst thing you can ever see out your windshield, and that's a very close second place to a mountain in your face, is an F-16 out your side window and another out the other side. You feel 'em first, heavy in the sky, and when you look over all you see looking back at you is nothing more than a mask and goggles with a thumbs down. Suddenly this A36 dream machine I'm in felt like a baby's toy.

There's a specific intercept procedure to follow at times like this. The interceptors don't always have civilian band radio capability so you just do the wing wag thing and follow or die. I knew they weren't going to shoot me down, but there's still that visceral memory. The F-16 isn't designed to be a friendly looking escort. It wasn't another minute before center came on and cleared me into Mountain Home AFB outside of Boise. Talking about visceral memories. What about this was so much like other times when the colonel was somewhere else and I was in his shit? I must have been on internal autopilot as I changed course because all I could think of was kidnapping, illegal imprisonment, international transport of an illegal detainee, illegal border crossing, jail, the general, the damn colonel, my lost life. I felt like I had gone back in time. What do they say, same old story, new set of words? At least this time I wouldn't be getting my balls fried. At least I don't think they do that in Idaho.

By the time I taxied to the ramp all that pleasant nostalgia was gone and replaced by the friendly picture of men with weapons drawn. I was done, at least for a minute, kicking myself in the teeth for fighting a war against an overwhelming enemy without any chance of success. But I knew that the second I learned who daddy was, day before yesterday. I wasn't kidding myself. I had nothing to say. Just following orders doesn't apply to civilians when given orders by civilians. I had nothing to fall back on but a hopeless sea of deep kimchee. Focus.

The MPs took the kid out the back and when the sergeant in charge had to cut those zip ties I could feel him cut right into me. Thanks to God for military discipline, at least for the minute. His sidearm never left his holster. When I started to unbuckle all I heard from him was, "stand fast, sir," and that was right up with the last thing I could have imagined. They closed the door and two MPs took up station with their backs to me outside the plane. I couldn't be certain, but I sure thought I saw a set of four stars sitting in the Hummer they took the kid to.

You learn to wait in the military and you try to keep your imagination in check. Maybe you BS with the guys. Or smoke. Some guys can sleep on cue. I just waited, but the imagination didn't check. That's when it's the worst. That's one of the techniques they teach you about way back in survival and escape school. How you'll be left alone, sometimes with the lights always on, sometimes always off. Real life is just a little worse than training, though. They don't tell you that. Lights off was the worst. You hear things, but you don't know if they're in your head or crawling around on the ground for real. Then you feel something crawl across you. Still not always sure if that was in your head. When you wake up with teeth marks around a festering wound, you know it wasn't in your head.

I spent some time looking around and knowing I was sitting in the Bonanza at Mountain Home with a couple of MPs outside and that I was about to be nailed to the cross, but my mind kept slipping into what I knew was the past and behind me. I've spent my life washing away everything—the past, the future, the now. I guess it didn't work.

Sat there on the ramp about three hours. Felt more than sorry for the two chumps standing outside guarding the plane. Glad it was November and not August. At least had a blanket in the plane. My mind took my emotions up and down about a thousand times before the Hummer finally came back around. Here it is, I thought, time to pay for my sins.

I had a girlfriend once a long time ago who used to get on me that I always thought I knew exactly what was ahead. She'd try to tell me that I limited myself too much by limiting the outcomes that were possible. I guess I thought I knew all the sorry possibilities up ahead and none of them were much to think of anyway. She got tired of it all, and me, after a while.

In the last few days each minute has shown me things that were so far out of my world of possibilities that they just wouldn't fit in my head anymore. I mean the colonel crying, the general's son in my zip ties, F-16 taking me to jail. What the hell's next? Does God Almighty exist just to screw with me?

There are things that you see when you're in the service and things you don't. And there are things that are so impossible that they can't be seen. And I don't know if God hates me or loves me, but I saw General Jack JB DeWitt, Chairman of the Joint Chiefs of Staff of the United States of America, four stars and all, get out of that Hummer and walk toward my aircraft. He stepped up on the wing, opened the door himself and asked, "permission to come aboard" and with a pause that wasn't accidental, "Colonel?" Then he stepped in and sat down in the right seat. I don't know if I was in shock or if I was ready to crawl out of my skin, and I don't know what hit me the hardest. I've been around plenty of generals, but I hadn't had anyone call me colonel in a long time. I didn't expect to ever hear that again.

"That is my boy you brought up, you know."

"Yes, general." You don't call a general *sir*, you call him *general*.

"Didn't hurt him then?"

"No, General."

"I don't carry any rank on you anymore, son. Call me Jack, and thank you for bringing him in safe, and thank you for not hurting him."

I didn't have anything to say to that, so I just sat. This was out of my control and well above my station and I sure didn't have any idea what was coming.

"You think all this could just go away, son?"

"I don't know what to think about any of this, Gen ... Jack" If you've never been there you don't know what it's like to call the man by his first name.

"Do you think I'm going to cover this all up, some kind of conspiracy, protect my boy against all things evil?"

Had I not been there with the man, I would have said *yes*. But in that second I saw everything that got me to apply to the Academy so many years before. Something that I lost over the years of bullshit and cover-ups and botched missions, and incompetent fools leading good men into battle. I saw the honor that I haven't believed in since I was a kid.

"No General, you're not. You're going to let me take him in and you're going to trust that justice will prevail, no matter what that is." And I meant every word of that as I looked in this man's face and saw a sadness that no man should have to feel. I saw it in the colonel's eyes two days ago and I saw it here. And I felt empty and knew that the mission always prevails.

He shook my hand and didn't say another word. Just got out of the plane and went back to the Hummer. The sergeant came back out and asked me if I'd like to go over to the mess hall and hit the head.

I was still in shock as we lifted off an hour later. Me on the instruments, and the kid zip tied to the back seat.

Mountain Home up to Sandpoint isn't a long flight, a few hours. But time isn't absolute. A few hours is all it takes sometimes. Still, nothing fit. This kid should be screaming at me long before now. Instead he just sat there still in the headlights. And I've felt that before, with the general. You can feel when they are only giving up just exactly what they want to give up and nothing more. He knew more than he told me, which was exactly nothing anyway.

I got the file back out and read through it again. Everything pointed to this kid. He had a history, and that's the first place you look. He was close to the colonel's daughter, and that's the first place you look. They had forensics on him, but I didn't have the detail, just the summary. He took off right after. Red flag. Ran to Mexico. Bright red flag. I looked through the photos again and I looked back at his face staring out the window, vacuous. That didn't fit. I remembered the general's face when he came back out and that didn't exactly fit. Maybe a little. A man like that doesn't give up tactics on his face, so no info there one way or the other.

When I cancelled IFR over Coeur d'Alene I had nothing, so I did the first thing a pilot does—fly the plane.

They met me at the Sandpoint airport again, like the last time, except this time there was the chief and the colonel as well as the same officer who met me before. Same kid came out and asked if I wanted fuel and if I wanted the hanger. Same answers. The officer took General DeWitt's son into his squad car, and I got in with the chief and colonel. I expected a barrage of questions, but got silence. What had happened in the last two days that I was in the dark about?

Back at the station the chief left us in the same room and the same officer brought in some coffee.

"It's done," the colonel told me. He wasn't asking.

"It's done, but I'm not comfortable with all this." He gave me that familiar face that said, keep talking. "Everything went by the numbers. The kid was right where you said he'd be. You do know that they put me down at Mountain Home?" He just kept listening. "General DeWitt thanked me and cut me loose. Is he planning anything? You know he can come down on you like a rock?" He still just kept listening so I realized this was just going to be a one-sided narrative on my part.

"That kid didn't run, he didn't cry. Nothin'. I don't know, I'm just not comfortable with it all. I don't have anything to go on. You're sure he's …?"

"He's the one all right. We've got him now. He's going down for this, and your job is done." I'd been in this seat with the man before. Dismissed with not so much as a job well done.

We sat there for a minute just looking at each other, then I stood up and we shook hands and I said I'd be heading home now. Felt unrequited, but what I felt wasn't his business. I got as far as the door, and he said, "Thank you …, Colonel," with the same pause the general had said it with. "You're welcome, Colonel," I said back, without the pause.

I was way over hours flown without rest, so I decided to see about a room before heading out. The officer at the front desk gave me the names of a couple places and promised both were within walking distance. Sand-point's a cute little town, right on a lake, mountains all around. I headed towards the lake, hoping for a room with a view. Found the hotel the ser-geant suggested, checked in and took a walk trying to not think things out. Found a little hole-in-the wall Mexican restaurant that had sit-down and take-out. Too cold by then to take it out so I got a burrito and sat down for the first good meal in a few days. Not much more to do so went back to the hotel, showered and fell asleep pretty quickly, and out of character as well.

Next day up early, some coffee, a couple doughnuts and I thought I'd look up the chief to put some things to rest in my mind. We spent a couple minutes talking and he seemed nice enough, though not particularly grate-ful, given that I'd just brought in his man while he sat on his butt. Told me to hang on for a few minutes more and that a possible witness was com-ing in to ID the kid. He didn't seem too jazzed about it, though. I got the feeling the witness wasn't anyone he considered reliable. I hung out about 15 minutes reading the bulletin board and drinking another cup of coffee when a patrolman ushered in a good looking woman about my age. I didn't pick up anything that remotely felt unreliable or histrionic, so I figured I'd hang back and see what she said. Took her about a second to say the kid was not the man she saw in her neighborhood. They cut her loose and she was gone before I got a chance to talk with her, and since the chief was sud-denly nowhere to be found, I took off for the airport.

One thing you learn in the service is what is yours and what's not. This was no longer mine. Not a bad flight back. Hit clear skies a few hours south and cancelled IFR. Dropped down low for the last few hundred miles. Nap-of-the-earth, and in a Bonanza to boot. That felt good and I wasn't paying for the fuel anyway. At a hundred feet up and 150 knots you're not thinking of your problems, just feeling the terrain. Wasn't 500 knots in an F-16, but then I'm not a young man anymore, either. Reflexes are slowed down, vision is worse, and decisions come way slower. It's a young man's world. Us old guys are just still living in it.

St. George looked as beautiful as ever. Vast, wide-open space as far as you can see. Time to go back to life and file away another mission where I never knew the why, just the how, where, when, who. Been a long time since anyone called *me* colonel, though.

9

Just then, in the midst of reflection, the phone rang. It was someone from the police station asking if I could come down and identify the driver I saw from Friday. Seems they had already apprehended him. I was surprised, mostly because I did not think they gave any credence to my statement, or believed I recalled enough to be helpful. I drove down anyway. On my way, I felt an uneasiness. Could this cold-blooded killer have been so careless as to have been caught so quickly? It felt sloppy, and that guy was far from sloppy. I kept my thoughts on the road, trying not to imagine the upcoming encounter with these torturously demented eyes. I hoped they would have a one-way window like in the movies. I did not want him looking back at me.

Walking into the station, everyone was very kind and accommodating. They ushered me to a darkened staging area of sorts and I was asked to look through a one-way mirror to a guy in a small room. Bracing myself for the Eyes to be burning their evil into my eye sockets, I tentatively turned toward the window. What I saw was a punk, a young, probably entitled, lazy, undignified guy. Not that he was a bad guy, he just was far from the Eyes. He held no personal power and certainly did not seem capable of brutal murder, or much else other than partying and skiing. I was probably exaggerating. I guess I was just expecting something much more intense, yes, intense. He was not intense.

A voice asked him to look up at the mirror, which I assumed was for my benefit and I saw his eyes. Harmless, bored, a little scared, but definitely not the guy I saw fleeing the mountain behind me last Friday. I shared this information with the officer attending to me and they took some notes, had me sign a few things and said I could go.

As I turned to go, I observed a tall, focused and confident man standing in the shadows behind me. Feeling his energy, he was as much or more capable of murder than the guy I was just looking at. He smiled a half smile from behind his shadows and I could feel his warmth. OK, so that was harsh, no mass murderer then, in fact, his smile betrayed a sweet sensitivity behind that rugged and authoritative exterior.

That was weird, I thought to myself as I exited the station. That was the man they thought capable of a cruel and evil murder? Admittedly, I knew nothing about criminal investigations, but I knew energy and that guy did not carry the energy signature of a killer of anything but time. Shaking my head, I thought to myself, well, I guess I can feel safe now that the murderer to which I am the only eyewitness, assuming the man I saw was indeed dropping off his cargo, has been imprisoned and will be justly tried. Oh boy, my tax dollars are hard at work. What did I know? Maybe he was a schizophrenic.

Several evenings later, having forgotten about my near self-observation, I was soaking blissfully in my hot tub. The tub sits on a ridge near my house overlooking a valley and mountains in both directions. This night, it was deeply dark and starless. The intense quiet of a thick night sky, not a sound, rarely even a bristle of wind, left only the feeling of total undisturbed silence. This night I let everything go. It felt relaxing, my body responded to my mind's suggestions. I observed the silence of the night, the total darkness. I usually can see some lights from houses in the valley below, but the dense fog made it impossible to see anything. With the lights in the house turned off, it was completely dark. I waited to get my night vision, but there was nothing to focus my eyes on. It was rather eerie. I did not let myself give over any power to fear. Yet I sensed something. In the total darkness, it felt as if I had a visitor.

Something I had not invited was present, something that definitely did not live here, yet not totally unfamiliar either. Waiting for a connection, I opened my mind to receive a message, if that is what you could say about it. Tonight I felt I had a visitor that was either lost or needed my assistance. The energy did not feel like it wanted to connect for teaching or learning, it actually felt sinister. This definitely alerted the immediacy of tuning in.

Then I felt that thing that was blocking what I was about to uncover about myself days ago. It was palpable. In the thick dark clouds, it was something I could almost touch. It appeared as if to say, *this obstacle you encountered is real. And not only real, it is living and dangerous.*

I remember sitting up straight in the tub, as if somehow it were a more defensible position. All sensors were on alert. I still could not see with my physical eyes, yet physical eyes can only show you physical things. If you want to see the non-material world, you must employ a different set of eyes. These were activated. Suddenly the itchy feeling of not being able to put my finger on something, or scratch an unconscious itch was returning. The memory of my questions resurfaced. Normally, I welcome an opportunity to learn something, to uncover a saboteur, but tonight alone in this dense and silent darkness, surrounded by a dark and starless visitor, I felt a discomfort that longed for relief. Somehow I knew relief was not on *this* side of an encounter, but the other.

I knew this energy, or being, had participated in my story before. I did not resist the connection. Running into the house was really no solution. This was no coyote or wolf, but a non-physical being composed of something sinister and dark. Running would not help. I reminded myself of my primary tool: my open heart. I breathed in my own knowing, in contrast to the burgeoning heaviness, recaptured a sense of lightness within my being. Yet I felt isolated, cut off from the herd, alone in my light. I must have appeared like a lone lighthouse, not connected to any other light or skyline.

The sinister presence enveloped me, above, below and in all points of direction. My lighthouse stood firm, even though unsupported in any other way other than my own will to survive. If I had let myself, I could have felt the chills that were intended for me. A feeling of dread and hopelessness fell upon my extending light of love. Were I to let myself remember experiences when I myself have felt these two emotions, I knew I would lose my ability to be the lighthouse. So I disengaged my sentimental self and cut off all connection to my sensory self. I knew I was invulnerable as long as I did not waver in my one single mission of being open-hearted. Yet I could feel myself being investigated, something looking for my weak spot, a way in. I did not let my mind wander to where that might be. I only held the truth strong in my heart. The continued presence of dread and hopelessness had fallen like dew onto me. I did not have to *become* that dew, but knew I needed to remain the singular lighthouse in a sea of darkness, shining not for lost seamen, but for me.

Focusing all of my attention and energy on this one task, I was unaware of anything else save for staving off a sea of darkness so encompassing I may never resurface from its undertow. I knew I could not make this darkness my enemy or I would essentially give it the power of being a worthy adversary, and yet wasn't it? Where could my mind go to find information or inspiration to help me see this sinister guest as welcome? I could not find anything. I knew this was a source of my weakness and resumed my strength of purpose in extending light. I allowed my heart to well up with love for all those I had known and knew that I adored. I remembered moments of happiness and fun. My heart began to brighten and swell. I knew I was taking a risk stepping into my memories because my conscious mind knew there were ones already labeled *dread* and *hopeless*. I steered clear of those, opening only the boxes of sentiment with joy and love on the top. It was working, I found myself half forgetting I was surrounded by a very intelligent dark entity looking for entry.

Just then I became aware of Hilde. She was sitting right on the step to the hot tub, resting her nose on the rim, making a low, soothing whine. She was holding court with me. There she was with me, knowing something was there in the dark, yet not leaving for safer havens. I was aware that I was aware of her, which meant I was capable of splitting my attention. Taking an energetic pulse of the surrounding area, I sensed immediately it was gone. Just like it had never been here and it left nothing behind. The darkness that descended lifted as silently and I was left wondering what had just happened. Had I just accomplished a serious feat? As soon as I thought that, I knew I had not accomplished anything. I had not defeated any Great Darkness. It had simply probed my beingness and then left. I knew that if it had wanted in, it would have found a way.

Breathing a sigh, but also knowing I had not experienced the last of it, I suddenly realized the water was getting cool. I stepped out, pulled on my robe and went inside. A sense of dread was intermingling with a sense of accomplishment, seeming to cancel each other out. Then that sense of familiarity returned, where had I encountered that exact energy? If only it had a face, and I could remember the profile, look into the eyes.

The next morning the snow began falling, gently at first, then with greater gusto and larger and larger flakes. As it started to accumulate, the landscape rearranged itself before me. The view from my house is expansive, in fact, that was the singular word that I used to describe to the realtor in narrowing down options that led us to this place. To the southeast, there is a wide river valley capped with a mountain range and Montana. To the northwest, the river takes its origination so the valley grows narrow and high, the rugged peaks of the Selkirks and Canada on the other side of them. As the landscape changes, it's as if someone is painting the entire world white, all at once, not like a painter who begins in one part of the canvas and moves on to the next. Everything was becoming monochromatic. Only faded memories of the colors they had been. The mountains are a cool payne's gray and the bare trees a pale mix of burnt umber and sienna, now sprinkled with white dust. Before long, they will all be a solid white, at least, by day. By night, especially on clear full moon winter nights, the snow is blue, unmistakably and beautifully blue.

I spent years trying to encourage my art students to seek options for shadows other than black or gray—watered down black. Then one day I just went through my supply of paints and removed every tube of black that was in there. The first class I had after that—I had forgotten I had done it—I commented to a woman about her painting, how awe-inspiring her purple shadows were. I asked what propelled her to choose that color, to which she replied, "I couldn't find any BLACK!" Eureka! Success! So even though many people categorize things in terms of just black, actually, very few things in nature are really black. There is always some color in there. My mind reflected on the darkness in the Eyes. Was there some color there? Or only black? I hoped I knew the answer. I was warming inside, but winter was approaching outside.

10

Merkle! …

I'd been deep in the soup for about two hours with my eyes glued to a partial panel of instruments after multiple failures. Best decision would have been to divert to the closest airport, but there was that little bit of macho bullshit pushing me on. Steering a course with the magnetic compass instead of the directional gyro, and keeping wings level with the turn coordinator instead of the attitude indicator. That's what it's all about to an instrument pilot. This new generation of pilots is so plugged into GPS and high-tech glass panels with backups up the wazoo, that most would have been at the end of a death spiral by now. And that is just what it sounds like. Your internal balance mechanism slips just a little bit and you gently spiral down and down and then check out fast with the last thing you ever see being the ground in your windshield.

Actually, I was feeling pretty big of myself after two hours with about half an hour to go. I expected enough weather clearing at my destination that I wouldn't need an instrument approach anyway. Half the time I have that voice in my head telling me to stop taking any of these delivery jobs for guys who can afford to buy a plane, but don't have the know-how to fly it home themselves. The delivery pilot shows up, trusts the logbooks and that the last annual inspection wasn't bullshit, takes off, always has some glitches, delivers the plane to the happy owner and collects way less than it was worth. Less than it was worth in cash, but nothing equals being in the air, even in a junk bucket like this one. What I'd give for an autopilot about now.

Anyway, after so long with so much concentration your mind drifts back and forth; side to side; future, past, other dimensions. Conversations you'll never have, then suddenly back in the cockpit trying to make sense of the instruments. Getting back on course, staying wings level. Shocked back to life with the voice of the controller in your headset.

Hans Merkle. He always insisted that we call him Hank. I think he was trying to erase his past, but we all knew who and what he was. Efficient to a level way beyond any machine, dedicated, focused to perfection. Relentless. Driven. All that packed way too tight. No more morality and ethics than a machine, either.

He was with us from time to time. Nobody could ever figure out how he got attached to the unit or who was pulling the strings when he was. The colonel never liked him, but used him when he had him. Usually on the dirtiest missions, the ones none of us retold later around a few beers. I hadn't thought of him in so long that I wasn't sure he existed at all. After a few hours in your own head the line between reality and memory fuzzes.

I don't know if the name jumped into my head first, or if I saw his face in my head then heard the name. No, I didn't see his face, not clearly at all. It's like I saw his eyes all of a sudden, right in front of me. Nothing but white outside the windscreen for the last two hours and the drone of the engine, then in an instant I see his eyes right at me, and I'm in a full-on sympathetic nervous system reaction—*fight or flight*. Oily sweat, little chilled, heart pumping louder than the engine and perfect mental clarity. Perfect clarity. Merkle's not dead. I knew that as clear as I know I'm sitting in this airplane. I know that so much that every debrief I wrote and read and heard about his death welled up in me like the biggest lie of my life.

My mind went way past redline, and suddenly I'm futzing with everything I can get my hands on trying to speed this tub up and get on the ground. Maybe 15 minutes 'till I expect to begin descent and I'm crawling out of my skin.

Three months of nothingness followed by more nothing. Some instruction, a few deliveries, couple of test flights, going here and there, a few dates with a few women I can't remember. That's the last three months of my life. One sentence, that's all. That's what a whole life comes down to. What a total loser. You could have taught a monkey to do every single thing I've done since flying out of Sandpoint. I left that place and the colonel and the general and that home-town chief like you end a meal that you looked forward to and waited for and then ate the last bite and had no taste for—cardboard. Like tofu right out of the package. I hadn't done anything to look more into anything. Hadn't heard from the colonel, nothing. I think I must have jettisoned my give a damn on the way back.

I did hear that they cleared that kid I brought back from Mexico. Total screw up! Total, absolute waste of my time. I still wake up thinking of what General DeWitt thinks of me for dragging his kid back up. Makes you feel like the first pawn sacrificed early in the game. Makes you feel like a pawn and makes me know that I've been a pawn my whole life.

Walked away from that woman I saw in the station, too. Could have talked to her, but didn't even give it the effort. And, for the life of me, can't even remember her name. I know I heard the cop say it, but just can't remember. Damn, missed opportunities.

That's my last three months.

Hans Merkle. Clarity. Of course if there's clarity and purity, it's Merkle.

Came down hard and fast. Cleared the clouds and landed hard, too. Taxied too fast. Guy was waiting with a shit-eating grin on his face. Happiest day of his life. Here's your plane, fly safe, thanks for the cash, where's the commercial terminal, goodbye. I don't think he noticed me at all.

Few hours back on Delta gave me time to do some internet research. First off, anything I could find on Merkle, which was nothing—of course. Then on to the Sandpoint thing. Tried to look up the woman from the police station. Wracked my brain trying to remember her last name, right on the tip of my tongue the whole time. Googled everything that sounded close and finally got a hit after about a million spelling variations. Strange name that, Wexler. Wow, not what I expected, pages and pages. Definitely not a flake. Who is this woman? Got lost in her website checking everything out. She was into some strange stuff. That's for sure. I was still reading some of the articles she'd written when they turned off the Wi-Fi before landing. I definitely have some more research to do. But not before I get back to work. Merkle is out there.

11

Tomorrow begins the final intensive week of a year and a half program aimed at consistently taking the higher perspective. Rosa, my devoted cook, was preparing the kitchen for the group to arrive. She would prepare delicious Mexican meals passed down from her grandmother and mother. I watched as she unloaded all the vegetables, meats and her usual 50 pounds of flour. She loves making cinnamon rolls for the first morning, her delightful way of greeting these seeking souls and a welcome warmth in mid-February. Seeing Rosa there with her curly black hair and warm smile, delicious curves and cowgirl boots under a mini skirt, I remembered why we all love her so much. She loves to be noticed and to live all of life, not just a smidgen of it. Not only would we have Mexican meals, but she loved to cook Greek food, Thai, Italian, you name it, she cooks it. And she cooks it all with such love for cooking and love for the recipients of her delicious and abundant food. I cleared space for her to set up all her special cooking appliances and implements. She always made herself comfortable as she claimed the kitchen for herself.

While she was doing that, I got out of her hair and went upstairs to my loft office to call my sister. I knew I wouldn't have a chance to talk to her all week, and wanted to connect with her. I looked at the time, calculating the three hours ahead she is and settled into my chair. I put on the headset I use when working with clients. As soon as I placed the headband on my head, I was struck by lightning in my mind. I cried out! Something had pierced me through the brain. Before I could register what it was, my *eyes* felt the bolt of electricity too, like an instant migraine. My first thought was an aneurism, but before I could react to that thought, a visual began to play out in my mind's eye. At first only partial seconds of flashes; a woman screaming, then red blood, dark evil. I could feel intense anger, silver reflecting light, a man's voice.

I tried to breathe deeply to make it stop, but it only seemed to bring it into clearer focus. It was now as if I had a camera on the scene of a brutal ... Brutal what? Oh, make it go away. *I paint peace and beauty and nature, ahhh!* It hurt my soul, it offended my essence. I was being ravaged by this uninvited vision, complete with emotions, feelings, even smells as I would later recall. I began to see a young, terrified woman with long dark hair. If she were acting, it was the most convincing thing I had ever witnessed. *What* was I witnessing? The jab of violence cut through me again, piercing my heart, again and again, causing real, physical pain. I grabbed my chest, crying out. The pain was sharp and excruciating, yet the spiritual offense was worse. I had been so open and available as I was preparing for my group, it was as if someone had chosen the most vulnerable moment possible to strike at me. And it did feel like a strike, again and again. I was weakened. I could no longer see my desk, the mountains in the distance or the carpeting below me. I had no vision for my physical world. All those senses were completely cut off. I was weeping now, unable to control the offense to my being, to the tenderness of my heart, to the empathy for other living beings. A deep and powerful darkness was yanking my eyes as if it had my optic nerve and was rewiring the objects I could focus on. I had no control, the images continued. More dark red blood, a deep and heinous laugh and a woman's shivering and begging. I realized then, I was seeing the *woman*, not the man that belonged to the voice. Was I inside the man? Was I seeing as *he* was seeing? The thought made me wretch. I turned to my side, clutching my stomach. Filled with the stench of bodily fluids, the scent of fear, and adrenaline sweat. I was becoming nauseous. How much more must I watch? I tried to scream for help myself, but have no idea what, if anything, came out. I could only hear the scene I was being forced to witness.

The next thing I remember was Rosa, shaking me, saying something sacred sounding in Spanish. The look on her face told a tale in itself since I have never seen anything unnerve the woman. At first I thought something was wrong with *her* and asked what was wrong. She looked at me like I was insane. "*Wrong? You tell me, woman, what is wrong?* Why were you lying on the floor, screaming, clutching yourself? I have never heard sounds like that before and I could not get you to respond. I have been calling your name 100 times ... *Dios mio, Dios mio.*"

Was I recalling the event of last fall? I had pretty much forgotten all about the woman who had been murdered and dumped a few miles from my house. I had not heard another thing about it, so consequently I just assumed the killer had been tried and that was the end of it. I pulled myself up from the floor with Rosa's help. I was covered with sweat, exhausted. Nothing like this had ever happened to me before. I am not an empath. I have control over the energy I work with, well, usually. What just happened? I felt spent and exhausted at every level of my being. Had I had a bad dream? No, I was just about to call Janni. Did I dial the number? Was I electrocuted by a defective headset?

It occurred to me that I needed to see the face of the woman brutally murdered last November 10th. How had I recalled the date so effortlessly? I noted that. I went to my computer and pulled up the internet. I typed in the date and the newspaper and the subject. Instantly, there was the face of a young woman posing for a senior picture or something. A beautiful woman, but very blonde, not the woman I had seen. I knew that. Not at all. My stomach wrenched again. Rosa sat by my side still trying to figure out if I was possessed and what this picture of a smiling woman had to do with my situation. I could tell she was praying for me. I could feel the blessing and appreciated it as I looked through my desk drawer for the card of the policeman who came to see me last November.

He wasn't in, but they said he would be back in the office within the hour. I decided to drive into town to wait for him. It would take half an hour to get there, and the drive would help calm me down. I could try to piece together the story so it sounded coherent. What was I going to say to him anyway? And why would he believe me? What was the point? I knew I needed to do it, that's all. I drove the winding road to the highway trying not to recall the graphicness of the images, but to try and piece together anything that could be useful. Was there something identifying I might be able to share? About what? A murder that happened in my cerebral cortex? I still felt I had to go. If for nothing more than to assuage my conscience, to give the images to someone else whose job it was to collect them. I had enough for one lifetime.

Two hours later I was driving back up the mountain road to my house. That was a complete waste of time. If I thought he didn't believe me before, I am pretty sure I just fell into the nutcase category of someone who has watched one too many sci-fi movies. What's weird is that I am used to people actually believing me. Many people give credence to things that happen in the mind. After all, as I am so fond of saying, everything begins as an idea and where do ideas begin? In the mind. That whole thing would have been lost to Captain Strickland, or was it Sergeant Strickland? I never can remember what the hierarchy is. Doesn't matter now, doubt that I will ever have intentional contact with him or anyone from his department, whatever their rank. It's just as well. It did suffice in shifting my energy. I had felt that it was somehow very real, and now, thanks to Major Captain Strickland, it no longer feels like anything except a bizarre fantasy of someone who has a grand and over-active imagination. I needed to get back in my own space for tomorrow anyway.

My intuition and inner world shaken, I began to ponder the efficacy of many of the guided explorations I have led over the years. Did I need to validate myself after my encounter with the unbeliever? I recalled many people who have had meaningful and emotional experiences in guided visualizations in their own minds, allowing a space for forgiveness and reconciliation that would never have happened otherwise. Not really knowing where to put everything, I brought my mind back to the task at hand. I had never been to a police station, and Rosa reminded me of this as she greeted me. She asked me how I did in this reality. I'm sure I looked confused because then she just laughed, "Woman, I have never known you in any place other than the spirit world. What on earth did they think of you at the *real* police station?" She wasn't really looking for an answer as much as entertaining herself with the visual of the scene, I think.

With that familiar laughter, I saw Rosa's concern relax and she regained her normal composure. She said we had some work to do, so I rolled up my sleeves and got into the tasks at hand.

12

"Well, I hear they cleared the kid?" I asked the colonel as soon as he answered the phone.

"Little shit, yea. Should'a burned him when you picked him up." He let his bad mood come right across.

"For what? He didn't have anything to do with your daughter ..." I started to say when he cut me off.

"Hell he didn't! He was bad for her from the git-go. Never should have been with him in the first place. Just a punk going nowhere."

"I meant he didn't kill your daughter and you know it. You know it now for sure and you knew it then. Soon as I brought him in you knew it. You knew it before I got him there." Just a pause on the line, no response.

"How's it with General Jack?"

"He thinks I should crawl back in my hole. He's probably right." The colonel let on just a little remorse. Just a little.

"You're not going to. You're going to get whoever did it, right?"

"There was another one." He said without answering my question.

"Another killer? How do they know?" I didn't have any idea about this.

"Another girl."

"Another ..." I had no idea. I'd been in the dark for three months. I mean really in the dark. The darkness. I hadn't even thought to follow up on the whole fiasco in Sandpoint. The continued silence on his part was indictment enough. I had a job to do, didn't, and didn't even try to follow up. This call was turning from bad to worse, quickly. My self-respect was going with it, too.

"Well?" He finally asked.

"Well what?"

"Well, what the hell do you want? We've got nothing. The locals have nothing to go on. There's some nut job out there and my daughter's dead and we've got nothing. So what the hell do you want and what can you do to help? Clear enough for you, mister?"

I had heard that voice before.

"Who is the second girl? Any connection?"

"Took you long enough to ask that, didn't it?" I wasn't taking that bait so I just waited. Silent. "She was Becky's college roommate. You wouldn't have known her. Girl named Samantha." There was something in his voice that told me there was more than just her name.

"And?" Talking with the man was like prying open the jaws of a dog with a bone. He never came straight on with anything.

"And?" he still held back. "And who the hell is she other than a roommate? There's more, Colonel. There's a hell of a lot more than you're telling me and I'm getting really tired of all this shit. Nothing here has anything to do with me except that I know you and because that I knew Becky and she was a great kid. Hell of a lot nicer than you. I am tired, and I am tired of playing games. We've all played enough bullshit games for a lifetime. How about leveling with me on this one?" Gets old sometimes. Payback time was coming to an end for me and I was feeling like I didn't owe the man anything any more. And I hadn't even got to what I called for in the first place.

"Samantha DeWitt." In a tone that was as dead as can be. I had no place to put that. I had no idea about the second murder in the first place and I had no idea how much all this was entwined. I completely had no idea about the connection between Jack DeWitt and the colonel, and even less about the girls. Made sense, though. They all went back to about the same time. Ran in the same circles. Circles way the hell up in the stratosphere. No wonder the general gave me a break back at Mountain Home. Something was so far wrong that there was only one answer, clarity. Absolute clarity.

We didn't speak for a minute or so, but I could tell he was waiting for me. I could feel he had nothing and for some crazy reason still held onto me for an answer. It wasn't the first time we played this out. He lived at a place with a higher vantage point than I did. All those guys did. The general lived way out of my scope. But I was the guy those guys came to. For a minute, I wasn't sure if I wanted to play that part again. I had been certain when I called, but there was a part of me that kept saying, "let it go." I wanted to believe it wasn't my fight. We sat there each with a phone in his ear listening to nothing. No breathing, no sighs, no opening. I think this was a moment in my life when I had two choices and neither was worth a damn. A lifetime of duty, honor, country. The mission. A lifetime of bullshit. Really. I knew that then. I hadn't when I was young, but that excuse ran out a long time ago.

"Merkle." I dropped without any explanation.

There was no sound and no response. And there wasn't any indication that he heard me or was even on the line. He could have put the phone down and been in the crapper. It was that quiet. But I could see inside that brain of his in those moments. I could see the same memories he was seeing and feel the same guilt that he felt. We had all been part of the same shit. Maybe there was always someone higher up the chain making the decisions, but we all carried the same guilt. Give the order, follow the order. Go to hell all together.

I knew his mind went right to that first mission when we got Merkle attached to our unit in Panama when Noriega was somewhere between our friend and our enemy. No shit, we had a board that had photos tacked up with the South American yahoo politicians and we'd stick a smiley face on their faces when we were told they were friends of the US and we'd stick a frowny face when they told us they had become the bad guys. I really don't remember what face Noriega had on that day.

I saw inside his head and we both saw Hans Merkle walk in with his orders attaching him to us for one mission. I remember the colonel reading the orders and I saw his face when his eyes got to the signature on the order. I'll never know who signed it. But it was enough to see those eye slits open wider than I'd ever seen before.

Creepy dude and that was the truth. He was kind of like the Terminator in the first movie. I mean after he had taken a few hits and his skin was starting to rot off. I remember us joking about that scene when Schwarzenegger was in the hotel room and the super knocks and asks, "Hey buddy, you got a dead cat in there, or what?" Great movie and funny as hell. Well, Merkle wasn't rotting at the flesh, but they could have been brothers. At least that's what we used to say.

It was a twisted time, that mission. Maybe two weeks, day or so more or less. Merkle had some kind of inside connection, we all were told, and that's why he was with us. We all thought we could have done it without him, but when it all started and all went to hell from the git-go, we all knew we'd have been in the shit if he wasn't there. Every time you'd call him Hans, he'd say, "call me Hank," with that creepy smile and his hand out like he wanted to shake. Nobody ever did, though. You couldn't. He was no Hank. No way. We actually called him the Terminator when he wasn't around. I always wondered if he would have minded that. Word was that he was ex-Stasi or East German special forces. You just didn't ask, and didn't believe what you heard anyway. He was clearly not one of us and didn't make any moves to be part of the team.

In the action he was right on, though. You knew that he'd be there where he said he'd be and he'd do exactly what he was supposed to do. It was how he did it that bothered us all when it was over. He was a cold, brutal killer. All the way through. That's what he was. We were glad when it was over and I know everyone was glad when he left the unit, and just as not glad when he was reattached a few more times for no apparent reasons. Not to us at least. No teary farewells or reunions between any of the guys on that note. Glad to be alive. Glad to have not dropped the ball any more than we did. Glad it was over. Sick how it was done though. He was not like us. Death is not all the same.

I don't know how I knew that was what the colonel was seeing, but I think it was. After a long time of total silence all I heard was, "Merkle's dead. Honduras, 1997. You know that."

I knew that. I had signed off on everything. I was there. Hans Merkle was cut into little pieces by Sanchez's men after the screw up mission of the decade. We lost 3 men including Merkle. I was there.

"No Colonel, this is Merkle's work. This is payback and Becky was just the first." I expected an outburst, some denials, impossible … What I got was a curt, "Hold." Then the line went quiet again. This time I could tell I was on hold. Not the most polite way to deal with a caller, but some things you learn to accept.

It was maybe 15 minutes when he came back on the line. He could have called me back but then he would have had to be someone else, and that wasn't happening in this life.

"Can you get down to Nellis?" He asked. That would be Nellis Air Force base in Las Vegas, which is about an hour south of me. I don't think

I ever heard him put a qualifier like *can* in front of a sentence. There was more here than was visible on the surface.

"I'm about an hour if I leave now."

"No need. Tomorrow 0800. Major Ben Morgan is your man. He'll be in from Virginia. Just check in at the gate with that and let me know what you find." And that was the end of that call, and the beginning, or continuation of what had begun a long time ago and seemed to be coming to a head now. Interesting how he just said Virginia. My first thought went into the Pentagon, but I lost track after about twenty other military and intelligence possibilities HQ'd in Virginia. I always questioned the intelligence of putting the entire command structure of the entire nation within a stone's throw of each other. Like a bad Monopoly board. Not defensible at any level. Anyway, just more BS above my pay grade. But that thought left me back at square one. What was my pay grade? And do I have a pay grade? I've been out of the game for long enough that my uniforms have all been sold and resold at thrift stores and are now probably just dish rags. And what am I doing in this river anyway? I got a beer out of the fridge and sat looking out over the vista. Beautiful red rock and sunsets beyond your wildest imagination. I've got a life filled with leaving beauty and going into the shit. Not the smartest kid on the block, that's for sure.

———————————

Up and on the road for the smooth drive down to Nellis, just outside Las Vegas. You've got fighters in the sky and NASCAR right below. Can almost smell the testosterone in the air.

"Nick Drake?"

"Glad to meet you, Major." We shook hands and I followed him into an office that clearly wasn't his. "You're in from the Pentagon?" I tried with the subtlety of a rank amateur. He just smiled and pulled out a file from his briefcase.

"Sorry, Nick, but this isn't my office so we'll just have to wing it. Would you like a coffee or anything? There's an orderly outside who seems gung-ho to meet my desires."

Guy was trying to be smooth all the way through.

There are people you meet who you instantly know are completely in charge of their emotions and comfortable in their environment. This guy fit the bill, but didn't look the part. You spend enough time around personnel in uniform, you know when someone is wearing one that isn't his. This *major* wasn't USAF. So it wasn't the Pentagon he was from. My ego chalked up one for my side. Maybe intelligence, but no field experience. Probably had some comfortable office in some gray building back in Virginia. Not my problem or interest. I was just glad to still be able to pick out something that was clearly out of place. Not dead yet. I felt better about myself already.

"That gets a blanket yes from me. Sugar and half & half, or milk if he doesn't have any."

He was gone for long enough for me to open the file and realize that he wasn't trying to hide anything in it. First page let me know that I wasn't the first off the blocks with Merkle's resurrection. Every new day makes you realize nothing's new under the sun. The first guy to discover something finds that somebody else has already been there and gone. I got lost in Merkle's file for long enough to lose time, then when I looked up there was very stern looking, and attractive, in a uniform sort of way, major standing looking at me with a fine balance between questioning and being put off by me. And this major definitely fit into her uniform like she was made for it.

"Sir? ..." She addressed me with a big question mark across her face.

"Uhuh." I answered, not quite knowing what was up, or where was my phony major and what was up with the no coffee anyway.

"Excuse me, sir, but that's my desk." She still was being as polite and controlled as possible, probably not knowing if I was in her chain of command, and who the hell was I anyway. I mean sitting in her office on Nellis Air Force Base in civilian clothes. When you wear the uniform, you never know who's your boss unless they're wearing one too.

"Oh, sorry," I stood up as I folded up the file and almost tripped over my own shoes. At least that brought a smile to the sternness. She was like some bad librarian or something and suddenly I felt like I was in the reserve section without a pass. "I was just waiting for Major Morgan and a cup of coffee." Which seemed to confuse her even more. Testing her patience? I wasn't sure.

"I don't think we have a Major Morgan in this squadron, sir." At least she hadn't dropped the sir. I knew I wasn't in trouble, yet.

"Oh, I know that, we were just using the desk." Which was probably the wrong thing to say. And where the hell was Morgan?

"Sir, this is not a classified area, but that still is my desk and this still is my office, and no one informed me of anyone being authorized to be here. And, there is no major Morgan in this squadron. And, the mess hall is three buildings to your left. This isn't the cafeteria." Ouch. Took me a second to reach up and erase that chalk mark. The little shit must be intelligence and he played me, somehow. Only the *why* wasn't clear.

"Ma'am, I am sorry. And I am confused. I guess he meant for me to wait for him somewhere else. My mistake, and …" I started to walk around and out, but the librarian formed some kind of force field.

"Sir, I'll have to ask you to wait just a minute while I clear this up. Please. I mean, a civilian sitting in my chair, alone in my office, on base. Give me a break here." Then she went back out and I spent a frantic two minutes imagining myself jumping out her window and running, but the wiser part of me realized that I hadn't done anything wrong. Then my eyes fell to that broad red stripe across the file marked *Top Secret*. I think half my life has been in places I can't explain being in. Does someone on high have it out for me? I just sat down and figured everything would work out.

Couple of minutes later Major Librarian came back in with an over-worked, underpaid sergeant with a brace of paperwork.

"Sorry sir. I've been half way around the base looking for you," he said while she stood behind with that same question mark on her face. "they just dumped this on me an hour ago and I've had the damnedest time. Never seen anything like this. We got a shitload of paperwork for you to sign." He said as he looked behind at her with a half-hearted shrug of apology for the curse.

"What pap …" I tried to ask before he cut me off like I was a new recruit being processed.

"Says here you're attached to the 24th Special Tactics Squadron and reinstated to your previous rank and pay grade of O-6 for …" as I heard the name of *that* squadron and *that* rank my heart skipped the proverbial beat, and I could see the major step back like someone just popped her in the nose—O-6, Full Bird Colonel.

"Wait a minute sergeant, I'm no O-6. I …"

"Sir, says right here on these orders, *Reinstated to previous rank and pay grade of O-6.* I didn't type this up, sir. Way I read it, that means you were Colonel Drake once upon a time. I can't demote you, sir. And I can't do anything but ask you to sign every one of these documents. You know how it is, sir. You've got to know my job here. Please don't make it harder. I don't understand this and I've never seen anything like this, but it's in front of me and you can see by this signature right here," he pointed at the authorization and I skipped the next proverbial beat, "that this is what we're both going to do. Right now."

Damn me for asking about pay grade. At least I wasn't on my own on this thing. I had official recourse and that felt better. I don't know if that meant official protection on what I was about to do, or not. Maybe it just meant the chance of official punishment if I screwed up.

Of course I signed and signed, and got everything in order and when I saw my clearance I calmed down about having that top secret file still in my left hand all the while. Wasn't going to jail for that, after all. As I walked back to my car three hours later, I had just the tiniest little twinge of disappointment that I was a couple grades above the librarian. I think we could have had some fun there for a while. I started to open the car door when I saw her walking up to me with a stern smile on her face.

"Colonel?"

"Major."

"Sir, it's clear that you're not in my chain of command. I don't understand any of what just went on, but it doesn't look like you're in anyone's chain of command. So I think we can find that cup of coffee for you." And I did like that smile.

13

The music of Simon and Garfunkel came on and suddenly the *Sounds of Silence* took on a completely different meaning than when I listened to it as a child. I pressed replay and listened to the words a second and then a third time. The music was haunting and eerie. Yet now it felt like the lyrics delivered a message personally to me, defining my situation. I felt that *Darkness* actually had come to talk with me. And that it had really planted a seed while I was sleeping. There was no doubt that something remained. But what? During this week of great clarity, community and love, the seed had not been watered or tended, but it was still there. Perhaps we all have it and that is what the story about the two wolves within each of us is about; which one do you feed? Something about the now, though, felt like it had come to my attention: *deal with the seed.* You cannot ignore this forever, you must … what? Fighting is never the answer. You cannot beat the darkness, it isn't about destroying the darkness, *it is about understanding why the light is missing.*

I could feel the destiny in my thoughts. I knew the timing was right, yet why now? What had happened that made me think I was ready on some level? Had I unintentionally opened a karmic Pandora's box? I could hear my own voice admonish me about getting entangled in the *whys* instead of just accepting the task before me.

Allowing my mind to let patterns and messages, metaphors and experiences, quotes, songs, and images all swirl together, a painting was beginning to form in my mind's eye. One of great inspiration and brightness, created out of deep sadness or great trauma, I could feel the empowerment of it, the radiant glory. It was as if I could flip ahead to the fabulous ending, but couldn't actually be done with the story yet. I could only have a sense that what was to come would be worth it. Yet I also knew that what stood between me and it was a deep crevasse and I breathed a heavy sigh. As much as I believed this life was a dream and we were the main characters, it is times like this I wish it were not so. I wished I could fast forward to the end and just watch. Being the main character now in my own play was taking a dark turn, one I was not completely convinced I could succeed in.

I looked at the time, it was time to round everyone up and get a project underway. Tonight's project involved a presentation of one woman's journey in the form of a book that she was presenting to a woman's group several miles away. The evening unfolded beautifully. Everyone in the group was sparkling, radiant and genuinely connecting. After all, they had been together in a space of genuine spirit for almost a week. It was contagious and the sparkle got on everyone else. Several of the guests had asked who we were. What was creating such a joyful sparkle?

We left in two cars and on the way back to my retreat center, we were stopped by a train. It was late and dark, cold and crisp, yet we were all high from the connection and experience we had just shared. The train stopped just a few cars before it had cleared the road. We sat there waiting and talking, then our sister car came up alongside us after about 5 minutes, wondering what to do. We had brownies left in our car from the event and passed them back and forth from window to window. We all laughed and joked like teen girls at a slumber party. They all provoked me to move the train with my thoughts. I laughed at them. I did take a quick energetic assessment of the situation to see if we would be better served to go back the extra 15 minutes to another crossing. Gaining a swift inner positive response, we made a U-turn and headed back. No sign of anything but pure joy tonight. I made a note, as if looking for the seed to have somehow grown on its own.

That night as I was filled with gratitude for these wonderful souls and for the unexpected emotional experience of the evening, I wondered why I felt so unprepared to meet this darkness. Did I have a knowing of who or what it was? It felt overwhelming, as if I had played this drama before and failed. Yet, would we be tasked or taken somewhere that we were not capable of succeeding? It does not mean we necessarily will, only that we *can*. It may require more than we think we have. It may require acceptance, transformation, letting go of something we hold valuable, but I knew I was giving some power away already, even before I knew who my opponent was. *Or did I already know?* And with this thought a chill ran down my spine.

I silently asked for assistance. I knew I was encountering someone I had left unresolved, and for good reason. Gratitude filled my heart for my non-physical assistance, along with the knowing I would forget these joyful moments when I was lost in darkness. The next few days were glorious, joyful and powerful. Unknowingly, I was charging my batteries for what lay ahead.

14

Driving north out of Vegas the next day gave me a little time to think about things. The desert there has its own special beauty. So many people feel the desert is dead, but they're just looking in the wrong place. You won't see green, but there's plenty of life. I don't just mean reptiles and scrub brush. There's just a life that you feel when you look out over the vastness and rock formations. Any time I fly someone over Nevada I always get the same reaction. "I never knew Nevada had so many mountains!" When you go over Wheeler Peak on the Utah-Nevada border, you're going over a glacier at 13,000 feet. That's a surprise to everyone.

I love Las Vegas! It's my roach motel. Traffic is steady from Southern California all the way up into Vegas, then it's mostly gone from Vegas north up to St. George. They come in, but they don't go out. At least not north, anyway.

After a bit on the road, cruise control set at 82, I started going back over time. Felt strange to have a stack of paperwork that would get me a paycheck from the Air Force. Nothing in me felt like a full bird colonel. Nothing. Not now, not then. Just a carrot and manipulation. Now and then. Not hard to put that one out of my mind. Maybe a little hard. Just a mild sense of irritation. It helped when I thought of an old Larry Bond book I had read forever ago. Main character was an ex-New York detective, but now a recovering alcoholic private investigator with a pragmatic view of life. "Man hands you some money, put it in your pocket." I always took that to be good advice. You don't put it in your pocket, you set yourself out to be different, or better than them. Maybe you're ready to head off to Internal Affairs in his world, or some office of investigators in my world. Nothing's clear, just all shades of gray. Who hasn't done something for expediency at one time or the other? Maybe that's why I like Southern

Utah so much. The sky is crystal blue most of the time. I guess I'm tired of shades of gray.

Happy for the pay grade, the paycheck at least. It's not like I'm rolling in the big bucks sitting in the right seat of a Cessna with some kid in the left. You pay the price of admission when you get into aviation. Seems like the forces of the universe figure that flying is so great that just doing it is reward in itself. Most people would be shocked out of their seats if they knew how little the guys in the front cabin were getting paid. It's like it's so cool to be doing it at all, nobody thinks of paying much for it. I guess I'm happy for the doors that automatically open to a full bird colonel. Really happy for that signature on my special orders. Open doors all the way. Not stupid enough to be happy for the future when they hang me out to dry, though. What the hell, not doing anything important these days anyway.

Pulling into St. George about an hour later and honestly can't remember what I had been thinking about. It does get harder to keep it together as you age. As I get home and heft out all my paperwork, and that red-stripped file, I start to get anxious about what's ahead. That perfect clarity about Merkle is getting pushed to the back. When I first remembered him and knew it was him out there, my mind was suddenly back in the day when I was doing what I did. And did it really well. This isn't my stuff. I'm not an investigator. I have no idea what to do first. You can read all the investigator books in the world, but that doesn't make you one.

Cup of coffee and the whole file spread out on the table. Mission prep. That's all this is. I'm not a cop, not an investigator, but I can plan, equip, and execute a mission. First thing up, what is the mission? The mission is always paramount.

Mission: Find and eliminate Hans Merkle.

What I can't do is bring back the girls. I can't do anything directly for the fathers. I can't change the past. I don't really care why the very dead Merkle is very much alive. Stop.

Question: Do I know this is Merkle. Yes! No. No, I don't know it is Merkle. I have more evidence that tells me he's dead than alive.

Question: Why Merkle? The clarity when his eyes bore into me in the cockpit day before yesterday. Perfect clarity—knowing the truth. Knowing the truth? No. What then? … Feeling Merkle.

Question: Feeling or knowing? Same thing. Is it? That one took me a while, then—yes.

Question: What is the mission? Find and eliminate the threat. OK that feels better. But, threat to what? To the colonel or the general? No. Whoever did this would not have gone after the girls if that's who they wanted. Whoever did this wanted to make a point, a statement. Maybe a challenge to someone.

Question: Is this related or are the two deaths coincidental? I've got to choose one and go with it, so I choose related.

Follow the trail, where is the relationship? Both military. Both about same age. Relatively similar careers, but the general was way cleaner than the colonel. Crossed paths? Stop, unknown. Above my need to know. Time for the birds that I won't wear on my shoulders to go to work.

Now that one stopped me in my tracks. Want to feel old? Just try to remember who did what back when. I couldn't think of where the hell personnel was headquartered. Then, bam, I'm in the 21st century—Google it. Who handles personnel for the USAF? And in a millisecond I'm on the Air Force Personnel Center website. What the hell is that? We always joked that the Air Force was just some big-assed corporation, but this is ridiculous. Took me a little digging and a couple of calls down to Randolph AFB in Texas and I was on my way.

I knew of General Jack, who doesn't, as Chairman of the JCS, but never followed his career. Those guys spend a little time everywhere and there's always a stint or two with one foot in politics and one in uniform. Looks like he headed up the early days of the War on Drugs for Bush in '89.

Holy shit! Slap in the teeth right there. Man was my boss! Man was the colonel's boss. He was pulling the strings on all of us. He was the big man and if you look high enough, he was Merkle's puppet master. Had to be. Who else could it have been?

Quick call.

"Richards." Always that same clear statement, right on the first ring. No *hello*. No, *Colonel Frank Richards speaking*. Just, *Richards*. Must be hell of a lot of fun to play golf with the man.

"Who's signature was on Merkle's orders?" No need to explain that question. I knew his memory was right in line with my own. Just the slightest pause, then, "DeWitt." I hung up and sat there at my kitchen table just feeling the quiver roll through my body. Had to shake out the wetness in my eyes and blow my nose after that one. What kind of force in the universe is suddenly bringing us all back in time? What the hell is going on? We're talking 20 plus years ago. Another life ago. Jack JB DeWitt has got to be the squeakiest clean mama's boy in the whole damn service. I did another Google and checked on his confirmation hearings. He slid through congressional interviews like it was preordained by God almighty. Nobody challenged his appointment. What the hell is happening here?

Question: What is the mission? Eliminate the threat. To what? To … I just don't know.

I spent the next few hours drawing out an action plan. Felt good. Definitely something I'd left long behind, but I felt fully tasked for the first time in a long time. Flying had moments of total demand, but mostly was hours of boredom with a view.

First thing up was a trip to Maryland. No problem getting another instructor to cover for me. It's that freedom I've liked since getting out of the service. Nobody telling me where to go, or even if I could go at all. Sometimes with what feels like total freedom you get restrictions as well. When you can go everywhere, do you go anywhere?

Back on Delta to Reagan National. Little Embraer Turboprop to Salt Lake then a 757 non stop. That Embraer is one shaky piece of work. Sad thing that the mighty US of A has to go with the best of Brazilian aerospace to stay cost effective. At least Delta was flying a Boeing and not some piece of garbage Airbus.

Samantha lived alone in a little berg called Crofton and commuted to work at the naval Academy in Annapolis. What a burr in the butt that must have been for the old man. He was big green from birth, born in an Army hospital and never fell far from the tree after that. Must have killed him to see her working for the navy. She was doing an internship for some program in grad school. Wonder if she did it to get at him. I dropped that line right away. No need to lose respect for their lives. I knew there was no dirt here, just some old vendetta. Had to be.

There were a few agencies involved in the murder investigation, as you can imagine. Lots of turf protection. I didn't need much, so I figured I could be in and out and not step on any toes. I was about 40% right on that. Took me a day that started at seven in the morning and got me back to the hotel outside Reagan at eleven that night. Lots of calls, plenty of waiting for the sake of waiting for the sake of someone having the power to make me wait no matter what signatures I had on whatever the hell pieces of paper I had. So much military in that part of the world, my invisible shoulder birds just would have made me part of the flock anyway, so I didn't try to pull that card. Mostly, I tried to be respectful and demonstrate the superiority of any civil servant standing between me and what I needed.

They were all in full heat looking where they were trained to look, for what they were trained to look. You only find what you're looking for, so I knew nobody out there would find anything even close. I wouldn't say any of them; local, state, federal, or military were incompetent in the slightest way. I just knew that who they were looking for was long gone into another realm of existence.

Finally boarded a 5:00 am flight out of Reagan with two stops and one plane change to Spokane. I needed to go there before my next move. Probably could have gotten the whole file Fedex'd to me, but I needed to walk the property. Just like out here in Maryland. No matter what the technology, you've got to walk on the same ground as your enemy. He always leaves a trail. Maybe you can't see it, but it's there.

One tiring over-long trip later I'm in a rental car on the way to Sandpoint, about two hours from Spokane. Now that's an easy airport, may I never set foot in Reagan again.

Chief Longfellow was nice enough after the initial shock and anger. I'll give him credit for not killing the messenger. And for understanding that nobody had found the link between the girls—yet. A week is a long time with this kind of thing and I wondered why neither the colonel nor the general had directed the investigation in Maryland out this way. Actually, I didn't wonder that much. I was too used to working with only partial knowledge under men with more pieces of the puzzle than I.

He jumped at the chance of first knowledge when I offered him Samantha's file in exchange for Becky's. I knew I wouldn't even make it to the parking lot before he'd be on the phone to whatever federal asshole had tried to break his back in the past. I figured anyone who ever called him a small town bumpkin was going to get the chief's foot up his butt. There's nothing like being the guy to figure out a connection all the other boys are missing. He knew right off I wasn't looking for any credit and was giving him one hell of a meaty bone. I didn't know if I'd need him anymore, but you never know how many cards you'll need to play your hand.

Once again I was feeling pretty full of myself, but as the chief started flipping through the file, the look on his face took away any points I thought I had. He punched his intercom and called. Detective named Strickland came in, and the chief asked him about that same Wexler woman I had seen when I brought the kid in a few months ago. I didn't understand the connection at first. They had her come in because she had seen some guy up on her road, which was the same road Becky was found on. She had come into the station and I remember standing behind her when the general's son was asked to turn towards the window we were behind. I didn't need to see him, I'd just spent a long trip back with him zip tied in my back seat. I watched her from behind and a little to the side. There was no mistaking that the kid was not at all who she had seen on that road. Everyone, especially the colonel who wanted it to be a closed case, just blew it off. Maybe she did see some ominous dark figure out there at the same time as the murder, but it wasn't that kid, so the dark-eyed guy she described must not have been the killer. That sure proved to be some bass-ackward reasoning.

Turned out that it wasn't the kid and that I had wasted a few days and broken some federal laws for absolutely nothing. They cut him loose a few days later and everyone went home.

What were they talking to her about, anyway? Chief Longfellow sent Strickland out to get her and bring her in to see these photos of Samantha. I just sat there completely stumped.

"Chief. What's up? This girl was killed in Maryland. That woman seemed like a nice person to me. Why do you want her to see this mess?" I was feeling instantly protective of … what? I think it was purity. I think I just didn't want to expose her to something this gruesome. Maybe the chief just had it out for her. I recalled that he seemed embarrassed by her definitiveness about it not being the kid when she came in last time. She sure was right and we sure as hell were wrong. "I think you should leave her out of this."

"Well, Nick, I think you should read this." He gave me a two-page transcript of what she had described to them six days ago. I started reading it not expecting anything one way or the other, but right away started to get a bad, bad feeling. I read a little then picked up the photos I had brought from Maryland. I read, then looked, then read, then looked, then just stopped reading and sat there. That same dizzy, sweaty, eye-watering, sick feeling. I was reading a textual description of the photos I was looking at.

Took me a minute to get my bearings.

"Chief, you got any coffee around here?" He got up and brought me back a mug himself. I just looked at him and asked, "got anything to sweeten this up?" He looked at me for a full 30 seconds then bent down and pulled a pint of Jack Daniels out from his lower drawer and poured a dose in the cup.

"Can I use your phone, chief?" He pushed it over to me and within 5 minutes I was connected with some guy named Higgs, FBI, who started a full search on all the airlines and any other form of transportation to see if this woman had taken a trip out to Maryland recently. He said they would run all her bank and credit accounts to see about purchases as well. I trusted he'd look for more than I knew to ask him to look for.

"She just showed up last week with this crazy story about some dream or vision or whatever she called it. We listened to her. Why not? Not like we're over worked around here. Seemed like quite a story then. Just one more nut case, know what I mean?" I did know what he meant, but I didn't exactly know what I was feeling or what to think of this. I had seen her for what, ten minutes max? I even checked out her whole web page, all the stuff she does. This wasn't fitting.

We just sat there and drank JD flavored coffee for the next hour while we waited for Strickland to get her back in.

15

The last thing I expected the day after my program ended, as Rosa and I were cleaning up from the group, was a call from the station. Yes, the very station where all the ranked individuals who thought I was daft reported for duty. The professional voice on the other end asked if I could please come back down to the station, they had some things to talk to me about. I certainly could not imagine what, perhaps one of the cops on his nights off was writing a thriller and wanted some of my overactive imagination. I laughed to myself. Did I have any outstanding tickets or anything else it could be? Could not think of anything, so I left Rosa to the rest of the straightening and packing her truck, bid her a warm thank you followed by a genuine hug and went into town.

During the intensive, I was so completely present to the work we were doing together that it seemed like we were above all the mundanities of social regulations and rules. When it was over, I came back into civilization again. Strange to come back the same way I went in, with a trip to the same police station, that up until last November I had never even been inside. I recalled Rosa's comment about me being in the police station. That didn't help me feel terribly confident about going back again.

The week had been so powerful, so full of rich experiences and healing transformation that no matter what the police investigator said, I was confident that what happens in my mind is *real*. I spent the better part of the drive down into town having a purely cerebral conversation with Mister Strickland, sharing the wisdom of someone who does not see things as he does. I imagined his face comprehend and nod, ask questions and listen politely while I further explain that we are creating our own realities through our very thoughts. And that whether we were conscious of it or not, we would draw things to us or repel them depending upon our deepest fears or loves. At that point, I laughed out loud at the absurdity of it. *I would be happy to accommodate any way I could, and keep my beliefs to myself,* I promised the invisible Strickland.

The faces that greeted me were not what I expected. I had just come from a group of completely open and expansive people so the contrast was painful. What stood before me were several people who as a group had either just heard a really sorry story or watched someone's beloved dog get run over by a truck. Either option, I did not know why I had to be involved. Then I had a thought, they wanted me to find a missing child or something, like psychics do. They were going to give me her little blankie and I was supposed to close my eyes and find her. Oh brother. This was going to be fun. How was I going to break it to them that I was not a psychic? I was going through all this in my mind when I was greeted by the receptionist. I am making that assumption, perhaps she had a rank too, I don't know. She asked if I was Laura Wexler and I nodded. I followed her to a closed office at the back of the station. I hadn't noticed this office last time I was here. The name on the door said Longfellow. I pictured a long face on a long fellow. The door opened from the inside, as if someone knew exactly when my guide would touch the doorknob. I was escorted in.

The faces did not look much lighter in this room and in fact, if the man behind the desk was Longfellow, he indeed did look like a long fellow. It didn't take long to ascertain that a murder had occurred exactly as I described about a week ago and that Longfellow just found out about it this morning. I was stunned. Of course, I believed it was happening somewhere. I witnessed it. But so much of my work happens in places and realms that are not in the present, that I don't think it really occurred to me that the violent experience I had observed could actually have happened while I was witnessing it. It also didn't take long to ascertain that they thought I had something to do with it. That is a thought that had never entered my overactive imagination. *No good deed goes unpunished,* I could hear his familiar voice repeat to me more often than I wanted to recount. No kidding.

What now, I thought to myself? Wait a minute, Rosa was there, I had an alibi and then I had an entire group of people who could testify that I never left them all week. I felt the ability to breathe better gently wash through my muscles. But I knew I was locked into this case until they were done with me. Luckily it was late February and I did not have any events other than my usual clients until mid-April. I remember saying to myself I would be accommodating and helpful on the way down. I guess they were going to take me up on that.

A man I did not know handed me four pictures of women's faces. Similar to the one in the newspaper, they were smiling for the camera and all very pretty. I instantly recognized one of them and the rancor and nausea returned to my stomach. I held back a foul sensation in my mouth, as if acid had just released of its own accord. Holy ... Jeez, *there she was*, not just an image in my mind. I picked her out and handed the picture to the man who had offered the pictures to me. I looked at him. Who was he? It was not Longfellow, nor was it my own personal Strickland. I did not see any identifying marks on his outfit.

This guy wore no uniform or jumpsuit, but casual jeans and a leather jacket. He did not look like he had a rank, yet he looked capable of leading people. He returned my glance. Then I recognized the faint smile of the man in the shadows behind me when I had identified that kid last fall in this same police station. I also recognized his energy, but it wasn't so focused now, perhaps less capable of murder? I definitely could feel his weariness. Something about this whole affair, I had a feeling, took him out of his comfort zone. Longfellow started speaking to me. They were going to need everything I had. Did I really have to remember that scene again? I had purposefully given it to Strickland last week. It was his now, couldn't *he* give them everything they were going to need?

They wanted to show me the photographs of the woman's mutilated body, but I asked them to spare me from that. I really could not handle it. Could I simply tell them what I experienced and they could correlate the photos themselves? The guy in the leather bomber jacket said it was actually a good idea. I could tell he wasn't doing it to be sympathetic, he didn't necessarily believe me. He wanted to see what I was made of. He's the kind of guy I would fully expect to interview everyone in my group to make sure they were not covering for me.

My focus returned to the chief. What did he want to know? He was asking about what I do for a living. Funny, no one had asked me that before now. Perhaps that meant it never mattered, until now. I instinctively asked him, as it had just occurred to me this moment, *when did this guy get out of jail?* I thought the killer had been apprehended months ago and was in trial. Why was he released anyway?

I always loved that term pregnant pause, but never felt it so clearly as in this moment. No one offered the next syllable. There was only a space that hung in the air that was definitely pregnant. By that, I mean something was being born with the answer. Each man contemplated the answer as it applied to him; the implications, the effort, the work, the past waste of energy. All those things must go through your mind when you discover you are pregnant. The answer about what I did certainly was lost in that fertile space.

"It wasn't him." Seemed to just materialize, coming from no one in particular.

What did this mean? Did that mean that the murderer was still at large? How could this be? I was connected to both murders through the Eyes. Holy shit, this meant I was the only connection they had to the real murderer. I must have voiced all that in one run on sentence/question/concern that no one seemed to feel they had to answer and yet were all thinking the same thing. Was someone going to tell me I was the only witness to a brutal, now potentially serial crime? I do need protection now, don't I? Suddenly the gravity of the situation landed squarely in the pit of my stomach. I sensed that life as I had known it was not mine anymore. It belonged to the Eyes until I found him, or he found me.

We all sat quietly, pondering the next step. Each of us with our agendas, all breathing heavily, waiting for something to break, someone to enter with a piece of breaking news or some guy on some social media site to admit to the crimes so they could just go and arrest him. This guy was way too sophisticated and had no ego in these crimes. Something very dark began to descend on the inhabitants of this small, overcrowded room on Lake Street in this little mountain town. It was too large and too heavy for the chief. It was too much trouble for Strickland, and it was some kind of fire or vengeance for the guy with the bomber jacket. For me, it meant I was stepping into a lesson that I was not completely sure I was ready for, but then what kind of lessons are we ready for? Somehow I felt the responsibility in that room, I was the only one with the knowledge of what was behind that man's eyes, and what he was capable of, and what was required to satisfy it.

16

Not sure exactly how, but I found myself back in my own home in St. George after that crazy trip out to Maryland, and that even more bizarre stop in Sandpoint. Bone tired and fuzzy in the head with no more direction than I started with. All I could think of was to just sit there and start all over again. Spent one more sleepless night going over everything and still nothing made any more sense, no matter how many times I rearranged all the knowns, unknowns, facts, fictions, players, intel, and the data I had.

Must not have been totally sleepless though. Woke up the next morning still at the kitchen table buried in a stack of papers. Hot shower and a few cups and all I came up with was, *what the hell*.

You can plan as long as you'd like, but then you've got to move. Enough experience and you know you're never going to be ready just from a plan.

I didn't have much to tidy up on the home front before heading out. Not sure if that made me a little sad or not. How long had I been down in St. George now? Three years. Friends? Yea, sure. No, not really friends. A few guys I'd connect with at the airport. A few CFIs. Sam, the old mechanic, but that was just listening to his stories. Neighbors? Said, "hey" to on a regular basis. Mostly on the way in or out. Some small conversation on the course, then a handshake and, "nice game" on the 18th hole. Women? No complaints there, not really. Some serial relationships that didn't really run too long.

Maybe a little sad on assessment. Not really like I went looking for much companionship. Didn't run from it either. As I sat on the shuttle down to the Las Vegas airport, I couldn't think of too many specifics about the past three years. Didn't really feel wrong, though. Some moderately fulfilling experiences, some not. Enjoyed almost all the flying in the area, that one was for sure. Enjoyed the solitude of the desert. Enjoyed the times I was playing alone and the last guy on the course up in Hurricane. The front nine up there overlooks some incredible red bluffs, and when you catch that along with a sunset and you're sinking every shot, well that's the bomb. No small talk and no company, just the moment. Looking around at the Virgin River Gorge just into Nevada was fulfilling enough. Something about the beauty of this area, no doubt.

Finally down past Mesquite and the flat lands when I started wondering why the colonel hooked me up with Dim Wit. That's Derrick Whitkin, and he was *not* the go-to guy for intelligence back on the team. Colonel said he's a contractor now and is absolutely *the* go-to guy on this one. Man, times do change. And, what the hell is he doing down in Guatemala City? I'm so out of the world these days that I have no idea what we're doing in Guatemala. I thought those days were over. CIA did one hell of a number on that country, then hung them out to dry.

I spent a little time in the mountains down there in the late nineties after the peace agreements had been in affect for a few years. The government had waged war on the people for so long nobody knew how to have peace. The Mayans were some wonderful people. Still able to live and had a pretty good state of mind, in general. Guatemala City was no place to be then, and I imagine it's not much better now. Maybe OK, I'll see. Anyway, I should get all I need from Whitkin in short time.

Flying first class on the government tit. I'll probably hear some whining about the expense budget later, but this full colonel BS won't last anyway, so what can they do? Might as well enjoy the ride while it lasts. Heck of a lot nicer than the jump seats in the back of a transport. That's for sure.

Got off the plane actually feeling pretty rested. The plan didn't get any clearer, but at least I was moving. Sometimes you've got to follow the, "don't just do something, stand there," and other times you've got to just start moving and see what turns up around the next corner. Merkle fell off the world 15 years ago, and here I am clearing customs in Guatemala City on his trail. Old man must have known I didn't have much going on in my life to rope me into this royal mess.

Smiling little man pops out of the shadows out on the street and we're off to who knows where. Pleasant city—this is not. As we weave through the streets at some insane break-neck speed all I'm picking out are shotgun-armed police hanging out on most corners. We go though a guarded gate and barbed wire to get into what seems to be a fairly pleasant residential district. That's something you don't see up in Utah. Lots of armed men standing about for protection, but this doesn't really feel like the safest place to raise the kids.

Derrick Whitkin meets me out at the taxi and with one big-assed smile takes my bag with one hand and my hand with the other. That's weird in itself.

"How the hell are you, Nick?"

"Derrick," I'm still a little guarded, but I don't know why, "you're looking good. Doing something right? That's for sure." And he did look good. Confident. Had a presence that I didn't remember. I wouldn't have thought for a second to think of him as Dim Wit anymore. I guess you should leave things in the past where they belong.

"Nick, you know I am. Everything really. Come on in. Hell of a thing seeing you. Hell of a thing."

We went into a pretty nice little place. There were gratings on the windows, and a metal wrought iron grated screen door that looked pretty unobtrusive for the job it was designed to do. Through a small living room, down the hall and out into a shaded courtyard. Weather was perfect and the sun was shinning. I took the coffee he offered with an apology that Guatemalan coffee wasn't strong and he remembered how I'd liked coffee you could, "stand a spoon up in," back in the day. I took all this in without letting on that I was beyond amazed. I hadn't thought of him in years, and here he is remembering how I liked coffee. Felt a little bad about that.

"What's this about, Derrick? I mean, what are you doing in Guatemala? Last I saw you was …"

"Was when you stopped at the bottom of the ramp on that C-130 after that FUBAR mission in Ecuador and told me I was in the wrong line of business," he said with what sure looked like a sincere smile. I had really said that? I think I might have, now that I remember it. Must have blocked that out of my mind, because I probably wouldn't have come down here if I had remembered the bad blood. Like I said, he did have a nickname, and that didn't come out of nowhere. In that second I couldn't remember what he had or hadn't done, but that shadow was there somewhere in my memory.

"Ouch. Long time ago. Bad time, that. Bad time for sure." We had been tasked with some drug trafficking interdiction that went bad from the second boots hit the ground. I was part of air support and nobody, I mean nobody, had any intelligence that anyone down there had SAMs.

That's surface to air missiles that drug runners in the jungle "absolutely do not possess." There were a few seconds of my life that took a toll. I guess I did OK. We didn't die. That's one good thing. I guess Derrick was just at the wrong end of my needing to blame someone I could see. I'm sure later I knew it was some CIA puke who fed us that poor excuse for intelligence. Always was.

"Long time ago, Nick. You were right. You changed my life right then. It wasn't the work. I believed in the mission. Most of the time, anyway. I just didn't think we should be doing it for that kind of pay. You were the motivation for all of this. You planted the seed that night standing there. I owe you for all this." He said with that same big-assed smile. I really didn't see much in the *all this* thing, though.

I think he must have read my face, because he came right back.

"No, dude. Not *this*. This house and this shit-hole city." He waved his arms around like a symphony conductor.

"This is just one of my overnights for work down here. I've got places like this all the hell over down here. I'm serving the great Uncle Sam all over central America. Boots on the ground and all that bullshit." He must have read my face again, because he outlined his whole operation for me. I guess it wasn't classified or anything.

"We've got locals infiltrating damn near everything. Got the pulse on drug and weapons movements. We don't take any action, just feed up data. Don't even process it, just feed it up the chain. Honestly, I don't know if they do anything with it at all. I don't give a royal damn, either. You can't even imagine what they spend on this operation of mine. The money is in contracting, my friend. Take off the uniform, do the same thing, see the world, bill the Uncle. All because of you. I owe you, Nick." And I think he really meant it.

"Thanks for that, Derrick. No guilt, I'm glad I could help. I guess you just don't know who you affect, do you?"

"You sure don't. And that's for sure. Anyway, what's this bird colonel shit about?" I sure didn't know how he could have known I was back in uniform. Well, invisible uniform anyway.

"Just a carrot. It's not real" I tried to blow it off.

"It's real, and it was real back then, Nick." His smile was gone, and he was serious. "I know why they gave you those birds after Somalia. I know …"

"Was pure bullshit, Derrick. Always was. Now, tell me, why'd the colonel set me up with you?" Some topics aren't up for discussion. I could tell he caught that right off.

"Information, Nick. Information is my game, and have I got some for you."

17

I lay awake that night, not really sleepy, but not really wanting the day to last any longer. My mind naturally began to relive the scenes of today. I knew I was searching for inconsistencies, things that didn't match up, something that had fallen through the cracks at the time. Middle of the night was always a great time for discovering subtler things unknown that stronger or more powerful emotions may have overridden. Sometimes it was a time for creating unnecessary fears, too. So I just had to allow this sort of *following an energy trail* to take a life of its own. If I had an agenda, or was planning to be freaked out by something, that is exactly what I would find and validate very logically. Yet I would be way off mark. So as emotional as it had been today, I felt drained of any real attachment to anything. I wished someone were lying next to me in bed, holding me, cradling me in his strong and protective arms right now, taking this on with me. I closed my eyes and called him. I could feel his protective presence around me as if he were with me again. I could even *smell* him again. That was the detail that allowed me to drift into the neutral space of following the trail back into the experience of today. What isn't exactly right? Why? Why? *Let go of why, just allow the energy to find its natural course, like a serpentine river, flowing where it must.*

Following my thoughts back to the station, I recalled the weary eyes of the pilot, as I discovered was his occupation. I felt a familiar energy, yet somehow unique and of itself as well. A strength, even he does not know he possesses, is buried deep inside those eyes. I allowed myself permission to travel through them. I fell down and back, into something secret, or sacred. I was not sure. Perhaps both. There was much confusion, unclarity, errors, misunderstandings and in the end, he had closed the book. Whatever it was, it was unresolved. I became intrigued as to the details. This was my world now. I came alive in the presence of things unresolved, or resistances still held, and of unhealed stories. He had all three. I knew we had come together for a reason.

My mind looks for messages. Instead of looking directly at something, like a specific star in a dark sky, I soften my gaze and look causally to the side. Then I can see the star perfectly. But try and stare at it straight on, it is lost to the darkness. As I lay there looking into the dark night, I wondered about the story I had written and what I had to discover. What was I being taught? What do I need to learn?

Winter nights the sky is ink black. Tonight it sucked up all remnants of any dim light left over from a pale February sun. I felt the metaphor, but couldn't put words to it. I would come back to it. I allowed myself to return to the closed chapter in the background of the pilot. I could already feel a thread of energy from him to me. I softened as I thought about his personal life, imagined his story, allowed myself to drift off into a sweet space of healing with him. I recognized my process right away and curbed myself. I had no one to save or even help. He was perfectly capable of living his story exactly as he pleased, with no help from me. I felt a pulling in of the wandering tentacles of invasive thoughts. I knew my own history had schooled me and I did not need to repeat anything. I did not need to take this class again. I knew better than to try to substitute saving this guy for the one I could not.

Sleep began to claim me and I did not resist. Glad to end the day with clarity and a sense of being protected, I felt snug as a bug. No sooner than that feeling settled into my being than a contrary thought made its way to the front of my brain: *What about the murderer on the loose?* Are you simply going to fall into unconsciousness in the total darkness and forget about that? Put it that way, and it did seem somewhat irresponsible. And yet another wee voice said, let me go, let me go Home, I am ready. I knew this was the longing to return to those protective arms. Long ago I had to resolve whether I was staying or going and was finally convinced I was not yet finished with my story here.

Should I take action? Had I locked the doors? Even if I had, the doggy doors for Hilde to come and go as she pleased left the place pretty open to anyone with long arms. Should I get my gun out? Where was it anyway? And was I prepared to shoot someone to save my own life? I continued to lie there. Should I call the pilot? Why, because he is the closest thing to physical protection right now? He could not make the fears go away, only I could. So I let that thought go and started the familiar process of dispelling fears. Envisioning a sphere of light containing my kindest, brightest, most loving, and powerful Self, I then allowed myself to step into it and feel it … but something was tugging at this image. I pushed that thought out and returned to the radiance and peace … something definitely was entering this holy space. I asked for assistance. I knew what it was without even asking. It was always that way, as soon as I ask, I already know the answer. I think it is that way with most people, we just want verification because we don't trust ourselves.

This was the contact I suppose I was expecting. I knew we would have to find each other. How else could the story proceed? Every perpetrator secretly wants to be known just as every soul wants to be known. He was making first contact. I say he, but this was not a man, this was an energy. And not an energy I had recently come upon, that's for sure. In fact, looking back on it, I can see I was expecting it, but not consciously. The intrusion into my safest space surprised me. Only energy with that vibration can match that vibration, yet did it actually match it or just block it? And how did it find me there, accessing my own inner powers? That seems obvious now. Are we worthy adversaries? If so, it would know I would access my reserves and replenish my stores to better equip myself for this experience. One might think it was preventing me from rejuvenation, yet this was our playing field. Inner space was our venue.

I heard a voice, not one I had ever heard before. I knew this was not me because the voice was not only foreign to me, it was saying things I would not say, or even think. And it was also extending itself in a very powerful way, not my method. Part of me recognized something as if we had met many times before in many lives, and part of me sensed an unequal authority like a teacher that I had either avoided for lifetimes or had failed under. And another part of me simply went limp.

"Give it over to me." This was very clear. When I hear something only once, I can pretend it is an accident, but then I heard it a second and third time. "Give it over to me. Give it over to me." I felt the darkness and the power, no bluffing here. Yet it wasn't enough to scare me, after all I didn't know what it even meant; give what over to whom? But as soon as I pondered this question, the answer came … and the shivers and the coldness in my blood. "I came for what is mine." It chilled me to the bone to think we had once shared something so close that it would think anything I had belonged to it. I shuddered as I thought of the implications. It was not ambiguous, however, but extremely specific. It was aimed at me and it knew of my powers and it knew what I was capable of, probably more than I did. I was preparing to access my strength when it showed up. Had it been watching me, had it been monitoring my *progress*?

I found myself falling, falling out of my personal reality, out of my bed, into a long, dark and winding tunnel. I had no control to stop it at this point. I was being brought somewhere, and because so much of my work is done in the etheric worlds, it knew I knew it was real. I tried not to panic. The sense of being paralyzed was either coming from me or I perceived it was happening to me. I was not sure. Either way, the effect kept me spinning and falling. I saw spires of tall hoodoos, black and barren trees with gangly branches, and a misty coil surround me. I was intrigued by the colors, all the colors of the rainbow swirling together like a dancing ribbon. Yet they were made of mist. Still the energy of it was entrancing and containing at the same time. It was holding me. I was not afraid. I kept returning to my training, there is nothing to fear in this world, yet this was a different world, wasn't it? *There is nothing more powerful than an open heart.* As soon as I locked on to that thought, I landed immediately, no coincidence. I noted that. Beware. But keep the heart open. That is my only tool, my only protection.

I was out of my comfort zone. I was clearly being engaged by something I did not give permission, and yet, had I? How could this be happening if I had not left the door open to it? Was this the lesson I was being prepared for? If so, I was not ready. I wanted to regroup and regain composure. I wanted to say, "hold on here a minute," but no words would leave my mouth. Not for a long time actually.

There before me was a scene. It was one I had already witnessed energetically. A woman was being brutalized by what appeared to be a demon. I turned away. I knew I was being weakened by being shown things of a horrible and malicious vibration. When I looked to the side, there I saw another woman being tortured and mutilated. I closed my eyes. I asked for assistance. I tried to find my open heart, but everything in me wanted to close down shop and seal up the doors and windows. My heart was aching, yet I managed to keep it open. I knew these things were stories, as cruel and evil as they were, they were simply options in an infinite world. I felt compassion for the women and also for the demonic being involved. I knew these images were being exaggerated to shock me. I had a handle on my being ... until I saw *him*. I saw him with a pistol in his hand and I saw him hold it to his mouth and I saw him pull the trigger. *I lost it*. I saw the blood and brains fly everywhere. I began to sob, to gasp with disbelief. It was my worst nightmare. I had avoided this image for seven years. Yet there it was as if it were being pulled from my memory as clear as yesterday.

I was lost, spinning out of control again, the image and the man falling with me. He was calling my name, begging for help, calling my name. I was mortified. I could not help him. He was falling too, but not within arms' reach. I tried to see him, to grab for him, but he kept falling behind me and as I twisted to catch another glimpse of him, all I could see was the blood and the brains. Or the act again and again, the bullet ripping through his skull, again and again until I could not see. My eyes were filled with tears. I was sobbing and retching, nausea completely overcame me. Why this image? There was no wonder why this image. It was the only one that could unglue me. And it did.

I woke up hours later in my bed, sweating, eyes crusted and swollen. Had I dreamed all that? Was it just a bizarre compilation of all my subconscious fears put into one demonic nightmare? That was not the answer. Yet I didn't know what to do. I lay there seeking connection, not to the demon or the voice, but to my highest self, my reserves, my source of power, my open heart. It was there. I could access it and feel it. What had happened? *Stay in this sacred space first. Absorb the healing. Fill your being with calm.*

As I breathed in the comfort of this peace, I began to wonder if my need to help the one I loved the most was now my Achilles' heel. Was this my lesson? Did I need to let go of my desire to help other people? Before I wandered too far down that train of thought, I recognized my need to focus and gain some clarity.

Let's go back to the case, I thought. Something feels backwards about this whole thing. It's as if I am looking too hard at one thing and need to look somewhere else, like with the star.

What do the police have? A killer who left no evidence, no fingerprints, nothing incriminating. They imagine him a real pro.

What do I have? For whatever reason, the killer and I have some kind of psychic connection, as odd as that is for me to comprehend. What enables us to connect like this?

Taking a more logical approach, I backed up. Could I have simply stumbled upon a time bubble with this murderer in it? Is there any way I might have picked up a signal that was not meant for me?

I don't think so. It has never worked like that before. I don't go snooping into places I don't belong. Plus I know I consciously turn off my energy tentacles when I am not using them.

Think. How could I have gotten this information about this murder on the other side of the country downloaded into me as it was happening? What sorts of things link people to each other energetically?

A story. For example, if one person is playing the role of a Rescuer, they might be drawn to a prisoner story or damsel in distress. In the case of the Eyes, he needed someone who knew how powerful he was without giving himself away. I was that person because I recognized the inherent energy as a deep and dark possession of the man in the truck. So the being, if that is what you want to call him, found a way to be known without being found. We have the components to be in each other's story. I recognize energy and the Eyes were definitely energy that wanted to be recognized.

Just then, my next coherent thought was, could I find him again? And I remembered I already had. Or rather, *he found me*.

As soon as that thought hit me, I suddenly came back to the reality of my own bedroom. I sat straight up. Yes, I needed to understand what this connection was. I began to follow the energy trail of how I could locate this being. I knew that if I didn't take matters in my own hands, I would be left with simply the police work of Longfellow et al., and they were not equipped to locate this being. I am not one to shy away from a challenge, yet I also don't go prying into dark alleys. I had no choice now, it seemed. I wished I could call a wizard friend for brainstorming, yet I knew that only happened in the movies. Here and now, it was only me, and I had to be conscientious about this whole process or I would find myself in way over my head. I had to be focused. And my intention had to be clear.

What was my intention? Locate a dark teacher ... as I said these words to myself, I could feel another voice finish it for me ... *that you have unfinished business with*. What? Startled momentarily, I knew it was true, in the core of me. I knew that energy. That is why it was so powerful to me. That is why I channeled it. That is why it nearly knocked me down. I thought of the Harry Potter stories and how Harry had been so connected all along to the Dark Lord Voldemort. Was it like that? No, it felt more like a teacher-student relationship. And I instantly knew who was the teacher and who was the student. That meant I was already working with an inequality of authority. Add that onto this insurmountable task, I felt overwhelmed. I supposed there comes a time in every student's apprenticeship when they must face the teacher in order to own his or her own power, even if it was lifetimes later. But why now? The voice returned, *why not?*

That answer was not enough. I knew my heart and mind would be searching for a reason this had come into play. I think of the karmic world as a cone-shaped crater lake. Walking peacefully along the rim of the lake, looking into the deep blue water, the depth is incomprehensible from the top until something happens. You slip and in you go. You can't climb out of the karmic lake until you have gotten what you came for. I imagined I was in a swirling eddy in this deep and cold karmic crater lake. No sense fighting it. Where to go now?

I decided to go up to my office and sit with this. Pulling my sitting cushion up under me, I sat quietly for some time. Through long slow breaths, I gathered my strength. I allowed the quiet to calm me. Then I formed a question in my mind. It was directed to my highest guidance.

Do I know this dark teacher? Then I held the energy of the being who had possessed the man in the truck. Without a moment's hesitation, I knew the answer was *yes*.

Not really wanting to ask the next question, I was reminded about a wise man's admonition: Don't ask a question if you don't want to know the answer. I asked anyway. *How do I know this being?*

The answer came in a swirl, as if that karmic lake had a whirlpool in it and I was being sucked down into it.

Falling, feeling the floor fall from under me, I was losing a grasp on my sitting cushion, but I still grabbed onto its sides anyway. I allowed the answer to come. I allowed the visuals to make themselves known. I could feel different energies or presences. There were eyes staring at me, remembrances of relationships, all swirling around me, like being in a film where the camera is circling the subject, around and around. So much for being focused, I remember thinking. I could feel the energy shift as we got closer to the time bubble we were going to view. Perhaps *enter* is a better word. I knew I was doing more than just viewing. I was *revisiting*. As the energy began to stabilize, I could feel the presence of someone powerful and dark.

It was unlike anything I was familiar with in this life, yet it was very familiar. Very familiar.

I had arrived. Looking around, I wanted to see the presence, as if seeing it would help me understand everything I needed to know. But I only saw the place. I was alone. There was a darkish room, or was it a house, a workshop, not sure? I tried to allow the place to come into focus. I could see plants in lots of different containers. Perhaps we were in a greenhouse of sorts? No. That didn't feel right. My stomach was churning. Something I was going to see, or maybe the time bubble itself was not welcomed in my heart. Looking through the windows, I could see it was dusk outside. I could not get a clear view of what was out there. Trees, some things hanging down, perhaps Spanish Moss? Inside, I could now see more in focus. There was a large stone fireplace. There were nice objects all around me. Someone here had a taste for fine art and décor. That thought did not make me feel any more at ease. If anything, it made me feel closer to what I did not want to know. I knew I was somehow responsible for this luxury and the beautiful surroundings. I did not ask myself how.

Assuming I was a visitor, I continued to peruse the place. It became more comfortable and more familiar. I would see an object and instantly know what was in it and what it was used for. I was used to being a neutral observer in other people's time bubbles. This one was way too personal. There was no question, I was ready to turn back. Except to turn back meant I would leave so close to the answer and eventually have to come back again. Only the next time would be even more fearful at having run away once. I braced myself for what I was going to find out.

Just as my hand touched a white feather attached to a writing utensil, someone entered the room talking to someone else. My instinct was to freeze and cloak my presence. After all, I was not sure if I was actually there in their time bubble or if I was accessing it only through my memory. These two people were passionate and lively, talking with great animation, yet clearly not agreeing on the topic. I did not want to interfere at this point. No sense becoming the object of their increasing animosity.

Then I saw them. A tall statuesque woman, clearly in the powerful stage of her life, claiming her own with this man next to her, she was … *what?* She was … my heart leapt. I did not expect this. I did not expect to find this dark woman, poised and elegant, carrying a strong scent of mystery and poison, darkness and passion, focus and treachery, malice and evil, I did not expect that to be ... *me.* I blinked and recoiled. I had never owned that much personal power in this life. Where did it go? I stumbled backwards. I saw her look over as if an invisible curtain had been disturbed. Frozen in my spot, I did not breathe. I had to wake up. I had to return to my sitting cushion. That was enough. That was what I needed to know. Yet, was that the being I sensed in the Eyes? No. It was not. I must be patient. I was so close. I had to wait. Wait for it. Who is she talking to? Is this him? Who could possibly have enough guts and power to argue with *her*?

Then I saw him. I knew him immediately. I realize I could have described him in intimate detail before he walked into my vision. He was also tall, but not elegant like the woman. He was a force to be contended with. He was pure energy. He embodied life, passion and he had bottled and contained it. And perhaps some times it was too much for him, like a wild stallion, but he never let himself be thrown. His muscles were taut and strong. His jaw was fixed and angular from many, many years of holding his will against the world. His eyes were penetrating and fierce, yet there was a hint of laughter somewhere in there. What was I looking at? This was the being behind the Eyes, but he had become something else since this time bubble. What had transpired? Why was I being shown this now?

As soon as I formed that thought, the two became more animated than they already had been. I knew this was a moment in time where they reached an irreconcilable difference. This is when things took a turn. This is what was left unfinished perhaps?

"It isn't up to you, Raymond."

"Do you even think in the remotest recesses of your mind that I would leave this up to anyone, even you? You do not understand. You have always been so driven, you missed what this is about. This is bigger than either of us, my love. I have waited lifetimes for this. I am not about to join some group consensus to dissect this mammoth power into a million miniscule bits of nothingness."

She cut him off. "You arrogant bastard. You always planned to claim it for yourself, didn't you? Well, I will not let you do that."

He jumped right in without missing a syllable, "*Over your dead body, Leticia?*"

The room shifted for me, and maybe for them. I cannot be sure. I could tell I was not in the presence of two normal people. I had already known this, but up until now, nothing gave that away. The place reeked with poised threats of dark power. She did not back down, but neither did he. It was as if they called their potentiality to them to arm their resolve. The animated conversation came to a disturbing halt. They both knew they were no longer comrades, but powerful foes. To share anything else meant to give information to the enemy. It wasn't quiet that descended upon them, it was the absence of any energy whatsoever. It was as if they were both claiming all the air and energy in the room to arm themselves. Even the energy of the objects and furniture was taking sides, lining up with one force or another. I felt a dread and tenseness overcome my being. I knew this was not going to have a happy outcome.

The room began to fade. I felt myself lose my sense of connectedness to this time and place and I started to become aware of my own body there in my office, seated on my sitting cushion, knuckles white from clutching the sides. As I loosened my grip, I began to ponder what I had witnessed. I had a barrage of questions.

I breathed deeply for the first time since I had entered the karmic space of Raymond and Leticia. I took notes, scribbling all the details I could remember from the experience. Raymond and Leticia. Odd. I had always used the name Raymond Bagdad as a fantasy character when I was young, pretending to have a foreign romance, when I was really too embarrassingly shy to even speak to a boy. Had I recalled this name from my past? So much more to contemplate. Somehow I felt I had gained access to something helpful, but at the same time, I had taken the bait that he had set for me. Did I even have a choice? *Why are you talking like that? He does NOT own you, Leticia.* As I said that name, I froze in shock. Why did I call myself Leticia? Maybe it was somehow true in the bigger sense, but not in this time bubble. I must still have strings of attachment to these characters, but how? I suddenly realized that this whole experience had much more to do with me than just locating a murderer.

Would it mean regaining that power? I shuddered. How could I want that? It was so dark and foul with suspicion and deceit. It was not love. I did not want it. And yet, did I need it? Was I saying I did not want it like so many sour grapes? Was this the next step in my own spiritual journey? So many conflicting feelings and emotions. I needed to find balance. I could feel my heart close when I began to think of the power that was once mine. But why would my heart close unless I had instructed it to do so? Is there anything inherently wrong with power? Isn't it required to truly know you carry all possible potentiality within? Who was speaking in me, where was my own truth? Everything was making sense and not, and as much as I did not want to know it, I knew I had only begun to find out what was behind the Eyes and my relationship with him. I also had a premonition it was not going to be effortless. In fact, this was indeed uncharted territory. If I could always stay in the Lighthouse, I would be safe. I would be the light that signals lost souls to shore and safety. Yet now I was being asked to venture into the deep blue, beyond shore's sight. I needed to reclaim something that belonged to me far from the safety of land. Yet did it? Was it someone else's? Did I need to return something? I was beyond confused.

18

Derek talked nonstop for about three hours and left my head filled with one heck of a complex bunch of operations all going this way and that, headed by one guy, one cartel, funded by some other program, government, mega-corporation, half the alphabet departments of the USA. Drugs moving here, there, everywhere. More money than you can imagine. Lots of double dealings. But mostly, one sophisticated network where it was impossible to know who the bad guys were. The war on drugs was good money all around.

I listened and tried to take in as much as I could. I think Derrick was just trying to impress me. I imagine some of it was even true. Hell, who knows, maybe it was all true. But it wasn't all seminal to my mission so I glazed over most of it in my mind. I had no interest in picking a war with the way things are. I wasn't down here to be any kind of hero, and I wasn't here at all on a mission from Uncle Sam. Invisible uniform or not. I knew they were playing me with the reinstatement and all. I knew that they'd hang me out to dry if it served the greater good. Or any good, for that matter. Right now I was the go-to boy for the colonel and the general. I had some lift under my wings with the O-6 thing, and I had access to all kinds of intel and access to more sub-departments than I ever had when I was in uniform.

We went out for a couple of beers after Derrick's briefing and then he cut me loose back at the house. Said his man would collect me at seven the next morning. Then he was gone.

I was tired and not just a little bit overwhelmed by the whole thing as I came back into the house and heard that metal grate close over the front door. Everything in my body wanted a hot shower and a bed. Everything. I must have stood there about a minute before I shook it off, went back to my room and grabbed my bag. I was out the door and down the street before anyone could even plan to come. Not saying that anyone was coming, but if there were some bad men with ugly guns, they'd wait 'till three or four in the morning. You've got to listen to the small, quiet voice in your gut. Act first, think later. Hear a shot, hit the ground, then look up to see if it was just a backfire from some cab. You can't do it the other way.

I was still breathing the next day, so I'll never know if there was anything in store for me or not. Does not go the other way. Can't say, 'now I'm dead, I guess I should'a prepared for that one.'

Had one hell of a hot shower in the airport Hilton and was out quicker than I can ever remember before. Not typical for me to fall asleep so quickly or sleep so deeply.

Next thing I knew was my cell phone ringing in my head.

"Nick, you SOB!" Derrick's voice was way too chipper for a Hilton wake up call. "My man didn't find anything but this number pasted to the front door. What were you thinking, man? Old Derrick was setting you up?" He went on for a bit and sounded generally hurt. I couldn't make out anything in his voice.

"No, Derrick. Nothing like that. Just some barking dog. It was him or me, and I'm not going to jail in this town for taking out a dog." I said without missing a beat. I'm generally pretty quick with the words.

"Dog? Dog! Holy shit. I'm sorry Nick. I thought I was doing you a favor with the house and all. Sorry Nick. Where the hell are you anyway? You've got to get going. My man is ready, and the meet is set. This isn't one you want to be late. Lack of respect."

Respect. That wasn't my highest priority for where I was heading today.

"Radisson. Give me thirty minutes. I'll be out front."

"Twenty minutes, Nick. He'll be there first." I could tell he knew I wasn't at the Radisson.

The games men play ... I rolled over and sure wanted to go back to sleep. Two minutes for a shower, cup of java in the lobby and twenty bucks got the airport shuttle to take me over. I had time enough to walk through the front door and back out just as the same guy who picked me up yesterday pulled up, one big-assed grin and all. "Where to, señor?" He asked like it was some private joke.

"How 'bout you just drive and let me get some more sleep." I think I hurt his feelings because he didn't say a word for the next hour as we wound out of town and up into the mountains. Guatemala City is not what you'd call a prime tourist destination.

I didn't sleep. Time to plan, get in character. I've been in a lot of bad places over the years, but this was the World Series of them all. I wasn't sure if this was sanctioned, but I wasn't sure if it wasn't, either. I had travel orders, but no mission orders. I was looking for someone who was officially dead, but when he was alive worked for us. I was in enemy territory. That was a certainty. Last time I was in a place like this I had lots of armed men with me, and we were all trying to do serious harm to the men I was going to meet now. I was a lot older now. Slower. Out of touch. Hell, I don't even know who's friend and who's foe. About all I knew about these guys was that after the peace treaty, all the bad guys changed faces. The old government oppressors became the new drug oppressors and the old footmen became the new footmen. I wasn't going into a dirt village with a bunch of bumpkins. Most of the widespread criminal element in the drug pipeline was formed of ex-soldiers and special forces. These guys were better trained and better armed than the police or even the military. I still remember swallowing my stomach when that SAM came up on that mission in Ecuador. They sure as hell weren't supposed to have SAMs.

A four-hour drive is a long time to think, and that's what I did—mostly. What the hell was I doing, anyway? Sounded like a good idea at the time. I guess I share some of the responsibility for Merkle and that last mission we were on. We all share it. Colonel more than me. That's for sure. The general. Now I know it's on his shoulders, too. No doubt about it. None at all. But then why am I the guy who's about an hour away from being put in a fifty-gallon drum filled with gasoline? At least that's the image that keeps popping into my head. Don't even know where that one came from. Don't even know if that that happens in real life. I heard it somewhere that they put this DEA agent into a drum of gasoline and set him on fire. Maybe it was just some sick-ass movie. Never really happened in real life. Maybe not.

By the time we were pretty well into the mountains Carlos, the driver, was warming up again and we tried to make small talk. My Spanish is pretty good, and I was enjoying talking about nothing. Just enjoying the language.

We were going on about how corrupt the government was when all of a sudden he turned cold and slowed. I hadn't been paying much attention, but when I looked up I think I was somehow comically relieved to see three big shinny black Chevy Suburbans ahead. The more sinister they tried to look the more I felt like laughing. I watch a lot of movies and wonder if these guys get their ideas from Hollywood, or if it's the other way around.

"This is it, señor," Carlos smiled and looked concerned and even caring. He shook my hand and I felt as if he knew I was off on a one-way mission. Didn't even say anything about picking me back up.

"Two hours, Carlos. Right here. Two hours. I'm not walking back to town." He nodded his assent, but I didn't get the feeling he was planning anything other that a fast trip back to the city.

I got out of the car and walked straight to the first Suburban. Nothing happened for the obligatory minute or so as they established that their dicks were much bigger than mine. I was biting the inside of my lip to keep from smirking. These guys may be battle hardened ex-special forces or maybe just punks influenced by Hollywood, but either way they sure as hell outgunned me. That's like 200 to zero, by the way. So I thought better of pissing off anyone's ego.

Finally, the back door on the side opposite where I was standing opened, but nobody got out. I stood for a few seconds, waiting, then walked around and got in. No hellos, no words at all. And no pat-down, either. Maybe they were making the point that to pat me down implied they were in the least bit concerned for their own welfare.

Took about another hour even farther up into the mountains. I was a little concerned that they didn't hood me, either. Maybe they weren't concerned about me coming back and giving up their location. Maybe they weren't concerned with me coming back at all. Beautiful countryside on the way up. Kind of like the high mountains up in Montana, actually. Very comfortable in the Suburban, air conditioning on full blast. I wouldn't have thought to bring a jacket. After the initial settling in, the ride wasn't bad. Nobody spoke a word. I started to imagine the drug lord's mansion. Like in the movies. Long drive up through sculptured lawns after we got through the fortified gate. Armed guards with automatic weapons everywhere. A beautiful wife slinking around, proud, but deferent to the master. Maybe we'd have an affair when he was out surveying his coca plants or the production of thousands of kilos of cocaine. I was getting a little lost in my fantasy and getting not just a little sleepy, when we turned off the road and came around to a small, but very serene clearing at the side of a creek.

One suburban stopped back closer to the road, and mine and the other one pulled up under a huge shade tree. The guy sitting next to me reached across my body and opened the door and with a nod signaled me to get out. As I did, there was a young man, about mid-thirties, I'd guess, getting out of the other suburban. Nobody else got out, and nobody opened any of the windows. He stretched, smiled and came over to me with his hand out.

I don't think anything could have been as unbalancing as that. He looked genuinely friendly and gave me a very sincere handshake.

"Señor Drake, allow me to introduce myself. My name is Marco Sanchez. I apologize for the long day we've put you though. I hope you understand that you cannot come to my home, and I had no wish to humiliate you with a hood over your head or even to dishonor you with a physical pat-down of your body." He stood perfectly still with an unwavering gaze into my eyes.

"I'm …" I couldn't think of a thing to say to that, "thank you. Thank you for that."

"Shall we sit by the river?" He turned and walked toward some large rocks overlooking the stream. I didn't know if there was someone with a bead on me from the suburban, but even if there was, he would have to shoot through the glass, and I could have taken this guy out well before that, had I been armed.

We sat by the water a little while without talking. He seemed to be comfortable there and completely unconcerned. I felt the wind leaking out of my sails. Right about the time I was wondering if I was going to be able to say my, "bring down the wrath of God," line on him for the murder of the daughter of the man who controlled the greatest armed force in the world, he said, "Señor Drake, or should I call you Colonel Drake? May I congratulate you on your promotion? Full colonel is a rank of great responsibility and honor." And he laid an almost delicate hand on mine.

For the second time I felt like a mouth full of cotton was choking me, "How did you … Thank you, the rank does carry some responsibility with it."

"And power, no?"

"Power. Yea, I guess you could say that. But in our military, power is very compartmentalized. I answer to someone who answers to someone who implements government policy. But yea, I guess I have more autonomy in decision making as a colonel."

"Why did you leave the service? If I may pry? But, please, tell me if it is none of my business." Mostly I just thought without replying. First thing that came to my mind was trying to answer that question. I've tried for lots of years—without success. But then the question of how the hell he knew any of this and what was it his business anyway?

"Thank you for meeting with me. We're not exactly on the same side of the law, you know." He nodded a resigned affirmation. "Can we get to business?"

"Business?" He seemed genuinely confused

"Business. Get down to business. What we came here to talk about."

"Oh, business!" He exclaimed up with a broad smile. "Forgive me. When I get down to business, it is not with a man such as yourself." He was still smiling, "and I mean that as the greatest compliment." I suddenly understood what business meant to this man.

"I won't insult you with any background on my mission. I don't know how, but I know your intel far out-shines my own on this. I'm down here in the dark. I'm looking for a man and the forces behind me are relentless. I'm just a small cog in this search."

"Pardon me, Colonel Drake. My intel, as you put it certainly does put me in a position to know you are not a cog at all. I do not think that the great General DeWitt would send a mere lackey in the search for the man who murdered his only daughter. And Colonel Richards, what can I say about that man?" He didn't need to have that question answered.

I realized that we were sitting at Yalta, at the end of World War II. We were in the negotiations that would either bring down the *wrath of God* as I had rehearsed the line, or see to the laying down of swords. They failed at Yalta, and the cold war was born. This man who could buy and sell half the countries in the world was sitting here by a creek in the mountains of Guatemala to prevent a war that he, or we, for that matter, could not win.

"Colonel Drake, I know what happened to those two unfortunate women and I beg you to convey my deepest and most sincere condolences to the fathers. Allow me to tell you everything I know. I am certain you will leave this place with more than you came looking for and we will all go back to our lives. I am sorry that does not apply to Rebecca and Samantha."

I was beyond being surprised by the time he said their names. What didn't he know?

I'm not a chatty man, but I'm not a silent one either. But for the next hour the story he told me left me with nothing to say. No response. This was the mission, and I didn't glaze over any of it in my mind. I could tell when he had said all he had come to say. He looked over towards the suburban with the most subtle nod and then sat looking at me with finality. I don't think he had any need for my response. I was once again in the place I lived. Enough data for action, but never enough for the whole picture. My place on the food chain. Higher than most, lower than some.

It was only about five minutes from when he nodded that I heard it. First just the chirp of a songbird, then the thunder of a Dolphin 65. Twin turbines, 175 knots. Used by the coast guard as their primary chase and attack helicopter. About $10 million depending on equipment.

"Please accept this convenience as my final apology for your long day. My helicopter will take you to the airport in much more comfort than your journey out here." And with that he got up, we shook hands, and he walked back to the suburban. They drove off as I stood there wondering what was in store for me next. I walked over and climbed aboard and we were off the ground before I sat down.

We got to altitude and hit 145 knots indicated. The sound of the engine faded into the background as I felt myself falling back in time to Marco's story. I had remembered the first part of it differently. I guess everyone sees what they see only through their own eyes. I could see that I was in the chain of command back then, but not as much a player as I thought. The colonel carried the most responsibility even though his hand was never on a trigger. The general was the puppet master as far as I could tell, but after hearing more, I even began to doubt that. Someone was pulling his strings, but that was so far up the chain I'd never know who.

We had been tasked with drug interdiction along the Honduran- Nicaraguan border. Mountainous terrain but nothing too impossible. We had pretty good air cover, and that was my primary responsibility. 37 guys with boots on the ground. A strange number I thought then, and still remember to this day. We had high cover with a U-2 tasked from Beale AFB, for the silent eye in the sky. The U-2 seemed a bit overkill back then, but I had the idea they wanted to make this one work for the media. Prime time stuff to show the world we were winning the war on drugs. These were the pre-drone days. Nowadays we'd have some kid back at Nellis sitting in front of a computer controlling a Predator or something. We were still in the bad old days, 1997. Hell, that's already 15 years. Merkle's been gone 15 years? I made a note to check my dates, or at least my memory. Doesn't seem like 15 years. I had two Cobra gunships armed to the hilt. That was still one kickass machine of death in those days even though it already had 30 years in service. After the episode with the SAMs in Ecuador, we had to re-evaluate our tactics. I was flying with a captain from the Honduran air force. A Gonzales or something like that. Maybe Cardenas. Not a friendly guy at all. I had rank on him, but it was his airplane. Old story.

The conventional wisdom of the day was that since we had a presence in Honduras, we would do interdiction from there. One bad day intel came across that the Columbians were running a pipeline out of a little shit-hole called Tolu about 60 miles due south of Cartagena. Crazy thing. Nowadays Columbia is a great tourist destination. Back then they kept us busy. The more things change … They were supposed to be heading out to sea, passing Panama and Costa Rica then right into Bluefields in Nicaragua. Then overland to the bay northwest of Chinandega, then back to sea across the bay into El Salvador at El Tamarindo, then across El Salvador through Metapan and across the border. From there, right across the middle of Guatemala to southern Mexico a little east of Comitan. I remember Master Sergeant Danfort snorting and almost spitting out that soggy cigar of his when I first sat down with him and this crap pack of intel. Went something like, "Well sir. That's damn near 500 nautical miles across open seas, then another 300 minimum to Chinandega. You've got another water crossing and a border after that. Up to the Guatemala border … Sir, what the hell is this? Who the hell would take that route when they could just go straight on up to Mexico, or just all the way to Texas, Florida, wherever the hell they want?"

I don't remember the exact words, but Danfort wasn't one to mince words about.

"That's pure hooey, sir. If you ask me." And he knew I was always asking him. It was our asses on the line—always. We both read the glowing reports of how we had the gulf routes all tied up tight, forcing everything overland. Nothing but success stories to prove we were winning the war on drugs. I didn't like that Nicaraguan connection at all. Sounded a lot like the drug pipeline built with US money to the contras in the '80s. Maybe this didn't have anything to do with that, but neither of us liked what was ahead.

"Where'd this pile of intel come from this time, sir?" Then we'd be off on our typical assessment of the CIA pukes who came up with the shit that got us in trouble more often than not. I never could figure if they were just stupid, or corrupt, or just on their own agendas that we weren't privy to.

We planned and prepped for the mission, and it really wasn't much deeper than that. Well, until now. Today I learned what someone sure as hell could have told me back then; that not only the central region of Guatemala, which I knew, but also that northern Honduras was controlled by the Iron Fist. Had been General Umberto Sanchez of the Guatemalan army, and who controlled what our guys said was the most brutal of the special forces who erased town after town over the twenty years prior to the peace treaty. I mean erased as in about 300,000 civilian deaths and the destruction of over 200 towns and cities. This was a very bad man. Evil in every way. And evil like that doesn't just disappear, it just changes faces. The peace treaty changed all the faces. Guatemala is really a very nice place, comparatively, these days. At least the Mayans aren't being tortured and raped as an official government policy anymore. General Umberto Sanchez—a man I would never want to meet. And I had just had a pleasant sit down with his son Marco. And I was still sitting in his 10 million dollar helicopter on the way to the airport.

Life sure as hell has its way.

Mission details weren't that important, but it was that mission where Merkle was cut to pieces. It was times like that, that probably put the images in my head of men in burning barrels of gasoline. Only it was machetes for Merkle. We lost three men on the assault of a convoy of trucks carrying drugs. Only they weren't drugs. They were some pretty high-tech ex-Soviet anti-personnel weapons. We were outgunned and out-positioned on the ground. Still not in Guatemala, but inside Sanchez's lands. Luckily there wasn't much in the way of surface-to-air, but that didn't help the guys on the ground. There was no chance in hell to retrieve the bodies. Not without losing more. I called a bug out and a couple Black Hawks did the pickup. The Cobras tore the hell out of everything they could see and we were gone. All I had after were some grainy photos from that U-2 that the analysts swore was three of our guys being dismembered in the center of a group of soldiers. Merkle was a head above the next tallest guy in the outfit and we all must have seen just what we thought we saw. I know I saw Hank Merkle die that day along with two other of my men.

We were hell of in the wrong place at the wrong time. Worst thing about the whole thing was that wasn't the last time in my life I've been in the wrong place at the wrong time.

Marco Sanchez was in his early 30s when that mission took place, so he must be about 50 now. I had pegged him for late 30s. Shows what I know. I could tell that he was making it clear to me, and maybe to my masters, that he was not his father. But at the same time he was his father's son and not to be trifled with. I didn't need to hear that because when he turned his back to me and walked to the river, I knew that he knew that if I were armed and here to kill him, he'd be dead. Me too, but he'd be dead first. He showed me that he wasn't afraid of me or of the United States. He just didn't want a war, and wanted his business to go on as usual. I guess he assumed I'd go back and make a full report. He was wrong about that. I may be wearing the eagles again, but I wasn't here for my masters, wasn't some errand boy.

Apparently his father had watched as the first two of my men lost were chopped to death. The old man, who must have been at least 70 at the time, and who had supervised one of the greatest mass genocides in history, watched with no emotion, Marco told me that was how he heard of it later. The men cried in fear, and begged as any normal man would, but the one man, Merkle, showed no emotion. Just looked straight into the old man's eyes as he stood watching. When it was Merkle's time to die, the old man yelled to stop and took the machete himself. He cleaved through Merkle's left arm cleanly severing it at the elbow. Marco told me that as the story was retold, it grew each time. Merkle, standing unmoving, blood spurting from the stump. The old man stared back, transfixed and then suddenly took off his own belt and wrapped it around the arm as a tourniquet. Merkle by that time had passed out from lack of blood and the old man himself lowered him to the ground. He ordered his men to carry Merkle into his truck and they drove off. Marco said he had heard the story many times over the years, but never from his father.

The old man was incensed at the attack on his cargo. Marco said that he took it as a personal attack against his own honor, that it had been the Americans who gave him the power in the first place. I had some knowledge about the CIA's involvement in setting up a military junta in the mid 50s and that regime had been the birth of what was later the genocide against the people. Stinking CIA. Man, I always hated those guys. It had to have been *big* money. American Fruit Company maybe. Their monopoly for years, maybe drugs. What the hell were we into back in the 50s? I promised myself I'd look into it when I got back. I knew I wouldn't. I had enough blood on my hands from being a puppet. I led enough missions myself that led to nothing but death and the change of one bad man for another, with the only benefit being that the new guy was *our* bad man.

The general stewed in his affront and Marco felt that was the beginning of the end for him. Only the end took 15 years in coming. He said that it was out of proportion to anything he'd ever seen from his father. He thought that it was because, in his own way, his father felt that the Americans were his friends and supported what he did. It was the Americans who gave him power in the first place. It was only when the truth came and the world outcry became so loud that they turned on him and denounced what he had done. He felt the Americans were cowards and liars and that one day he would punish them for what they had done to him and to his country. He took Merkle on as his number one man and they became like father and son. The more vengeful and hateful his father became, the more Merkle grew closer and the farther Marco became. Marco Sanchez made no apologies for the business that he became ever more a part of running, all the while his father and Merkle spent time together. The old man never released his iron fist, Marco was clear on that. And even though he was no longer in charge of atrocities, he still made it perfectly clear that no man would ever wrong him again. He didn't elaborate on what that meant, but I felt that Merkle was part of it. At least part of the enforcement, and maybe even the planning.

It was during the last years of the old man's life that more and more of Merkle's true self surfaced and it was here that he felt the stage was set for the horrors that befell the daughters of General DeWitt and Colonel Richards. As the old man grew ever more vengeful of the memory of the Americans' attack, Merkle also grew to hate those who, he felt, were responsible for his lost arm and lost honor. That, not only did they take his arm, they abandoned him. He never attributed the loss of his arm to Marco's father. His hatred was squarely set upon the colonel and General DeWitt who had masterminded the attack in the first place. Together they seemed to forge an ever entwining memory of the wrongs that befell them that day. And

Merkle never lost the pain in his arm. Marco told me that his father spent endless money on doctors the world over in trying to erase the phantom limb pain that woke him screaming in pain nearly every night. The pain twisted him and forged his hatred of the masters who deserted him.

When he told me that, he could see, or feel the change in me. I don't think it was fear, but I wouldn't swear by that. I knew I was dead center in that chain of command and responsibility. I took my orders and it was no one other than me who put Merkle and the other men on the ground on that mission. Marco then turned and looked at me with the most caring eyes I could ever imagine and said that I had nothing to fear. That over the years he knew Hans Merkle there were rare occasions when the man would seem to soften and warm, even become melancholy. In those times he spoke of his commanding officer, that was me, in the most honored of ways. He told me that in Merkle's twisted mind, it was I alone who protected and cared for him. That it was I who was wronged and used by my masters and that had there been any way under heaven, that I would have rescued him, but that since I did not, that I was as wronged as he was. I knew then he had gone completely insane. I had imagined he was on the verge of insanity when he was first attached to our unit by the general's orders, but I never would have imagined how far it would go.

Derrick Witkin told me that the general's organization was still the primary transfer apparatus of the most significant pipeline of drugs coming from South America on their way north, but that it was Marco Sanchez who was the brains behind the growth of the empire. But nobody ever mistook who was the force behind it and why it was never challenged, even by our *war on drugs* apparatus. It seemed that there was a strange kind of truce. Right there I was again way above my pay grade and this was someone else's war.

The familiar sound of the rotors changing pitch pulled me back to reality as we approached the airport. I could see we were about to set down next to a Gulfstream biz jet, which I imagined to be another of Marco's conveniences for me. Man hands you ten dollars, you put it in your pocket. But this time I begged off with a, "no thanks," and headed to the commercial terminal. Flying in the man's helicopter out of the mountains was one thing, but I wasn't going to be chauffeured home in his jet. Got to the terminal, but there was nothing else heading out tonight. I just grabbed the shuttle back to the Hilton. I could use another night to think, anyway.

19

It suddenly occurred to me that I may have an advantage here. I was presently *in a body* and Raymond was not. If he were, he would not have had to occupy the man I saw in that truck. There was no question, the man himself was no Raymond. He was nothing but a puppet. For the first time in a long time, I felt a bit euphoric at uncovering a trump card. But it did not take a moment as I turned the card over, to realize this could be my greatest disadvantage. I was findable. I was flesh and blood. I could be hurt and clearly I had the limitations of time, space and matter. He could *not* be hurt. He could vacate any body he chose to inhabit, and did *not* have the limitations of time, space and matter. I was back to where I started, yet it had evoked a question in my mind, "Why would he want to finish this now, when he was not capable of physically containing the power he so wanted for himself?"

I remember the feeling years ago when I first learned how to open the doors to the non-physical world. I felt like a blind person trying to define an unimaginable landscape. Just when I thought I had everything figured out, I would drop into a Grand Canyon of incomprehensible depth and breadth. Early on in my work I came to understood that exactly as in this world, there are no free lunches. Energy is power and we are living beings of vital energy.

I reminded myself of this as I thought of the power I registered in the time bubble of Raymond and Leticia. Both would energetically register as demonic forces while *in* a body. Outside of a body, what would that vital and powerful energy feel like? I already had enough of a taste to know that it was certainly foreboding.

Tomorrow began a weekend workshop where I was teaching astrology to understand your spiritual journey. I needed to focus on that and get my handouts ready. Putting my fascination with power aside, I then started to wonder if I could locate anything in my own chart that would offer an advantage here. I left this thought to search my computer for the list of glyphs of planets and signs and began to print and collate the papers for the group tomorrow evening. As my mind turned to something lighter, I felt a heavy burden temporarily lift. I reminded myself that I was just a simple person with unusual gifts. I did not have to save the world from evil demons. I was simply resolving unfinished business. That's right, I convinced myself.

Just as I attempted to sort out my papers and locate my own natal chart for demonstration purposes, I saw Pluto rear up from the paper wheel chart and glare at me in the eyes. What? I had looked at my astrological chart a hundred times, yet this time Pluto seemed to have moved. I know it hadn't, but it felt so unfamiliar in this location that I swore I had never seen it before. I felt the familiar twinge of intuition and paid attention. I grabbed my best book on interpreting Pluto. Pluto represents the underworld, the dark places in your being, the unresolved parts of your psyche and the places where we hold secrets. It would be like me to avoid this planet. I'm pretty simple, I think. Seems like secrets don't find their way to me. I think of secrets like cats, and I am more like a dog. Yet it felt like I was being told *some secrets we don't even know we have.*

I was reminded of the style of art that I suddenly started painting a few years ago, very different than anything I'd done before, much darker and soulful. This feeling somehow felt just like that, that I had some very dark secrets, filled with anguish and despair. There in my mind's eye was the painting of a gnomish creature of such pain, then one of a little girl bolting up from a nightmare, evil still swirling in the darkness around her. I do remember a witch and her pointed hat in the background, one of those unintentional strokes of paint that created something from the deep subconscious. I had not intended to paint any of the dark creatures in the background. But there they were nonetheless. Was my subconscious mind trying to unearth something for me then? Prepare me for what lay ahead? Warn me I had unresolved darkness afoot?

Pluto, what are you doing to me? I opened Jeff Green's book, *Pluto*, to the house placement of this mysterious planet in my birth chart.

"The need to know and expand constantly undermines the security created by the knowledge accumulated ... I got that indeed ... *there's a need to understand the world in a larger and larger framework ...* I certainly was beginning to see my world from a more encompassing viewpoint, past,

present and future lives!... *evolution occurs by progressively teaching the whole truth, essentially that all paths lead to the realization of Truth* ... this felt right, deep in my bones ... it felt like an arrow for me right now ... *can expose underlying issues* ..." there, I knew it. I knew there was an Ace in here somewhere. I stopped reading and focused on the truth, the knowing that no matter what happens it brings us all to our highest potential eventually. Eventually.

I read on. *"Surrender to the universal spirit and you will possess an inner light that transcends rational explanation."* My heart locked onto this. My mind needed something to hold on to, but my heart had found what it was looking for. What Pluto was illuminating for me was the message of our inner light. Do not lose sight of that.

My eyes caught the last paragraph, *"... resonates with an electrical field of another to trigger a neurological response that alerts to their needs."* Wow, I had felt that, not only with my clients, but with the Eyes. Raymond. Yes, the Eyes were Raymond. I now had a name and as ancient lore suggests, uncover their name and you have taken some of their mystery and power. And I had just been armed by validating some innate gifts. They would serve me well in this strange, other-worldly adventure. At least I hoped I could still call it an adventure later. My gut told me this might be classified as an adventure, but not of the Disney variety.

Surrender to the Universal Spirit would be my mantra, I knew that much.

20

Pretty late by the time I checked in and showered. Had a moderately tasteless Reuben with fries and a beer, then went back to work.

Lots of info, most of which was not seminal to the mission, but that's always the case. Data comes in loads. The task is to separate out the chaff. Set it aside. My mind was cycling through all Marco had told me, playing it back on endless loop. The emotions were feeding that, I'm sure. Lots of guilt in there, too. I knew that was a bad mission, knew it at the time. The chief knew it too. Only difference was that he just took orders. It was me who gave them, especially the bug out. And it was only me who carried that.

No matter. Not now. I pushed that pain back down in deep and cleared my mind and started making out my chart.

Thesis: Merkle and General Sanchez—revenge

Known players: Dewitt and the colonel. They were clearly the chain of command who put it all together at the level I knew about then. Me too, but Marco cleared me in Merkle's mind, logical or not. Not logical in any way or form, but set that one aside for now. Don't discount it.

The connection was too clear. I felt silly writing it all out, building my background framework for the mission. Sanchez was wronged, went over the edge, let that hate build up for years, but never did anything about it except talk. Who cares why, maybe the time wasn't right. Maybe his mind just wasn't right. Merkle. Went nuts as well, but he was on the edge of that before he came into the unit. I did a Google search on phantom limb pain. You hear about that, but never really give it any thought. Seems that the body is wired everywhere with nerves that originate in the brain and through their network connect to every cell in the body. Where they connect in the brain is called the homunculus and it's like some kind of representative picture of the body. It's distorted, though. The hands are huge because there are so many neurons connecting to the hands and fingers. That's why we have such fine tactile sense and fine motor control with our hands. A place like the middle of the back is small in the Homunculus because we don't have many neurons there. Sensations are not very discernable in the middle of the back. Not like the fingers. When you lose an arm, the severed endings of all those neurons that went to the hands are still sending signals up to the homunculus, even though there's nothing down there. The brain sometimes can't process that, and doesn't know how to shut off the traffic. In the worst case, it's like the itch you can never scratch. But the way Marco described Merkle, it wasn't an itch he couldn't scratch, it was more like having that arm cut off that he couldn't stop feeling—ever. I'm sure as hell not the guy to fault him for going insane. Not with that pain going on. I got into wondering why he never attributed that pain to Sanchez, but that's off track so it went deep along with the other memories.

So, here I have the seed planted. Way back in the mid-fifties, the CIA engineers a coup of the Guatemalan government and it's replaced with a military junta that evolves into one of the greatest monsters in history. Sanchez is part of that. Like the great America just gave him a country. He wasn't a politician, per se, but sure was positioned to grab more and more military power. Nobody knew much about the Guatemalan genocide until the early 80s, so his power just kept growing. But he was one hell of a bad man from the beginning.

Second, there's Merkle, and I never did know much about his background. But from the scuttlebutt, he was no Mother Teresa. Sanchez must have passed on the seed to him over the years, but in some crazy way just by them being together they must have checked any action. Unknown, can't be known—pass. It just happened that way.

Next, old man Sanchez finally dies and that lets the dog off the leash. Fifteen years of blame growing in an insane mind. Merkle only knows of the immediate chain of command. Me, the colonel, the general. But he shouldn't have known of the general. That's beyond his purview. But then why was it the general's signature on his original orders? What did they have in common? Those orders should have come from way lower down the chain. I went around that one for a while and got nowhere.

I went around all of them and got nowhere. About three in the morning threw in the towel and hit the bed, but all I got was a replay of the bug out.

I know I made the right call. That didn't help. Don't think I slept, but the start I got when the wakeup call came at 4:00 am proved me wrong.

Got to the airport and who was there with that grin on his face? Derrick.

"Nick, you look like shit warmed over, but I'm glad you're still breathing! Wasn't my first choice sending you to Marco Sanchez."

"Seemed like a nice fellow," I couldn't think of anything else to say.

"Like a panther, maybe. Nice to look at and pet, but watch out for those claws when he takes your face off."

"I got all I needed from him, Derrick. Thanks for the meet. I owe you on this one."

"You call me anytime, Nick. Any time. Draw a line from Tijuana to Matamoras, take it down to Natal in Brazil, know where that is? Then on down to Tierra Del Fuego, I know you know where that is. Now that's my house, Nick." He just smiled at me. "You have a question about my house, you just call me. It was you who changed my course in life. Right down at the bottom of that ramp." I still didn't know what to say. "Where to now?"

"Not sure. Not completely. Flight's headed to DC, but that's just 'cause I can't think of anything else. Whole damn thing is too crazy. I'll just climb up the ladder 'till I find something that looks good. I'm stumped here, Derrick. Right now I've got too much history in my head and nowhere to take it." I tried to be polite, but time was getting short.

"Looks like you better move your butt, time's short." He genuinely smiled and stepped up to give me a hug. As I cleared customs, that hug was about the weirdest thing about this whole damn trip.

21

The morning sun was attempting in vain to make its way through the dark winter night. It seemed like hours that I lay in bed watching the window's outline. It was just a rectangle barely one shade lighter than the blackness of the room. Then many, many moments later it suggested a slightly lighter shade onto the rectangle. The darkness of the winter night was tenacious, holding on to its domain. The longer I watched, the more it felt like I was watching myself watch the window, seeking the light. My consciousness felt one step removed from the body it was supposed to occupy. Eyes open, my pupils awaited their natural awakening from the rising sun. Darkness still reigned. Why didn't I fall back to sleep until the sun came? Why must I watch for it? These thoughts the watcher of the watcher had. The one lying in bed only seemed occupied with holding the place marker for a sun to appear.

As I watched along with my body, it occurred to me that there was a silence in my mind. The familiar ever-present voice of my guidance was ... quiet. Quiet? Or gone? At this point in the winter sun's feeble attempt, if I turned on a light inside, it only made it appear much darker outside. So I just waited in the mostly dark, knowing that if I stared at the window frame, it would bring morning. Eventually.

I searched the winter months in my mind. There must have been indicators all along that slipped past me to bring me to this place of such heaviness. My mind's eye recalled one morning some time ago when I had been preparing for clients. The familiar ritual of step-by-step preparation had felt comforting. Yet had I forgotten something important, a vital step? I tried to remember, then caught it, but like a fish sliding back into the water, I only had the fading impression of something there and then gone. Realizing now it was that I had forgotten to do the ever important system check on myself before I began any work on another person. I could see where I had begun to grow cloudy. This check is where I focus on my own energy and balance, then I begin to look for any breaks in the ... had I watered the plants yesterday? Oh yes, I remember I had looked over at my drooping creeping charlie. The water container was downstairs. I had gotten up from my desk to go fetch it. Once there in the kitchen, I decided to add some fertilizer. And then some pistachios caught my eye at the end of the counter. I proceeded to lose myself in the menial task of cracking open each shell to find the fleshy nut inside. My lucid mind started to search for the metaphor there, but returned to the simple task that it was. Thinking back on it all, I realize I had been completely unaware that I was suffering an insidious and slow redirection of my energies.

Then later, was it the same day or a week later, I remember calling a client back in New Jersey, listening to his accent, connecting, but just dutifully fulfilling the tasks of the day. Scheduling, reminding, organizing and so on. Where was my passion? Lying in bed, I tried to ascertain where it went and why I had not noticed anything wrong.

Those days progressed like that, simply, naturally, without a difficulty, in fact, without anything. The watcher of the watcher could feel the discomfort. There was no passionate joy, no deep connection, no constant conversation with guidance, but the one at the desk felt snug as a bug. It felt like the rubber band connection of the one watching was being pulled tighter into the watcher. The capability of seeing what was happening from a higher perspective had steadily grown slimmer.

My inner movie projector rolled a scene where I had been lying in bed early one morning as the sun worked its way through the thick fog. I seemed to remember something was missing. A feeling more than anything, wasn't there something I usually did or created? Or felt anyway? It felt like emptiness, no sense of anxiety or angst, only of a nagging feeling underneath that I had forgotten someone I knew, or some thoughts that usually accompanied me were just gone. My mind had spaced out into the blue and white swirls of the ceiling. Thoughts swirled in like the blues above me, reminding me of why I had originally painted them. The feeling of helplessness came in on that same tide. The color blue did not seem to have any purpose now, except to make me feel blue. It certainly had not helped the one I painted that false sky for feel more positive, as my motivation had hoped it would. I was watching scenes rerun in my mind's eye, and observing how I had lost the thread to my purpose.

Each day started that way, without a sense of purpose or passion. Doing my work seemed automatic, something I was grateful for at least, but it seems in retrospect I should have known something was happening to me. A slow debilitating disease had crept in on me, consuming me from the inside. And it had happened so slowly that it did not set off any alarms. But I was still a long way off from identifying the soul-eating bacteria. So now I see that each day was just one more in what was to become a long downward slide with no cognizant way of stopping what I did not even know was happening.

I recalled that several weeks later my dreams had become very dark and foreboding. Noting that now made me feel a little more powerless. How had I so easily forgotten I had methods to investigate the inner me? This one evening I was at a friend's house for a wake and was introduced to an older gentleman. He was kind of shy and even though he had been introduced with many credentials and accomplishments, I directed our conversation somewhere other than his past. It was a comfortable and easy conversation. Then he asked me what I thought about dreams.

His voice got a few decibels lower and he whispered close to me that he had a belief that something else happens to you in dreamtime. I figured he wanted to tell me, since he brought it up, so I asked if he would be willing to share his theory. He came in close and related an experience he had as a young man. He said he was a child in his mother's kitchen in this dream and there were all sorts of gnomish looking characters there. He asked what they were doing and one said, "We are living here." He asked, "Who are you guys?" The smallish character who had offered the first answer was quickly cut off by an older, taller one saying he could not tell the truth to this child, because he would know who they were. They all sat quietly and smiled, not betraying their purpose in his dream, but he had the distinct feeling that this was *not* a metaphor. This was something entirely else. He said this had opened him up to reading a great deal about the idea that our sleep time is not our own. It belongs to those who would take it and use it. And if we don't know this is happening, we leave ourselves open to who knows what.

I remember leaving there pondering his theory. At first it felt very fear-based and I discounted it as the thoughts of someone with nothing left to explore in his professional life, since he had done so much. Later though I felt the similarity to my own situation. Had something been usurping my energy during my dreamtime? Was someone planting something, or rather, reaping something I had planted? My mind held onto this idea. When I got home, I took out a journal to write some thoughts. So often this winter, as soon as I began to ponder something, the intricacy of the weaving threads slipped from my conscious mind. I wrote some thoughts about my own vacuous feeling dreams. That night I asked to see my gnomes, if there were any, living in my dream kitchen. Then I went to sleep. *Better watch what you ask for* were my final thoughts before sinking into a deep sleep.

The dream began with me and a group of four others, three women and a young boy. We had all been rounded up by some authority figures. I did not know why or what I had in common with these other people. We were placed in some dormitory setting, bunk beds for the other four, a single bed for me. And we were handcuffed to the bed frames so we would not leave. I didn't know what we had done wrong, then I discovered we were all being held because of our *special powers*. Each of us had some unique and unusual attribute that was native to us, but apparently was a threat to the rest of the world. Then the young boy, who I felt some responsibility for in the dream because he was so small, could see that the keys to our cuffs were fastened to the bottom of our bunks. He unlocked himself, then slipped the keys to the rest of us. He slid past the two guards and out the door without much commotion. Then as each of us unlocked our own hands, we enacted our own powers. Since mine was flying, I created a distraction for the others to get away in their own ways. The guards were trying to grab my legs as I flew up and past them and out the door.

I felt so free as I reached the street outside and quickly rose above it. Noticing I was creating a turmoil, I went invisible and was flying high above the street when I could see the two guards again running after me, pointing. I realized I had taken my sweater off once I got outside. In throwing it down, it got caught on my feet, which as I looked down were both in solid casts. I unhooked the sweater and threw it to the ground. Again, I felt confident I was safe in my invisibility, yet the double casts concerned me. Better to fly than to walk, obviously.

Still flying, I rose above the houses and through some neighborhoods, trees surrounding the balconies of the higher levels of the tall houses and buildings. I felt secure and landed briefly on a balcony that must have belonged to a gardener. It was covered with beautiful ornamental trees, beautiful flowering shrubs and pots of vegetables. I guess I thought I could rest there, but no sooner than I had touched down, a woman came running over to me asking what I was doing there and how did I get there? I simply asked her how she could see me. This must have appeared to be an odd question, since she was looking right at me. As I explained that she must also have super powers to be able to see me, she immediately relaxed and admitted that she did. At this point, I felt powerful and collaborative, set free and with my compatriots also released. Having now discovered another companion along this path, the dream felt empowering.

Perhaps that was the end of my own dreaming, because then the set changed dramatically and the woman disappeared as quickly as she had run out onto the deck. I went to try and lift off, but nothing happened. My casts were both heavy and clumsy and I could not imagine how to walk with them without a cane. As I looked around the deck for a doorway, everything vanished. All the beautiful plants were replaced with bare wooden walls, no curves, no ornamentation, only the definite feeling of a barrier. Each direction I turned was another wall, and they appeared to be closing in. I stood there, circling my spot wheeling around on one cast, examining my possibilities.

Usually, this is when I would wake up. But I still didn't know I was dreaming, so waking up was not an option. Just then through each wall all around me walked some ominous characters. They were not gnomes, if that is what I had been expecting. They were demons, ugly creatures sometimes on four legs, sometimes on two. They had large ears, beady eyes and carried the fear of death with them, yes, distinctly death, the smell and fear of it. They seemed so traditionally evil, like walking gargoyles, only the stench was not of stone. Certainly not. They created a circle around me. My heart began to pound. I couldn't lift off to escape them. I couldn't run away either. Even if there had been an opening I could run through, my two casts prevented that. Their laser-focused eyes were locked onto mine, as if a valuable treasure lay within and they would not be deterred from obtaining it. Even the ones behind me drilled penetrating holes through my head.

I stood frozen. Never had I experienced such pure and focused evil directed at me. Then they began to make small rumbling noises, little shrieks, as if they were getting excited, like coyotes during a kill. The energy heightened. My heart pounded in my chest. The fear was like nothing I had ever experienced. The sense of dread and of being the prey was as pure as destiny. Destiny, yes, that is what it felt like, which may have been why it never occurred to me to fight back or to protect myself. Just then the creatures simply walked up to me and right through me, no not through me, *into me*. They did not come out the other side. They had gotten in and the treasure they wanted was indeed inside and there was nothing I could do to stop them.

That night as I lay awake pondering the symbolism of the dream, I could not help hearing my new friend's warning that our dream time is not our own. Yet symbolism is the language of the soul, so I preferred to seek a reasonable understanding there. I could understand the meaning up until the little demon creatures appeared. The four people were the three women and one man in a group that we had just formed. I could see that *special powers* certainly might be these newfound spiritual gifts. Equally, I could make sense of the casts on my feet, that something weighed me down to this earthly world and there was something I wanted to release. The new woman on the deck, a fellow traveler and a welcome sanctuary. Perhaps someone I had not yet met or a part of me offering respite.

The fearful creatures of intense focus and evil intent … what could they be? A part of me, surrounding me, but for what purpose? What was the message? I lay there seeking some logical thought process to accompany this dream, yet my love of metaphors and puzzles wasn't helping me now. It was empty in there, and I was tired. The fear that had shot through me from the dream and created an adrenaline rush had now worked its way through me. I was spent. I just wanted to sleep again and soon. No matter how I tried to hang on to the thread of understanding, something to work with in the morning, I felt it slip away as gently as a mother wooing a child to sleep. Following this story along with the others, I could see I was losing my focus and clarity, something was numbing my acuteness. Something was gently keeping me asleep, yet there were so many moments where I should have paid attention. There was that feeling of destiny again.

The morning that followed that dream was like any other, or should I say, any other of that new variety of life. It was filled with routine and habit, but the passion of life had been polished off. In fact, the entire memory of the night's dream was simply deleted from my mind. It was only now that I could uncover this much of it. This was the day where a seed had been planted in me, or rather, that seed was beginning to grow and attract visitors

I then recalled one night after showering I noticed that my eyes had dark circles under them. I passed them off as signs of just being tired. Yet I was not really tired, I was ... what? I was preoccupied. I heard a voice deep within ask, *"Pre-occupied? Or occupied?"* But I remember, I did not answer.

Later another night, I remember it for sure, I woke up in the middle of the black winter darkness, outside in the snow, with my slippers on and a shovel in my hand. How could I have forgotten this? Had I been digging something, or burying something? I didn't know what it could have been and saw no evidence of anything physical. Hilde had not come outside with me, as she has every single day since we met. That alarmed me almost as much as waking up outside in the night with a shovel. I had never been known to sleep walk, so made a mental note to investigate this further the next morning. I knew something was going on that did not involve me at the helm. I recall how it concerned me. A lot. I even remember asking myself, "What could I do, what should I do? Where could I go to get away from it, especially if it is inside me? And what is it?" I had wanted someone to talk to, to sort this out, to help me make logic out of it, as I hoped someone could. I knew I could if only I had the rest of the facts, yet what facts?

I had gone back inside and made some tea. I was not going back to sleep, if that was even where I had been, until I could sort a few things out in my mind. I wrote some things down.

Sleepwalking, dreaming of evil, circles under my eyes, dark events in karmic sessions ... and as I wrote, I could feel a textbook case of possession unveil itself. But could this really be happening to *me*? I may have worked with that in my clients, but ... but what? Again, I continued, *mindless habitual living, little passion for my own creativity, feelings of being preoccupied.*

Perhaps I was being melodramatic, after all it was 4am. These were also symptoms of depression. Although that thought brought a wave of relief, it also brought the realization that it was a bigger shock than thinking I was possessed. My mind logically locked on to this idea that I was suffering from depression. I made a note to deal with it in the morning, turned off the teapot and went back to bed.

Of course, I made no attempt to face the depression situation the next morning, in fact, I forgot all about it and the sleepwalking. Even Hilde's distance from me went completely unnoticed, at least by the conscious mind. These incidents were all coming forward in my mind now, like duti-ful children, remaining quiet until called upon.

Images of things I had not experienced myself were common. I passed them off as processing other people's healing sessions. Speaking of which, I realized now I had not gotten a new client referred to me in some time. Somewhere inside there, I must have registered a concern and made a mental note to self, *check on that.* Where the note got filed, I cannot be sure. Flashes of light slivers, streaks of blood, and spears of sharpness pierced my mind occasionally.

My sister called me one day last month to say she had been checking on my energetic state for some time and things were progressively getting worse. I probed my mind for a thought, something to ask her about, to share with her, but I lost the thread. I listened to her. It felt so wonderful to have someone check on me. She suggested a karmic session was in order. Usually that meant that my karmic body was out of alignment for quite a few days running and I needed to see what was causing the imbalance. She offered to facilitate a session for me, as we often worked on each other. I did not make a response. She asked if I was still there. I said, "Yes, that sounds great, thank you. Yes. Perfect. Thank you." I could feel her smile from the other end of the line. "When?" she asked. When? "When do you think?" She said she could do it that very day, obviously, she was concerned enough to want to get right on it.

I paused and I could tell that in that pause she thought I was saying I wanted to do it myself. But that was not what the pause was about. She said, "Alright, you think about it and call me when you are ready, okay?" I agreed and we hung up. Something in me felt the rope just got pulled away. I wanted to call her right back and say, please help me, but I didn't know why. It felt foolish. Help me out of a karmic bond? How silly was that, yet as I thought it, it had a tingling ring of truth to it. A karmic bond. *Don't lose that thought, Laura, a karmic bond.* Something has you in a karmic bond, *please help me out of it.*

I could feel the crater lake with a cone-shaped body of water and a thin narrow ridgeline around it. I had gone walking along it and slipped into its karmic waters. I knew I was in until it spit me out. My destiny must run its course. Like a whirlpool, it had sucked me down until I could resolve what had brought me into it. I knew I had not resolved it, yet it was beginning to make sense in my mind. But as soon as sense began to make my mind clearer, a soft fuzziness of cloudy thinking continued to seep in through my ears. I wanted to plug my ears, to close my eyes, as if it were getting in through the orifices of my head. I knew it was already inside.

Yet even as I rewitnessed all these moments now, I knew I was claiming my own self back. I was allowing these non-conscious saboteurs to be known. In doing so, wasn't I disarming them, making other choices, alerting myself to the enemy within? But as much as I wanted to believe that was all that was required, I knew I still had to face the dark and formidable Raymond and no amount of thinking about it was going to make that any easier. And whatever had been planted inside me was going to continue to be my nemesis until that happened.

22

Had about 2 ½ hours left on the flight up to Miami on the way to DC and was too jacked up on coffee to go back to sleep. Spent more aimless time searching around the internet for whatever political history was going on back then. I doubt I could have told you what was happening then even if I went back in time. Never spent much time following the monkeys in Washington. I just couldn't think of anything else to do except go higher. Could Merkle be blaming Clinton? Was Chelsea next on the list? Crazy. But too crazy? Who else, and how could I get deeper into DeWitt's connection with Merkle before he attached him to our unit? I figured Washington was as good a place to start as any.

We're somewhere just past the Yucatan peninsula about an hour or so out of Miami when I finally dozed off. No idea how long I was out before something suddenly shoots me with a dose of adrenaline, right in the heart. Heartbeat goes right off the chart and I'm in a cold sweat everywhere. All I can see is the clearest picture of that woman back in Sandpoint then it's Merkle's face, and hers and his and I'm ready to climb into the cockpit and take this plane from the crew. Everything in me is being pulled towards Sandpoint. I'm out here in the middle of the goddamn Gulf of Mexico and I should be in Sandpoint. Flight attendant tells me we're an hour and ten minutes out of Miami. I can't believe it. Hour and ten minutes! I'm back on Expedia looking for a flight to Spokane. What the hell am I heading to Miami for? Why the hell was I headed for DC? Goddamn flight from Miami is 8 hours at the best, but that one doesn't leave for 5 more hours. Next flight is 14 hours. How the hell can they take 14 hours to get to Spokane? What the hell? That some kind of damn bus, or what? I'm back and forth on what to do until I think of Homestead. Homestead! Of course, that's the 482nd Fighter and South Command's Spec Ops. Shit hell, that's Walker. I'm on the horn trying to connect to Craig Walker in the next minute.

Fighting through the obligatory phone maze in what must have been two minutes but felt like hours.

"Craig, Nick Drake here."

"Nick lazy-ass Drake. You turncoat. I heard you was down teaching babies how to fly the mighty Cessna Skyhawk. Man oh man, wearing you out or what?" I deserved that.

"Craig, I'm glad as hell you picked up the phone. I'm sorry I fell off the radar. But right now we're going official." I could hear the silence on his end. You don't get a call like this every day and all he knew of me was that I disappeared and walked away from everything he held dear.

"Craig, I'm on United 1501 out of Guatemala City, arriving Miami at 10:05. That's 72 minutes. I need the fastest thing you've got. I know you have 16s, but I'm hell of out of currency. You got any old rust bucket 15s sitting out there needing a cross country?" I could hear a mixture of silence and stifled laughter that lasted a few seconds.

"Nick ... Nick. Umm, what?" In fairness, he couldn't have said anything else.

"Reinstated. Full Bird. I'm on one hell of a mission here, and I don't have more than about one more minute for this call." I gave him a number to call for verification. I knew he'd be on it as soon as we hung up. I knew he knew that I was no kind of practical joker and not the kind of guy to waste his time. We hung up and I was back on Expedia checking the Airnav website for the length of the Sandpoint runway. I really didn't care. Who the hell ever was going to take me out there at mach 1.5 was sure as hell going to put her down on that strip.

Just kept getting deeper. What on earth does this woman have to do with all this? I mean she lives near where Merkle killed Becky, but lots of other people live up in those same mountains. She supposedly saw someone drive up and thought there might be a connection, but that's a stretch. She couldn't ID the kid, but that's right on. Kid wasn't the guy. She perfectly describes Samantha's murder like she's got a camera on scene or something. And she goes and tells the police all about it! And worst of all, I'm trying like hell to get back to crazy-town instead of heading the other way.

Why am I seeing her face and Merkle's? What's the connection? I get nothing more on her from Google so I escalate it. Back on the phone with less than an hour to go before touchdown and I can't sit still. I decide to try out just how big the orders I'm carrying are. First call gets me slowed up a bit at the Air Force Personnel center. Not sure where to go, so I start there anyway. Someone checks my credentials and orders, then comes back on the line with a lot more respect. Couple more minutes and I'm on with some old-timer, chief master sergeant. I love those guys. They run the show, but are usually nice enough to pretend we officers do. He listens to my strange story for a minute, then, unfazed starts clicking the hell away at some keyboard. Comes back at me swearing up and down there's absolutely no military record. OK, OK what's next, I knew that. But I also knew he would know way more than me about tracking someone down.

"Assume civilian all the way, chief. Where do we go from here?" He's thinking for a second, then puts me on hold. Comes back in a minute. Says to hold fast while he widens his search a bit. Comes back with still no government ties at all. I ask him about any ties in South America? Nothing there. Chief says she's got lots of info online. Tells me lots of what I already found on my own. Maybe I'm not as bad at this as I thought.

Then he goes, "Oh, what have we here?" Like it's some kind of personal joke that I'm not in on. "Looks like she did a Master's degree in Soviet Policy Studies at the Monterey Institute of International Studies."

Now who does a degree on the Soviet Union, but has no government ties? I tell him to go on, ask him, "You mean the Defense Language Institute in Monterey?" I know about that school. Just about everyone has gone through one of their intensive programs for every language on Earth, it seems. Certainly the place you go when you're heading into intelligence.

"No sir, not the DLI. The Monterey Institute is private. Back when she was there it was obscure as hell. Nowadays it's a grad school for Middlebury College. More international business these days. Back then it was just a few hundred students in a bunch of old houses in Monterey." How can he be finding all this out so quickly? Internet. Unbelievable!

"Yea. So what of it?"

"Well, sir. When I was just an E3 they sent me down to the DLI. Thought they'd make me into a radioman and sit me in Germany. Sounded like an OK idea, so a year later I was fluent enough in German tank-driver profanity. Anyway, way we heard it, the Institute was just down the hill from us, was that the Monterey Institute was some kind of CIA recruiting school." What the hell? I'm thinking at hearing this. "It was a private school and most of the students were there for translation and interpretation— United Nations level stuff. Their program was different from what we went through. Everything we did was gutter level speak. All we were going to do was monitor East German tank traffic anyway. Down there they were a world upscale. Some of the guys had girlfriends from the college, but, all and all, we didn't mix much. So everything I'm telling you is second hand and 30 years old anyway.

"That's OK, chief. Go on." He had my interest. That's for sure.

"I think the program was all Master's level. I wasn't far out of high school, so it didn't interest me. Mostly it was foreign students and US students on the way to the foreign service. We had our opinion of the foreign service, if you know what I mean."

"Yea, what about this CIA thing?"

"Word was under the covers it was a watch ground for CIA recruiters. Mind if I try to take a deeper look into this, sir? This is one walk down memory lane for me. Beats what piled up on my desk this morning" Did I mind? Hell no.

"You're the man, chief. Do it. But I'm in more than a hurry here. This isn't casual interest for me. I want you to imagine this Laura Wexler is your sister and she's in some serious danger. I want everything, and if someone has more than you, I want them on the horn. Clear?"

"Yes, sir. You just made my day interesting. You're going to be surprised at what the old chief has up his sleeve."

"And, Chief?

"Yes, sir."

"Later on you're going to give me the back story on why I'm talking to a chief master sergeant here. Seems below your pay grade."

"Like I said, sir. You're going to be surprised at what the old chief has up his sleeve."

Now what the hell's going on here? Is there something I'm missing? Stupid question. There is something I'm missing. I've got Merkle heading back up the command line with some crazy agenda, and this nut-case chick out in the woods of Idaho with a history. Casual witness? Just a coincidence? I'm not feeling good about any of this and all I can do for the next 32 minutes into Miami is look at my phone every ten seconds.

I'm met at the door as soon as it opens and we go down and out the jetway. Nothing like righteous indignation from your fellow passengers and disbelief from the flight crew. Didn't bother me in the slightest. I have no idea how Craig Walker pulled this one off, but there's the sweetest look-ing Citation X sitting about a hundred feet away and nothing but wide-eyed ramp guys all around. We're wheels up six minutes after I get out of that airliner. Something to having some birds on the shoulder boards and one big-assed signature on my paperwork. I guess I was just in crazy-town when I asked for an F-15. Shows where my mind was. Must have slipped back into battle dress for a second. Old habits, I guess. Just wanted some excess firepower where I was going.

Flight crew's a couple youngsters who don't look long out of flight school in the front office, but with enough sense, or forewarning not to ask any questions. Maximum climb to altitude and we're off in the fastest business class jet made. Nice to know where all that taxpayer money goes. Ridiculously comfortable flight ahead in this baby, even with headwinds the whole way. He's bumping up on the shy side of mach 0.9 at flight level 400. That's impressive any day of the week. I make myself comfortable with some pre-packed lunch and try to put together what the hell's going on—no success there and no success trying to sleep.

About an hour into the flight from Miami, I get a call from some yahoo who says he's from the State Department. Right. They always say they're from *State*.

"Mr. Drake," he starts, and that pisses me of from the start, "I was informed that you have an interest in any government association of one Laura Wexler." I don't say anything because I know a load of it is on the way, and that kicks up every warning sign in my body.

"We have absolutely no record of Ms. Wexler's employment in any department of the United States. I believe Sergeant Johnson found the same in the DOD's records." That absolute smugness kicked up my will to attack, but I'd done the major part of my life under guys like this. And I had enough experience to know this guy wasn't *State*.

"Any thoughts on her degree at the Monterey Institute?"

"The what? Oh, yes, I see it here. The sergeant did mention that. I see from the sergeant's notes that she has a degree from MIIS. That seems to be a graduate school of business of Middlebury College. Middlebury in Vermont." I knew that and I knew this was going nowhere.

"Well, thank you, mister ..." I start.

"You're very welcome. Don't hesitate to contact me if you have any further questions." And the line went dead. Contact him? Now that's a good one.

He never said his name. I got back on the line to Johnson at personnel and put him back on the trail. He was not just a little miffed when I told him how little I just got. I needed someone higher up the food chain. I started wondering if I was in the middle of a pissing war between someone in the know and General DeWitt. Maybe just someone not even in the know. And I just handed over a bone they could play with. Maybe this was going nowhere because it had nowhere to go. Wouldn't be the first time I was working with insufficient data or led on a wild goose chase. Every department has its own intelligence arm, but the CIA thinks they sit at the top of the heap. I guess being the Chairman of the JCS didn't carry much weight with the boys at the *State Department*.

Johnson got back to me somewhere over Montana, about an hour out of Sandpoint. I'd been picking up bits and pieces along the way, but nothing meaningful.

"Don't ask where I got this, sir, but looks like your girl was on the way to the Directorate of Operations." He didn't have to clarify what that meant. The Directorate of Operations meant CIA, and that would have been as a field agent. They've beefed up their name to National Clandestine Service now, and we've got the Defense Clandestine Services. I'm not in love with either one, and this was not doing anything good for my heartburn. "Looks like she aced the Foreign Service exam and that would have set her up for a post of choice. She was fluent in French, German and Russian, so who knows where she was headed. Anyway, some old records a friend of mine dug up shows she was interviewed about a half a dozen times. Nothing covert, no secrets and this was no field recruitment. It was just like any other job. She was referred by some professor, no idea if he was in the company, then applied and was in the process of what ever the hell they do. Seems like she was cut loose at the last interview. I got nothing after that. Gal falls off the radar. I got an old graduation picture, but nothing after that."

I'm thinking, CIA. What? What is this about? My stomach has a knot that just keeps getting tighter. I'm looking at my watch and willing this plane to go faster. Was she involved in this? How can that be?

"Chief, you've been more help than you could know. You dig up anything more, you've got my number. Day or night."

"You got it, sir." And we were through.

I feel the pilot throttle back and we're into the descent. What am I going to find? Could this be the next link in the chain? Me, the colonel, the general. Was this mountain woman somewhere up in that crap? How could she be? Doesn't fit at all. I'm on the phone all the way to touchdown, but don't get anything of meaning. Feels like we're all swirling around in the same toilet bowl going towards the same hole.

23

The studio needed cleaning up before my group arrived the next evening, so Hilde and I headed down there to set things up and make sure there was coffee and enough chairs. My studio sits only about 100 yards from the house, but is completely surrounded by trees. Heading down there, Hilde went off barking with her hackles up past the studio into the woods. I didn't think anything about it. She is always warning moose and coyotes off her property. Yet she was going off in a direction that was unusual for her. The studio did need putting things in order. It had been a winter of many paintings and their parts and pieces. Palettes and tubes of paint lay scattered around.

I started putting unfinished pieces away, wrapping up unused paint and feeling quite energetic and constructive setting it all right again. Then I bumped my hand on the walnut trim of the shelves that run all along the wall next to my art table. A little blood got on the walnut and I stopped for a solid moment to contemplate this. Everything seemed to freeze as I looked in earnest at the beautiful, oiled walnut trim of this very basic wood shelf, built especially for me. One who expressed his love to me through acts of service had built it the exact length and height to my specific request. I stopped my busyness in the studio and just stared at the walnut trim. That had become his signature piece for me because it said in this one detail how much he loved me. My heart just ached. The weirdness of the winter and the murder so close, then the inner witnessing of the second murder made me realize how much I needed him. How much I had relied on him for comfort, security and support.

A part of me was grieving my loss, not his. I knew he was at peace. It had been my job to help him get all the way there. But now, it was *me* I was crying for. I really missed him. Seven years without his smell, without his tender touch, without his love, without his depression and anguish.

Yet, had I gone a day without connecting to him, without talking to him in my heart? I caressed the smooth edges of the walnut trim, remembering how he had sanded and oiled it to make it so smooth that I would never snag myself on it, remembering how he had done it as a surprise and how I loved it. I imagined my hands were touching the same spots he had.

Soon I had lost all desire to tidy up the studio. It all seemed so unimportant now. I had also lost most of my initiative to do much of anything. I decided to curl up on the couch. Hilde must still be outside, but I knew she would be safe in her bed in the garage. Having never turned the lights on because I started my cleaning when it was light, I did not have to get up to turn anything off. The heater was on low and there were plenty of blankets. Soon I let myself drift off to sleep, hoping he would visit me there.

The next morning found me in the same fetal position of the previous evening. As I began to open my eyes, to stretch from the tightness of sleeping on a too-short-for-my-legs couch, I wondered where I was and what I was doing in my studio. Then I recalled the previous evening. What was that about? I had not felt such an overwhelming sense of him in so long. In fact, I still felt the lingering of those protective arms around me again. Were they protecting me from some unknown danger? I guess I would never know. We used to imagine that if we made one decision, how would we know we had not missed something tragic or life-altering if we had made a *different* decision?

I examined the slight cut on my hand in the morning light. Then I noted that this light felt much brighter than the paleness of the morning. I glanced up to see the clock, but it was behind my art table. I lay there yawning until I could bring myself to get up. I shuffled into the bathroom and found myself lounging in an unusually long and hot shower, even though a cool and brisk one was my preference. Yet, it felt comforting and necessary. Nothing in me could move this mountain that appeared to be me today. When I finally did look at the time, I was shocked to see 12:45. That is in the pm. Holy cripes, people would start arriving in a few hours and I was far from ready.

Walking up to the house from the studio below, I began to ponder the strangeness of the day. There was a sense of uneasiness lingering in the background. Hilde came running up to greet me, not from the garage, but from outside. I looked up the outside stairs to my deck, a place I rarely go during the winter. I noticed a set of footprints in the icy snow. Trying to isolate a clear print, it looked like someone was trying to cover them. Lots of smudged dusting of the light snow still left on the stairs. They were clearly not mine. Not only were they bigger, but I knew I had not been up this way for weeks, maybe even a month. All prints would have blown, melted or been snowed away. I searched my mind. When was the last time someone was up here? Could it have been Kurt from down the road? He has big feet and checks on me from time to time. Looks like he might have dropped something on the stairs. Hilde was sniffing them and whining as if she did not like whatever smell they held.

All the things that usually calm my mind and rejuvenate my body did not seem to touch this edginess I was feeling. My mind returned to the question of what had happened to my power. Was that what was haunting me right now? As soon as I asked myself that question, I felt a sense of calmness. That was validation for me. But what to do now? It was too late to undertake any deep healing work right now, my group would be here before I knew it. I resolved to look into the matter tomorrow. Again, the anxiety returned. Couldn't this wait? Was I being tapped? Was something or someone instigating something that I was feeling? That did not feel exactly right. Did I need to seize this moment? There, the calm was returning. Seize what moment? I felt the answer, yet did not know what the question should be.

24

Dropped into Sandpoint a little under five hours after wheels up in Miami. Same kid standing there at the FBO, but with his jaw a little wider open. Must not see a Citation X every day. Rental car was waiting and took about a minute to sign the forms. Thank God for Hertz on-line check-in. I was able to get her address on the way from Miami. Seemed easy enough to find. Hell of up in the mountains though. This woman was some kind of hermit or something. After about five miles up some winding mountain road that seemed forever, the road really got rough. Seemed like they were growing big and bigger rocks right in the middle of the road. I wasn't much for slowing down and hoped the transmission wouldn't catch one of the boulders in the belly. I was just about ready to turn around, thinking I was lost, and of course had long since lost cell reception, when I saw her address ... with the gate wide open. How could you live in a place like this and have your gate open?

I knew I was blowing things out of proportion, but couldn't seem to slow myself down. I'd probably scare her to death as I came roaring up the driveway. Still couldn't see a house and hoped it wouldn't be much farther. I came around the corner and saw a pretty nice little place. Had the view to die for, that's for sure. Some crazy little hyena dog came running out barking like hell, but didn't carry any energy of danger. Just seemed to be barking like crazy. Dog was running around in circles like it didn't know what to do.

Front of the house was just garage doors so it looked like the stairs up to the deck must lead to the front door. I took them two at a time and was out of breath by the time I got to the top. As I climbed up I was overwhelmed by the view. This lady had every mountain in the world out her front window. I came around the corner onto the deck and ... my world stopped. It was the kind of stop you think must happen when you die.

Everything just stopped and the background seemed to just blur away and there on the deck standing like a deer in the headlights was Merkle. Older, looked bad. Looked like a zombie just standing there like he didn't know what was happening. But holding one big-assed silver revolver in his one hand. Just hanging down by his side.

I just stopped and stared. He just stood there and either looked right at me or was looking right through me. This was not the Hans Merkle I knew. The Merkle I knew would have had all six bullets in me by the second I saw him. This man was just standing there, dumbfounded. I should have been prepared. I mean I had been thinking of nothing else since waking up in shock half way across the Gulf of Mexico this morning. I knew that this was my last second on Earth. Somehow I just knew that big gun was going to come up on me. I couldn't move at all. I didn't even have any motivation to move. It was like I was seeing my brother. Except I hadn't seen him since I was ten years old before he left to die in Viet Nam. It just felt OK that I was going to die today.

Without thinking, I just reached out my hand and said, "Hank," and couldn't do anything more. He stood there for how long I don't know, and so softly I could hardly hear it, said, "Hank." Then in a few seconds more, said, "Hank. You called me Hank. Nick. I always wanted you to call me Hank." And the gun just slipped out of his hand and made the biggest clunk on the deck you could ever imagine. That seemed to wake us both out of our dream as we looked down at it just lying there by his foot. I started to back up towards the stairs and he just came at me. I don't know what I thought he was going to do. He didn't pick up the gun, just came straight at me with his arms out. I backed into the railing and suddenly heard that damn dog barking like crazy. Had it been barking the whole time? And Merkle just kept coming like in the zombie movies, just looking right into my eyes like I was some kind of something. I don't know. I'm afraid to say it, but it looked like he was looking at some kind of angel or something. Just as he got right up near me he seemed to just disappear from my sight. In a millisecond he just went down like the world was sucked out from under him. The next thing I saw was him tumbling head over heels all the way down those incredibly steep stairs. It was like some rag doll or something, and that fool dog was tumbling down right after him, yelping and squealing as it fell. He must have tripped over the dog. Hans Merkle must have tripped over this silly, noisy dog.

I just stood up there on the deck looking down on him at the bottom of the stairs. There was no life in that body. I looked around the valley and the mountains and had absolutely no idea what had just happened. The dog had its tail stuck up between its legs, but at least stopped barking. It was cowering a few feet from Merkle's body. I knew I should go down there and check the body, but I went to look in the house first. There was a glass door that wasn't even locked. Open gate, unlocked door, nut-case dog, Merkle standing there with a smoking gun. This was a very bad day.

I called into the house, but could feel it was totally silent. No life in this house at all. Lots of plants. Beautiful art all over the walls. A really nice place. Felt empty, though. I didn't see any signs of anything anywhere. Nothing was disturbed. I checked every room and then again. Nothing. I came back out and looked over the deck. Nothing. Where was she? "Where is she?" I must have asked aloud a hundred times. I saw that there was an outbuilding about a hundred yards away. "Maybe she's there." I didn't see anything happening so I went downstairs and he was as dead as I thought.

That's when the training kicks in. Once you have it, it doesn't go away. I had him in the trunk, swept up the tracks in the snow, then one last look around for anything out of place and we were gone down that driveway. Right before getting to the gate it hits me hard in the face. Laura! Shit, where's Laura. I slam on the breaks and almost skid off into the drainage ditch because of the snow. I'm back out of the car and running up the driveway before I know it. No reason to head back up to the house, I continue towards that out-building. I'm just about to crest the hill when I hear her calling for the dog. Like I said, you hear a shot, you hit the ground first, ask questions later. As soon as I hear that voice I'm sliding along, face hard on the ground without a thought. She never sees me. I stay down until she's out of sight on the way to the house. Then back down to the car as fast as I can move. Next thing I know, I'm flying down some rocky dirt road in the middle of the mountains with a dead Hans Merkle in my trunk, dead for the second time in his sorry life, and I have no idea what just went down.

I got slowed down enough to be invisible by the time I reached the pavement and crossed a pretty little river that ran through the valley she lived in. Still no cell reception and even less any ideas of what to do next. I kept thinking this wasn't what I signed up for that first day I showed up in Sandpoint. I told the colonel right then I wasn't going to kill anyone. So why the big rush to get out here today? What was I planning to do? What did I really think I'd do when I found Merkle? I was coming down and all I could think of was this was another case of jump in fast, figure it out later. I mean everything worked out for the best. What would have happened if I would have waited for a commercial flight? What was he doing up on that deck? Why wasn't she up there in the house? And the gun. What was he doing with a stainless-steel Colt Python? That's one nice gun, but not at all Merkle's weapon of choice. No way.

I got out on the highway and the phone lit up. Called the colonel.

"Richards."

"Your package will be in the trunk of a blue Taurus. Northeast corner of the Walmart parking lot across from Home Depot. Damaged beyond repair by an accident. Repeat, accident."

"Accident. Right. Good job."

"I said accident and I meant it. This is now out of my hands, but I need that car to be back to the local airport by tomorrow. And I do not want to pay extra so it's got to be perfectly clean, copy that?"

"Like I said, good job. We'll talk." And he was off the line in his typically abrupt way.

I walked away from that car 20 minutes later and when the cab driver asked where I wanted to go, didn't have an answer. He looked at me for a minute, and said, "Not from around here, ey?"

"Not at all."

"Car break down or what?"

"Marriage broke down."

"Oh, sorry man. Where to anyway?"

"Any nice hotels? Something with a view?"

"Oh yea," he smiled and we pulled out. Wasn't but five minutes later when he pulled into the same hotel overlooking Lake Pend Oreille I stayed in last time. How'd he know? Brought back those old memories of the instrument written exam. Looked at this chart a hundred times.

Checked in and checked out of consciousness ten minutes later. Best sleep I'd had in … how long? I didn't even remember.

25

Sitting on my familiar cushion, emptying myself of all expectations, I quieted my mind. There before me was a ribbon of energy. I grabbed it and followed. I could feel the vibration was power, yet the thread I was following was only a pathway. It was not the power itself. It was yanking me inward. I followed.

Breathing in and out slowly, I could feel something was occurring *right now*. I was taken inward to visit a present moment scene, but where and why? The questions left my mind as I observed a tall, thin man fondling a gun. He appeared to be quite intent upon the intricate details of this gun, which I knew to be a Python .357 because I owned one just like it. It had a stainless 4" barrel, exactly like mine. I didn't know him and he didn't seem to be a threat in any way. I was simply watching someone engaging in a very simple, yet meditative act. Around him was some sort of object. It was dark blue, and somewhat squarish. Not sure what it was exactly. I continued to observe, non-judgmentally, to witness. Why, I didn't know or question at this point. As the scene came more into focus, I could see he was looking into a compartment at one end of the dark blue object. There was the mangled body of a hard looking man, clearly deceased, stuffed into this container. Yet the tall man simply gazed at him as if he were looking at an abstract Picasso. I could feel no shift of energy, no surges of feeling toward the scene or the man inside.

My focus zeroed in on the standing man, his energy, his intent and mind. I followed the ribbon of energy through him. He felt like an empty shell, a hollow automaton. Curious, I thought, this scene appears to contain nothing. Just as I thought that, a suddenness of breath caught the man by surprise, as if he himself did not gasp, but something *in* him gasped *for* him. A strange energy swooped in from seemingly nowhere and now as I monitored this man, he felt completely different. He was certainly no longer empty. But the thing that now inhabited him was not *of* him, that much was for sure. It was intense and dark, deep and darkly powerful. This is why I had come now, to witness this ... *possession*? Was that what I was seeing, a full-on possession? One minute I was monitoring a simple man, focused and intent upon his bizarre package, then the next moment, he is a seething tiger, a demonic and turgid being capable of much more than this simple task. I instinctively knew he could lock those laser eyes on his prey and ferociously attack it.

My intuitive mind began to stir, to unlock images and faces, to send me notes and ideas about this man, the possessor and my own safety. I only half listened. I knew I was trying to solve a puzzle I did not have all the pieces for, but my task now was only to monitor this moment. So I did. I witnessed, for whom or why, I did not know, but I was being asked to observe this experience. Something in me knew I was safe as an observer, but as soon as I started fiddling with speculation, I would draw the very energy I wanted to avoid. Keeping my mind neutral, I continued to watch from the safety of my warm and quiet home. Yet my heart did not feel like I was in the safety of my home, it felt like I was being exposed to something capable of torture and malice.

The man moved away from the deep container with the mangled body, gripped his pistol tighter and made his way to the front of the dark blue box, a cat-like quality to his movements. It felt like he could instantly lurch onto an unsuspecting mouse with claws out and in one swift moment, the mouse would be dinner. I felt too close for comfort, like I might be dinner if I wasn't careful.

He stood deathly quiet, made no moves, except for his free hand. It was creating a fist ever so slowly and releasing it. That habit felt somehow very familiar, I had seen it before, many times. I watched his fist, clenching and releasing, stretching his ever ready hand muscles, waiting for an assignment. I slowed my mind from searching for its owner. I did not want to know right now. I was only here to observe. Just then he turned around. He was staring directly at me, as if I were actually there in the flesh with him. He walked closer towards my vantage point. As I watched, I naturally wanted to back up, creating more space between us, yet I could not draw back my view. It was as if my inner eye's camera was stuck in this position. I saw him draw the pistol that I recognized as my own and hold it up, square to my face. He took aim, *at me*, and pulled the trigger.

The shock wave of energy and the mental blast sent me reeling back into my own space. I fell off my sitting cushion and crashed onto the floor, ramming my shoulder into the carpeting. My eyes were still squinting shut from the gunpowder blast.

I collected myself, hoping to understand what had just transpired, then I felt the message. *I know you are here and I will use your own power against you.* Was I really seeing this event, or was it fabricated as a metaphor for me? My own Colt Python, the guy locking directly onto me, in the eyes … the *Eyes*. For a moment, I saw the eyes looking right at me. Were those Raymond's eyes? I could not be sure about the physical eyes, but the energy certainly was his.

I needed to understand what had just happened. It felt like someone had actually shot me. I felt as offended and shocked as if it had happened to my body, not just my mind. Yet I knew this was intended to unsettle me. *Lock onto that energy source. Where is it coming from? Who is generating this image for me? Who is puppeting this poor soul?* I knew I wasn't neutral. I could feel this was definitely the energy signature of Raymond. No doubt about that.

26

Woke up feeling great. That's not at all typical. Curtains open to the lake, stunning. These are the kind of days you live for.

I had a few minutes looking out the window, thinking of nothing at all, just waiting for the coffee to brew. Then, predictably, the debrief began in my head. Debriefing maybe is the most important part of the mission. Here's where you examine mistakes and good moves, good decisions and bad. Once the adrenaline wears off you can finally look for clarity. But what was I thinking? I'll never repeat this mission. This is not my game and I don't know why I was tagged as a player.

I felt relief, in a strange sort of way, that Merkle was gone. Not vengeful relief, that's for the colonel. Just relief that a burden was lifted. I didn't have any place in my head to put that scene on the deck. I knew the guy a long time ago, and that wasn't who I saw tumble down those stairs. Felt like he was being freed somehow. Not my place to tally up his sins. Not my place to punish him. Glad he's gone, that's all.

His going after the girls as a way to punish the colonel and general made enough sense that I felt I could let that train of thought go. No reason not to believe the whole thing died with Merkle. Felt good that the old Sanchez was dead. No reason for that, but still felt good. One less bad man in the world. That's got to be a good thing, right?

Coffee tasted like crap so I dumped it and headed out to look for a café. Hot cup and a donut sounded good right about then.

Crossed a little bridge on the way into the main part of town. I could get used to a place like this. The image of the young Sanchez confused the hell out of me. How could someone so gentle and caring live a life like that? There's more than meets the eye. That's for sure. How involved are we in the drug pipeline and the war on drugs both at the same time? I start going down some thought paths I haven't gone down in years. Nipped that one in the bud. Every one of those roads leads to crazy-town. I justified my life back in the day. Not willing to play justification any more. Maybe I'll mail these birds back to the colonel with a firm *up yours* attached.

What was that about? He, they, whoever *they* are, could have just given me an expense account. What's with this active duty reinstatement load of crap, anyway? Doesn't make any more sense than them tapping me way back when, right after flight school. Used to feel my life was like that Harry Chapin song where the girl was going to be an actress and he was going to learn to fly, or something like that. That's all I wanted back then, just like him. I heard that he had planned to go to the Air Force Academy, or actually did go, not sure. Anyway, what I got was, "No, son, you're going to do exactly what the hell we tell you to do." Never thought I was the right guy for the job. Strange career path. Colonel! That's the weirdest of them all. Here I'm wearing the same birds on my shoulders that the colonel wears. And I mean *the* colonel.

Walking out of this nice little place with a hot cup and a sweet roll, no donuts. Must be out of style to make good old fashion donuts anymore. And I get this picture. There are colonels who should be generals, and there are colonels who should be lieutenant colonels. I'm playing twenty questions with that one. Pretty clear who I am, and who *the* colonel is.

So what now? Beautiful place, beautiful day. Maybe I'll stop in, say bye to the chief. Maybe not. Probably should give the colonel a call. Probably should make sure my car got back safe. No, that should be a done deal. Not like I left the hardest part of the deal to who the hell ever the colonel sends in to clean up this mess. Kind of like my mom. She'd clean her house before the maid would show up. I didn't leave anything too messy.

Thinking that I could call Laura. Thinking probably not. Better to leave things alone. This will fade into nothingness for her. Chief will chase his tail around a bit, guys out in Maryland will end up with nothing, Laura goes back to her life. What the hell, I should just get some breakfast, say bye and admit my failure to the chief, and head home. Job well enough done.

27

As I picked up the receiver, I instantly recognized the voice of Sergeant Strickland from the police station. It was as if I had not put it as far out of my mind as I had hoped. He asked me if I would mind coming into the station. This did not feel good, felt like something really sticky had begun the *first* time I went down there, but I agreed.

"Have you picked up on anything unusual?" he asked me, getting right to the point as soon as I arrived.

"You mean like a murder?" My mind recalled the pistol going off in my own face, but I didn't really think this was what he wanted to talk to me about.

"Exactly."

"No, I have not. Why do you ask?"

He went on to explain that there had been another murder, but that it was highly unlikely that it was the same murderer. Just too odd that this little sleepy town would have two murders in one season. He thought maybe I had picked up on something. I guess I was the local psychic now.

"Why don't you think it is the same killer?" I asked.

"The weapon was a Colt Python .357, and it was a single shot to the head, no torture or anything, thank God."

I felt a creeping sensation crawl up my spine. A .357? What are the odds of that? I asked if they had any leads. He said he was hoping I could help in that department. This guy had been a real professional, no prints, no leads yet. Something in me wanted to share the dream-like story of the .357, yet I could not. I just shrugged and said I was sorry, no psychic connection to this guy, I guess. Yet, even as I said it, I knew that was not true. It wasn't the killers I had the connection to, it was the dark being that *inhabited* them.

"Where did you find her?" I had to know.

"Who?" Strickland saw I was no help and had gone back to his report or something.

"The woman who was murdered."

"It was a man," was all he said.

"Was it a 4-inch barrel or a 6-inch?" I found myself asking as I got up to leave.

Strickland looked confused, probably more because the question must have seemed out of character coming from what he thought was a bona fide liberal tree hugger crystal person, but said, "I don't know, I can ask forensics. The guy left the gun at the scene of the crime, can you believe it? *Wonder what that was about?*" He said the last statement more to himself than to me.

Leaving his office, I was struck by the fact that I normally would have been overcome by a barrage of feelings, from the murdered, the murderer, the impact in the community and so on. I would have asked about the guy, who he was, his parents, felt the grief deep in my heart, but I just got up and walked out. It felt cold, but at the same time freeing that those empathetic energies had not found me.

Just as I was leaving the station, I bumped into the pilot. He was carrying a cup of coffee and heading into Chief Longfellow's office. Some hot coffee spilled on my jacket sleeve. It shook me into recognition. I remembered the guy from the chief's office last November. I offered a brief smile of recognition. The coffee had not gone through my jacket and I was saying it was totally OK to his pleas of clumsiness and forgiveness. He must have remembered me, or else he knew Strickland was calling me in because he didn't even miss a beat calling me by name and asking if I wanted to go get a new cup of coffee with him. I found myself walking beside him out to the parking lot. I looked at him to identify what he was driving, but he just shrugged, said he had already turned in his rental car. Without missing a step, I pointed in the direction of my truck and we both got in.

For the first time in months, I felt safe. Not sure why, but sitting beside this pilot that I had forgotten his name, if I ever knew it, brought me a sense of well-being I had not felt for some time. As we drove, I tried to ascertain the feeling, then the energy or the memory, something that would explain the warm bath of protection. Nothing surfaced except that familiar feeling of fate I had been running into. The ridgeline above the karmic crater lake? It didn't matter, it felt so soothing. I was glad I did not resist. Did I even have a chance to? I don't remember. He was asking me something and I had to ask him to repeat it. Told me his name was Drake, Nick Drake.

"What were you doing in the station?"

He seemed genuinely concerned, but I didn't feel like going over the whole bizarre murder in my head, and how it had occurred again exactly as I *saw* it. This was starting to be a habit I needed to break. Anyway, I had just met the guy, so I said something like, "they were just looking for some psychic answers, guess I'm the new town freak."

"So, what is *your* connection to this case?" I felt comfortable enough to ask him. "What are you still doing in Sandpoint?"

He stared out the window to the steel blue lake beyond. The beautiful blue sky cast a mirror sheen on the surface of the water. The water was expansive and serene, yet it was not the lake he was looking at. His thoughts were within. He did not respond quickly. It was as if he had to find the answer himself before replying to my question.

He mumbled something about being unsure of the answer himself and I could tell he wasn't trying to brush me off as much as make sense of it himself.

Pretty soon he was asking about how I could have witnessed the death of the woman from Maryland and I guess I must have felt like I knew him well enough, so then shared the most recent installment of my remote murder viewing!

He asked if I could make out the face of the guy I had *seen* in my inner movie, before the gunshot to my head. As much as I didn't like returning to this scene, it was effortless. There was the tall, thin guy, fondling his gun again. Then the thought occurred to me though, why should he go to jail for what his possessor had done? Would he even have memory of the event? What were the odds that he was still possessed? Why would Raymond go to jail if he could just jump ship? So what if I located this innocent guy, well, innocent in some ways … it was all so confusing in the face of the law.

That's why the law never suited me because it was so black and white and life was never black and white. The pilot could see I was stalling, or pondering really. He waited and then asked what I was thinking. He seemed to be assessing the many options as well. How to proceed? And what was the goal? Perhaps for him it was to apprehend the killer or killers, but for me, it was more complex. This karmic web that I found myself in with some dark entity from my past was not something that could simply be *apprehended* and the story closed.

I shared my thoughts with pilot Nick including the fact that, as I thought about it, was sure it had been orchestrated for me to witness. First, the guy, then the possession and then his clear recognition of my energetic presence. *He was leading me into a trap, don't you think?* It suddenly occurred to me that I was thinking more clearly than I had in months. Things began to surface that I had been seeking for so long, but could not hold onto. I threw out all kinds of ideas, asked questions, got excited for the first time in a long while. I felt safe and strangely that I had an ally. It wasn't that I was solving anything as much as I was allowing myself to question what had been going on the past few months. Being in my truck with Nick was like being on home base, like when you're a kid playing tag, the one place where you could rest until you were ready to run again.

Maybe it wasn't being in the truck, maybe it was being with *him*. I did feel the karmic bells going off, the familiar knowing, the instant comfort and ease of being with him, the synchronous collaboration. I stared at him, hoping for some validation or recognition of some sort. I tried closing my eyes. I could feel his easy presence, but did not know where our meeting could have been. Then he took his sunglasses off. I looked into his eyes just then and I felt myself fall into the whirlpool. The karmic waters I often talked about had arrived and were taking me under. I did not resist either. Now I know why the ride feels inevitable. You don't *want* to stop it, it feels so good.

I had pulled into the coffee shop parking lot overlooking the lake some time ago, but neither of us made any moves to actually get out and go in. The warmth of the truck, the coziness, the intimacy and the expansiveness of the lake were all too addictive to leave.

A thousand stories all played simultaneously in my mind's eye; voices, laughter, smiles, scenes, crying, grief, touching, tenderness, anger … it kept going, experiences of life. Not just life though, these were memories of rich and joyful lives, filled with passion and love. It overwhelmed me. I felt emotional and vulnerable, as if someone were looking in on my most valuable and treasured memories, but it was *me* looking in … how did that work? The only validation I needed was the mist in the pilot's eyes. Whether he was in sympathetic resonance with my emotions, or he was seeing his own memories, it did not matter. He was confirming our connection. It was beyond sexual in nature, it was like going home. It felt so comfortable.

I have often thought that when you meet your soul companion it feels like you have found someone you have been waiting for and now you are both home. I didn't feel ready to voice this to the man sitting beside me, but felt pretty sure he was having some comfortable feelings of his own.

I then mentioned the detail of the Colt Python revolver that I witnessed that was identical to my own. I was connecting the metaphor for him of having my own power used against ... when he suddenly bolted upright in his seat and his demeanor changed instantly. His face grew red and tense and all sense of a soft connection became a distant dream. I think I could see the veins in his jaw.

"What?" I asked, slamming the lid shut on my karmic treasure chest.

"Can you take me to the airport? Now."

There was no please, no discussion, no explanation offered, just terse and authoritative. I could feel no opening to continue to talk even. I turned the truck around and headed the few miles over to the local airport. Driving into the flight center parking lot, he already had his seatbelt unbuckled before I even slowed down and I thought be might just jump and roll if I didn't hurry it up. He glanced back as he jumped out of the truck and efforted a smile, but it looked more like a grimace and then he was gone. Just like that. Ran sprinting into the building. Gone.

I turned to drive back up the highway to my turnoff, wondering what on earth had just happened. I tried to imagine what that was about, but didn't know him well enough to have a clue. Maybe I was getting too friendly and that bothered him. Or maybe the second story of witnessing a murder while it was happening somewhere else was just too weird for him. I don't know. I guess it might seem weird to someone who was not used to this sort of thing. It actually was weird to *me* and so what did that say? I just thought he understood. It really felt like he believed me.

But before I even reached the turnoff from the highway, all enthusiasm about having an ally were beginning to slip from my mind. I remember watching a movie years ago about a detective being held captive and drugged with heroin against his will. God, I hated that idea. I had recalled it over the years whenever I thought of my most dreaded scenario. That's how I felt now. The heroin was kicking in again. I tried in vain to fight it, but I had no resources available to me to resist. My mind grew cloudy and the passion I had about all my questions and my complex situation all began to loosen their grip on my brain. Like wet fingers trying to hold on to an oversized box, they finally gave out. I found myself turning up my road with the same monotony of someone who had done this day in and out for 30 years.

That night as I lay in bed even though confused and disappointed, something bright seemed to fill my heart. I looked to the window automatically to see if it was a star, but the clouds had rolled in this evening and it was starless. I knew better. The sky was not starless, I just couldn't *see* the stars right now. They were still somewhere up there shining. That made me smile and I fell asleep.

28

No fair! Why didn't my mother ever tell me life is not fair? That should be the first thing you tell your kids.

I must have been in some warm euphoria sitting in her truck, looking out over the lake, just listening to her voice. Can't remember much of what she said, I was just comfortable somehow. Felt like there was no other place in the world I needed to be. Can't say I ever felt that before.

When she told me that guy was murdered with Colt Python .357, I swear it felt like she actually slammed that cold piece of steel right into my face. There's no place for coincidences. Yea, maybe just yesterday I put a dead body and a Stainless Colt Python into the trunk of a car and left it for someone else to take care of, and today, just by the luck of the draw some other guy, totally unrelated, takes a shot to the forehead—same gun. Right. God, don't you have anything else to do? All I can think of is getting mobile again. Get another car, get some answers. All I come up with are questions.

What the hell's going on here? I was on the way home. Who is this woman, and why was I so comfortable with her? And why the hell couldn't I have met her before? Why this? Damn straight, unfair.

Cleared out the train of *whys*. That's always been my weak spot. Looking for *why* just gets you chasing your own tail.

Picked up the cell phone.

"Richards."

"What's going on, Colonel?"

"What's going on, how?" I didn't pick up anything in the voice, but that doesn't mean anything.

"How secure are we on this line?" That was a stupid question.

"That's a stupid question and you know it, Drake."

"Give me ten minutes and a secure number." He spit out another number and I figured the best I could do was a phone booth instead of my own cell. Now that's one ancient piece of history, a phone booth. Drove away from Hertz and up and down a few streets not seeing anything even resembling one. Figured I'd try inside a gas station. First two didn't have one, but the third did. Just a phone on the wall by the restrooms. Nobody around at the moment, luckily.

"Go."

"I just ran into that women we saw in the station, remember?" No answer, but I could tell he was with me. "I ran into her at the police station." Still no response. "She says her pistol is sitting in this same police station along with a dead body and I don't know what the hell's going on here."

"Go on." Go on. Doesn't this guy have emotions?

"Can't say we're connected. Says they called her in to see if she had any ideas."

"Why would they call her?"

"She didn't know. I think they're grasping at any connection they can get. She says Strickland, remember him, called this a professional hit. Not that these guys would know what that means. Says there was just a dead body, no prints, and that there was a Python .357 left at the scene."

"Why would they call that professional? The gun left at the scene, are you kidding me? And why do I care about this, Nick?"

"I checked with Hertz and the car was returned yesterday, clean. I didn't pick up anything when I called. Just some kid doing a job. Who'd you put on it?"

"You're not telling me why I care, here." It was my turn to stay silent. He didn't give for a bit, then said, "I got a call said job's done. All I know. What's this about a hand gun?" I told him what had happened on the deck, pistol and all. Sounded like he didn't really believe that Merkle tripped over a dog and died, but he didn't press me on that.

"You didn't say anything about a weapon in that trunk."

"I didn't say anything other than to clean it up. Looks like your boys screwed the pooch on this one, colonel." Not a wise thing to put the blame on him, but now I was beyond mad. He didn't come back at me, so I knew I wasn't too far off.

"I'll check it out, but so far nothing is out of order. All I know, and that's all I know, Drake, is that the job is done. For that we're both grateful

to you. You were wrong to walk away from that promotion four years ago."
He hadn't hit me with that one in a long time. "But you were right to accept
it this time around. You're the best I ever had and the game's a hell of a lot
more serious nowadays." Yea, yea, yea, and my country needs me ...

He hung up with that and I knew he'd be hotter than hell to find out
what went wrong on his end. I didn't sense anything on my end so I had
nothing to do but head back to the station. Time to see if there were any
fires I could put out.

Back out of Longfellow's office after making small talk and hoping
something would come up about this new murder. No way I could broach
the subject without suspicion. I shouldn't know a thing about it. Popped in
to say goodbye to Detective Strickland with the same hopes. Got nothing
there either. Damn. I thought I was on the way home.

After about an hour, which should be more than enough time for the
colonel, I gave him a call.

"Nothing yet." Not like the colonel at all. Was this going from bad to
worse?

"You'll call me?" He just hung up.

I couldn't think of anything to do at the moment, so I took a walk
along the lakefront. Still a beautiful day, but the sun was on the way down.
Where did this day go?

29

That next morning fog lay over the valley in a soft, serpentine blanket outlining the riverbed below. Sometimes the beauty of this place overwhelms me. I stood looking out the window for what seemed like a very long time. The quietness of the scene, the gentle almost imperceptible movement of the shifting fog was not lost to me. The opaqueness of the fog prevented the viewer from seeing anything below, only a hint of its shape. It could be a river underneath, but it could also have been a deep crevasse or a canyon. Those below the fog might be looking up at the sky feeling completely closed in and heavy, only a few etheric inches from the expansiveness above. I wasn't just looking though, all these thoughts were passing through me.

Absorbing the scene, inhaling it, memorizing it, painting it in my mind, it was becoming me. There it was again, the metaphor of being overwhelmed by something. I could touch it now, the memory. The knowing that I was not operating alone suddenly turned on as if a switch had just been flipped. Something popped the switch on and like a light, I could see. Feeling wholly capable and eager, I leapt up the stairs to my office, not wasting a minute. As I prepared myself, I could feel a calmness return to me.

I felt a peace and wholeness return I hadn't experienced in some time. Also, a sense of vitality and wonderment flushed my cheeks as I breathed in the precious morning air. Strange how possessed I had felt, yet hadn't even noticed it, if that makes any sense. Like you know something is wrong, but you can't seem to focus long enough to see *what*. I shook it off like a nonsensical dream, wondering how I could have been compromised for so long and why. Quickly I heard a familiar voice suggest that the why would not be appropriate, only the *what now*.

Yes, what now? I cleared my mind and laid it out for myself. A dark entity I may have, no, scratch that, I *do* have history with, has reappeared in my life. Something acting on its behalf has kept me blocked from my passion and my skills. This dark one has possessed others to do violence. This character holds the key to my own personal power ... *what?* What am I implying? I knew this was coming. I have to confront him and end this karmic tie, whatever that entails.

Pondering the outline I was presenting for myself, I remembered the pilot. Where did he fit in? He did, I knew this intuitively, yet how, where, why? Is there some past life connection to him? Why such instant ease and comfort with him? Was our meeting yesterday part of what turned the light on today and if so, why would that be? What is this connection and why is it important now? Why is he involved in this murder case anyway? It isn't his fight. I could feel something inside tenaciously seeking resolution. I felt like an invalid finally up and walking outdoors again, stretching tightened muscles, appreciating what was so taken for granted.

Ok, what now then? Create an experience where I can meet Raymond and settle my ancient affairs. That sounded like a good day's work. I smiled to myself thinking I wish it could be that easy. Yet, my mind at least had something to lock onto, something to focus its efforts on. Too long drugged and foggy, my mind was ready to uncover the source of so much violence and angst, but mostly for me, to finish what I must have started a long time ago.

Deciding to create a time-line and wanting to understand better, I began the process of delving into this thing energetically. The whole world is made up of energy. People always think I read minds, but I don't. I read energy and our minds are energy. Feelings are nothing more than waves of changing frequencies. They can be selected out of a chaotic mess and isolated. I do this with time bubbles, too. I simply choose the time period I want to examine and isolate that. It still exists since everything is happening all at once—in the infinite now. It never disappears, as you would be led to believe if limited by the concept of linear time. Energy is all around us and is never destroyed, so we cannot wipe our history clean like we can with a computer.

The timeline begins to unfold for me, mostly to help me have something to do and see physically while my tenacious seeker is inside collecting data.

Now I need to see how the Pilot fits in, if he does at all. I begin by focusing on him. This creates the energy that the mind can focus on. Hold that focus. It isn't hard. He is easy to remember, personable to be with and intriguing. I bring my wandering female mind back to the task at hand. As usual, I was recalling only the warm connection. Yes, focus. Ask questions. Which ones? Part of me very much wants to know, another is stalling. Once you know something, you cannot go back to unknowing, and I knew this.

I ask: Have I known the Pilot before this murder experience? I feel *yes*, definitely yes.

Does that mean a previous life experience? This time, *yes, yes*. Does this mean, yes, yes, or several life experiences?

I ask: How many different life experiences have I known the Pilot? I begin—one, two, three, four, five, the numbers just keep going. I get the point. OK. This is someone I would consider part of my soul group. I indulged my curious, female mind in wondering what roles we had played together and how often. Thinking of us as actors, we must have made quite a few movies together.

Returning to the task at hand—I know I am not here to play theoretical romance with him—but to ascertain the quality of our relationship and what skills we may have created together. I was going to need this more than anything at this point in the time-line.

I uncovered that we had mostly played supporting roles, which I had already assumed from our brief encounter. The information also indicated that we had been instrumental in uncovering things or creating transformation. I could feel the Scorpio nature of our relationship, seeking underneath the everyday accepted norm to reveal mystery, passion, and truth. I didn't know the exact context, and at this point that wasn't necessary.

Was he an asset that could assist me in uncovering Raymond? *Yes.* I could feel the yes, but tentatively. No explanation? I knew what this meant. Ask other questions, is what it meant. The feeling in my gut told me that his involvement would change his life and did I want to be responsible for that? Did I have a choice? *Yes.* I wasn't really asking, it was more of a rhetorical question, but I had to hear that answer, didn't I?

OK, I have one ally who is a novice in the energy world, and unfamiliar with dark entities. Would I have to educate him, or would that be necessary? Taking the last question alone, *no*. I figured. He had developed his own skills in this life. Besides flying, I was sure behind those capable eyes, he had bagged quite a few other talents he was not bragging about.

Confident that I had one ally, even though he didn't know it, I could move on to the more difficult situation. How do I create an experience with Raymond?

I turned inward to my guide. Suggestions? *Take a hike.* Not what I had expected, but excellent advice. I knew my best venue for letting go of brain ideas and gathering real inspiration was to get out of my head and into the woods. Hilde could feel the excitement rising as I raced down two flights of stairs to the garage and my hiking boots. She was tailing me, wagging hers as we went! Life felt so full of vigor again, so filled with excitement and joy, even if that joy meant meeting a very dark old friend. As I was tying my laces, I reminded myself Raymond and I had been friends and lovers once, didn't that account for something? I could feel, *no*, probably just the opposite.

Just then a bolt of lightning shot through my body. The next question paralyzed my being—*where is my gun?* I was shocked with the realization that I hadn't come home from the police station and looked for it that very moment. What was I thinking? I jumped up from my chair and ran over to the cabinet in the laundry room where I had kept my rarely used Colt Python. As I was running towards the cabinet, the implications of its not being there ran rampant through my brain. Oh my god, this was the thing that would … would what? Don't go there. All this talk about possession and not being the right vibration, sheesh, all winter I could have been available to do someone's bidding and perhaps wouldn't even remember! *Where was it?*

I opened the cabinet where the gun has always rested in its hard-shell case and there was the case. I breathed a sigh of momentary relief, but as I opened it, my mouth dropped. It was gone. How could that be? I had not used it in years and would have known if someone had come into my house. Nothing had been stolen, no one had entered my house. My mind followed the energy trail backwards through the entire winter. Had I detected even the faintest whiff of someone else? Only those footprints on the stairs that one day. Yet had I even been in a state of clarity much of the winter? How could I be sure of anything at this point?

I fell back against the wall and slid down to the floor. Looking up at the ceiling, I came to the only conclusion I could. *I had done this.* In my stupor this winter, ever since that dream where those gargoyle creatures went into me, I had become available for doing someone else's deeds. Yet what had I done with the gun? I recalled the detective saying that the killer had left the gun at the scene of the crime, didn't he say that? Didn't he also ask who would do that? *Me!* Not only was I a murderer, I was a really stupid one, too. This thought didn't make me laugh, not even a little.

Do you remember waking up with a shovel in your hand in the middle of the night? I ran outside, hoping for some clues. I looked all around the area where I had awakened with the shovel in my hand. The snow had all melted now and I could see only the faintest hint of soil disturbed. I got the shovel and began to dig. I dug all around that area, but it was clear this soil had not been disturbed all winter, it was hard packed and fall grasses lay brown and pressed from being under the deep snow.

I went inside, trying to think. When was the last time I had used the gun? Target shooting years ago with my husband. Did I leave it in the shop after I cleaned it? I ran down to the shop, hoping to find it there after seven years, lying on his workbench where I had cleaned it.

Turning over every box, every bin, looking behind things, trying in vain to follow an energy trail of something not there, it was nowhere to be found. My mind went through the possibilities of where it could be, but I knew the gun that killed that man was mine. That means, unless someone stole my gun, which I was not prepared to believe for a number of reasons, I had murdered this man in cold blood.

Had Raymond planned this to incarcerate me? To disempower me? Was I being framed? Why would I have left the gun at the scene of the crime? Had he jumped ship? If so, why did I not have any memory of anything other than being a witness? I knew this much, even when I am *slightly* compromised, like when I yell at someone I love, I hardly remember what I said. How could I then remember this incident? Did my mind play that back for me in my head the other day? Or was Raymond pulling it up and recalling it for me?

Yet, as I thought about the vantage point of the inner viewing, I could see *him*, the one *with* the gun. It was not coming *from* me, like in the case of the woman, which I had experienced from the perspective of the killer. I witnessed this killing from the vantage point of the victim. Yet could Raymond have pulled this image from the mind of the dead man, then played it back for me to see my own heinous crime?

What could I do? Was I prepared to turn myself in for something I only *suspected* I did? What if I didn't do it? The despair started to descend on me, like it had this winter. I could not afford that, yet wasn't this what Raymond wanted? He did not play fair, that was for sure. I knew I wasn't compromised at the moment, so I should not be a threat to anyone else. The sickness in my stomach started to make itself known. Why had I looked into those Eyes that day? My life felt like it had taken a slow, and now, not so slow, spiral downward ever since.

I went outside, trying to get clarity. What options did I have? Was there someone who might be able to sort this out with me who knew about these sorts of things? Should I be hypnotized to see if I had done it, yet would I recall that violent scene in my mind, as if it were happening?

Slowly, I walked back to the house, Hilde in tow. What had she seen? I recalled that night I was burying something she had not been there. Why? If only she could talk. Yet, on more than one occasion, I had communicated with her. Once, years ago, I had come home from town to find her running around like she was guilty about something, but at the same time delighted. I asked her what she had been up to while I was gone. When I finally hit upon the thing, she ran around as if to say, oh, dear, am I going to get in trouble for that? I asked her if Rusty had been up here? Rusty was a red heeler—the faithful dog of a friend of ours. "So, Rusty *has* been up here?" I laughed, but I knew he had. She had told me. I let her know there was nothing ever to feel guilty about.

A few days later, I got a call from Rusty's dad, saying he had come up on Tuesday to give me the trail map I had asked him about. I asked if he had Rusty with him, to which he said, as always. Did you let him out to play with Hilde? He said they had gotten along really well and had a great time!

What would she have to say now? Clearly the crime had been committed somewhere other than my property, which meant that Hilde would not have been present. Had someone come in while I was gone to steal the gun? Could someone from one of my groups have taken it? Highly unlikely.

Back to square one. I murdered a man in cold blood. I could not make it right and I didn't have anyone to help me. Just then, my mind directed me to the pilot, Nick. Sure, he could help me. I had already ascertained that he was a friendly. And if I did do it, he would be gentle about it with me. At least, I suspected he would. What would I tell him? Dialing his number, he had given it to me yesterday by the lake, I heard him pick up. Frozen, I now thought better of it after his disappearing act. Yet, these days, there was my name obviously announcing the caller on his phone for me.

"Laura?"

"Nick? Yes, Laura here," trying to appear calm. "Hi, I'm so sorry to bother you, but I was hoping you might offer a fresh perspective here. Remember the gun I told you about, the one that was just like mine, that I saw in the murder scene in my head?"

"Yea?..."

"I can't find it. Anywhere."

I heard a pause; do you *hear* a pause or witness a pause? Either way, I could tell my mind was working overtime. I don't remember exactly what he said. I am sure he was trying to assure me that it was there somewhere or something. At some point, I admitted I was afraid I had murdered that guy, unbeknownst to my conscious self. Again, I heard reassurances, which is no doubt why I had called him. He asked if I wanted him to come up and help me look, to which I replied an instantaneous *yes*. After giving him directions, and hanging up the phone, I sat there wondering what came next now that I had embroiled someone else in my troubles. Was he now an accomplice? My thoughts took me from bad to worse, still I felt like someone clear-headed was on the way and he could help me sort this out. Maybe there was a logical explanation for all this and I just needed to have a sounding board. Breathe, I reminded myself.

Quietly calming my mind, breathing slowly and deeply, things started coming into focus. Did I really think, in any part of me, that I could have been a willing vehicle to a murder? No, not at all. I allowed my mind to slow. Logic was not my friend just now, it was incriminating me. I had to focus on what I *knew*. And I knew I was not capable of murder, inhabited or not.

Yet hadn't I written a paper on monsters in society and how they experience themselves in a way that removes that need from the rest of us, that *anyone* could be capable of expressing themselves as a psychopathic murderer? Yes, I did write that. Breathe.

Hilde went out to greet the pilot and I noticed that she was quite friendly with him, as if they had met before. I asked if he was good with dogs because Hilde seemed to like him. He just smiled and walked up the steep steps to the deck where I was standing to greet him. And without much ado, as I knew he was a man with a purpose, I shared with him what I had already done, where I had looked, my thought process, even my concerns about having done it without having the memory of it. All the while, he just stood there listening, not shocked or afraid, not even seeming to flinch. His resolve was calming, but I wasn't sure where it was coming from. Did he hear what I was saying, did he not care? Had I read him totally incorrectly yesterday in my truck?

30

"Hello, Nick Drake." I saw Laura on the caller ID, but heard nothing on the line. "Hello," pause, "Hello. Is this Laura?" And then my world was once again tossed into the rapids. I wasn't ready for this.

This wasn't the same calm woman sitting together in the truck yesterday. She was frantic, or maybe not frantic, certainly unsettled as all hell. Telling me she buried her gun, that she can't find it, that she must have killed someone. I try as best as I can to calm her down then tell her I'll come right away.

On the way out to her house I was spinning a mile a second. How could she think she killed … and who would it be? Of course she'd think it! She saw, whatever that meant, her gun, and now can't find her gun at all. Of course she can't find her gun. I tossed it in the trunk. Who's dead? Merkle's dead, but sure as hell not by a bullet. Someone is dead, that's for sure. Chief didn't say a thing to me. Why should he? What's the colonel doing? Should have got back to me by now.

I already felt bad about the whole thing. Asking her for directions was the first lie. I sure as hell knew exactly where she lived. I hate lies. I hate that she's in the middle of this, and I sure hate not knowing if she belongs in the middle or not. Is she part of it all? Still no word back on anything to do with her ties to the CIA after that interview. Where the hell was she for ten years? And why can't I just go on home and be done once and for ever. I've got no ties to this commission. Didn't want it then, don't want it now.

Back up the dirt road. Up that driveway. Same dog running around in circles barking like hell. Laura comes down before I'm out of my car. Back up on that same porch. I can still feel Merkle standing there. She's sorry to bother me, sorry to get me so far out of town, but sure seems relieved to see me. Hardly the same woman I was with yesterday. After she goes on for about ten minutes without a breath, I'm feeling like crap. I hate lies. I hate what she's going through. I can't stand here and let her burn up inside.

"I know you didn't kill anyone." She just keeps going on about how she can't find her gun, but she didn't use it. Hasn't even had it out of the case for years.

"I know you didn't kill anyone." I think I finally get through. She just stares at me. I take her hand. I've just got to touch her. Don't know why. "You don't have to explain anything to me. I'm here. I know what's going on. No. No, I don't at all know what's going on, but I know you didn't kill anyone. You sure as heck didn't kill that dead guy down in the morgue." She's still just staring at me. How much can I not tell and still tell the truth. I hate lies. I hate cover-ups. I hate lies of omission where you tell yourself you're not lying. My whole career has been those. But how much can I tell her? Is any of this classified? After all these years? I feel like smacking myself in the face at that question. Why the hell would I care if anything's classified? This woman holding my hand and looking at me is dying here and I give a shit if anything is classified?

"Last Friday?" She nods just a little.

"Last Friday you weren't here?"

"I was here. I had a workshop. Why?"

"Here?" I point to the deck. "Right here? You were right here last Friday?"

"Yes. No. I was down in my studio. I had a workshop to prepare for and I slept down there. It's like a whole apartment. I just fell asleep like I was drugged or something. I was down there until late afternoon. But I was here. I'm always here. I don't go into town more than every few days …"

"Listen to my whole story, OK? The whole thing first, OK?" She just nodded a little bit.

"I was here." I pointed at the deck. She looked confused. "I was right here on this deck and a man I know from my past was here, too. Only he was standing right there with your gun in his hand." I was afraid she'd run away or pass out, but she didn't move. It was like it wasn't a surprise from way the hell out in left field like it should've been. "I've been on his trail since the first murder, last November. Remember when you were hiking and saw a man drive up behind you? I can't be sure, but I'll bet it was this man. His name was Hans Merkle and he worked with me in the military, a lifetime ago. We believe he killed both the girls. The one here and the one you described. He was right here when I got here."

"Did you kill him?" She asked without accusing.

"You won't believe me. I don't believe me. My boss doesn't believe me. But your dog killed him." She still didn't waver.

"He tripped over your dog. And I'm not making any of this up. I came here to kill him. That's for sure. If I would have killed him, I wouldn't feel bad about it. But it was your dog. He tripped right there and went down those stairs and the world is a better place for it."

31

So while I was sleeping in my studio that night, some Hans Merkle guy was somewhere on my property waiting for me, finding my gun? Wonder what he would have done? I remembered Hilde's odd directional barking that evening, but thought nothing of it at the time. Then the feeling of warm protection overwhelmed me as I recalled cutting my hand on the walnut trim and how it sent me into a series of events that seemed now to have possibly saved my life. I could feel my husband warm in my heart.

Nick then explained what had happened next, how it had been an accident and Hilde had unintentionally tripped the man who had fallen down the stairs and broken his neck. Was this the man I saw crumpled in the compartment? My mind corroborated the tracks on the stairs, why Hilde seemed to have known Nick, it all fit, yet it felt so weird. My mountain paradise, so quiet and serene, also a setting for a murder? What was he doing on my deck with my gun? What was he going to do? What was this vendetta about anyway? Perhaps I was simply the untidy witness that needed to be dispensed with, or perhaps Raymond was still using him to do his bidding.

Then he finished the story, with mist in his eyes, about how some redemption had occurred for them both. That felt like it had a place here, but not much else did. I sat down on the chair behind me, dumbfounded at all I was taking in. Right here, a death, a man holding my own gun, with the intention of what? Killing me, framing me, killing someone else? Planting the gun, stealing the gun?

A thousand questions raced through my mind, and all I could think about was how had he gotten the gun, as if his entry would have somehow violated my private world. Yet, it had certainly already been violated. I dropped that line of thinking. Then I began to wonder about this guy,

Nick. Who was he? Why was he on this case? What was the vendetta he was talking about? What sort of pilot was he and …

Just about that time, he began to share his past, at least enough of it that I got the sense that he knew what he was talking about and who this guy was. Still didn't answer my question about why he was on my deck yesterday.

"Where were you after you left the Institute?" he probed.

"What institute?" wondering if he had me confused with someone involved in this vendetta.

"The Monterey Institute of International Studies."

"How did you know about that?" I wondered what else he knew about me.

"Well, for one, it's on the back of your books, in the part about the author. But I was mostly interested in the CIA part."

He looked right into me, waiting for the truth. What truth? My memory took me back to the movie, *Marathon Man,* with Dustin Hoffman playing an innocent who was being tortured because someone thought he knew something. The torturers kept asking him if it was safe and he had no idea what was safe or not. At times, while they were drilling his teeth to extract the truth, he would yell, "YES, it's very safe, it's completely safe, it is so safe!" But they didn't stop. I returned to the question, more put out that I should have to answer that, but then also realizing I was the one who called him for help. How this was connected, I had no idea.

"I met my husband at MIIS, and after graduation we sailed around the world for about 10 years. I interviewed with the CIA for two years thinking that was the path I wanted to take. But at my last interview, we both, my interviewer and I, mutually decided I was not CIA material and there is no more to it than that, at least as far as I know." As far as I know, or as far as I am willing to know? I stopped my mind from probing into places I wouldn't go.

He looked relieved, but still waited for more, perhaps processing what I said against what he knew, registering the truth or the holes in the truth, I don't know. Finally, I invited him in. It was still cold outside, which would explain my shivering.

Over a cup of coffee, he explained his part in this case, the relationship with his colonel and the two women. It seemed like way more information than a guy like this would share with someone he barely knew, yet he seemed to trust me and to know I was telling the truth.

Relieved that I had not killed anyone, could I be convinced that I had not possessed the man who did? I put that aside for now. It was my turn to explain. He asked me why I was involved.

I knew I needed to start from the beginning. Not the beginning of the story, but of how to understand the energy world.

We talked for hours. I explained how we are made of energy and energy is power. And when we leave energetic doors open to that power, something is sure to be around to take advantage of it. I talked about dark intelligences and how people can be compromised by them. He really seemed to understand. He didn't smirk or grimace or even resist anything. I could see he was correlating what I was talking about with what he knew and had witnessed through his own experiences.

"The reason we are in this story together is that your man's vendetta created an opening to be compromised and the energy doing the compromising, or possessing, however you want to see it, is the one I happen to have some tangled karma with. So there are no coincidences that we are entangled in this story, both of us finishing out something from our own pasts."

He asked about what comes next. We speculated together, shared ideas, philosophies and theoretical solutions. Finally, it came down to this. I knew one thing. I had to keep an open heart throughout this next ordeal. That was critical.

I could feel how hard he wanted to understand, but he made it clear to me that he was a man more accustomed to battle than to peace. The very concept of maintaining an open heart in the face of the enemy didn't set well with him, "And what if you can't maintain this open heart thing? What then?"

He had an excellent point. I fail. Period. I cannot face a non-physical being with the power and darkness of Raymond while using only the assets of my physical self. That would be annihilation. Pure and simple. Yet I felt I didn't have a choice. Besides, and I did not explain this to the pilot, I knew this was my master's class test, to hold that space no matter *what*. I could sense his desire to protect me by talking me out of that exam.

32

Drove out of Laura's mountains about 2:00 am with every kind of thought and emotion possible. I've been in some deep shit in my career, but this one just moved to the top of the list. I couldn't exactly reconcile my thoughts with my emotions. Everything she told me was crazy, but at the same time this woman was not crazy at all. Face the enemy with an open heart? Something felt right about that, but I sure wouldn't take that one back to the base. Everything in my life says take him down hard and fast, without a thought. Overwhelming force—always. That's what I've carried with me on every mission. That's what the US Air Force is built on. Hell, that's what the whole damn country is built on. But that part of me deep down inside wouldn't shut up. *Has it worked? Ever?* I've spent the majority of my wasted life south of the border fighting a guerilla war against what? Drugs. Has it worked? And now what about this dark intelligence? *Who has the overwhelming force now?* I wasn't feeling too good as I drove out of that valley. Never been on the losing side. Or maybe I have. I just don't know anymore.

I was almost back to Sandpoint when I suddenly stopped myself thinking about all the crazy spirit-world stuff she told me about and came back hard to the *real world*. What the hell had I done? I put that FBI guy, Higgs, onto her trail after coming back from Maryland. I had completely forgotten that, until now. What did he find? Anything? Was Strickland planning to bring her back in again? Was she ever a serious suspect? Is she a suspect for the dead guy laying there with her gun? Is it really her gun? Damn it, what's happened in the last week? And why the hell haven't I heard back from the colonel? I suddenly felt way the hell out of the loop. Last thing I remember was patting myself on the back for a job well done. Now all this. Overwhelming force. No shit.

No matter what, it's always back to the mission. By the time I got back to the hotel I came up with; protect Laura, protect the general and colonel, clean up the whole damn mess, and get the hell out of Dodge before someone takes me down. Tried to get into bed after a hot shower, but was back up in a few minutes that seemed like hours. Finally at 5:00, 8:00 Eastern, I called Higgs to see if he ever came up with anything on Laura. Of course, whoever I got through to first told me he was in the San Diego office and shouldn't be available for three more hours. Great! I got into the restaurant's kitchen downstairs before they opened and a helpful young guy got me a cup. Took a walk along the lakefront and kept thinking this was supposed to be time for some R&R. No rest for the weary, I guess.

Finally at 8:00 got through to Higgs and that's when I lost it. He told me what they'd come up with. Who was this woman? I was just with her. I could feel the honesty. There was no way what he told me fit with who I just spent the evening with. I figured I should high tail it over to the station and see if I could spray it down before the fire started, but on the way over I just got the thought that I had to check out one more thing. Felt bad about the distrust, but I still had to know.

About two hours on the line with everyone and their third cousins when I finally got what I was looking for. When you've got every single military branch with its own intelligence arm, and every other government entity with its own intelligence arm, and nowadays Homeland Security trying to wrestle the CIA from its hallowed position right smack dab on the top of the heap … well, guess what?

I couldn't actually believe it when the guy himself answered the phone. I already talked myself into the fact that I'd just get a message, but here he was.

"Fred Goddard."

"Mr. Goddard, this is Colonel Nick Drake. I need a minute of your time."

"What branch you with there, Nick?" With all the hesitation you'd expect from a retired CIA guy.

"That's the Air Force, sir. I need to tell you straight off this is an official call, but there is nothing that remains classified."

"Official. Hell, I haven't been official in ten years, son. Least as not any more than I'm getting set to make an official 10:45 tee time. Sure, I'll give you a minute."

"One more thing, sir. I was given your number by Clariston in Ops, and told to tell you that you still owe him for that big-assed beer stein you broke over his head in Hamburg in '94"

"OK, OK. I know you're passed on for real. Thanks for the memory of the good old clandestine days. I'm just an old guy with a 28 handicap now, so let's get on with it." I was grateful he wasn't going to break my back. He sure wasn't under any obligation to talk to me at all. I kept an eye on the clock. Didn't want to get on his bad side by making him miss his tee time.

"Does the name Laura Wexler ring any bells from about twenty years ago?" There was a pause long enough to tell me that it rang one hell of a big bell, or that he was just senile.

"Laura Wexler." He paused again. "Ding. That does ring a bell, colonel."

"Nick, please."

"Nick, you're Air Force, right?"

"Yes, sir."

"Stop calling me sir. So you're Air Force. Clean billets, nice uniforms, pretty airplanes. You a pilot?"

"I am."

"Well then, you've had a pretty clean life of it, haven't you?" I could tell exactly where he was leading me. I had also just told him that nothing was classified on this call. My career had been everything under the sun, except clean.

"Fred, I can tell you that I know what you're asking, and I'm telling you my life has been squeaky clean to a fault." I answered with as much sarcastic inflection I could muster. That made him pause again, and I could tell he caught the innuendo. He knew we were from the same sordid undergrowth of the government.

"Good to hear. Well, not so good, but you know what I mean." I did. "Wexler never worked for me, but I still remember the name." Great. At least this call wouldn't be for nothing. "I drew her file in the late '80s. That's damn near 25 years ago, you know." I actually could count. "Maybe that tells you something. I can't remember where I put my dentures yesterday if you know what I mean." What I knew, was that he was trying his best to act a lot older and dumber than he was. I've seen this crap before. Always an agenda with these guys. "Got an initial from one of the professors down at a little place in Monterey, California."

"Monterey Institute of International Studies?"

"That's right. Have you been briefed on this already?"

"Yes, and no. What I need, is what only you've got."

"Figures. Anyway, I got this initial contact report, so I filed it away like we did back in those days. Just a heads-up to keep an eye out for a potential recruit. I remember needing to go to the DLI for some other business, that's the Defense Language Institute out there in Monterey as well." I was aware of that, but let him go on. Whatever was coming up was important enough to miss a tee time, because he just kept talking. "I figured I'd stop in and see this guy, he taught Eastern European Policy Studies, and actually was a pretty good talent spotter on the side. "So, the professor and I are sitting out in front of the student cafeteria just talking about the sorry state of world affairs, and checking out the coeds, when Laura Wexler goes walking right by us with an armful of mail. My guy points her out to me and says she's doing work-study in the library." I should have guessed I was in for the guy's whole life story at this point. "I don't know, but she sure didn't look like field agent material to me. No idea what hit me, but I filed it away."

"You were her recruiter, then?"

"No, like I said, she went through the basic process of applying, and the whole nine yards: interviews and the such. This was no field recruitment. Anyway, I dug a bit more into her file when I got back to the office. I reread her initial essay and saw the humanitarian I hadn't caught the first time I read it. That girl just wasn't field agent material. She was too naïve, if you know what I mean." I did. I'd just spent the evening with her, and I wasn't sure much had changed. "She had outstanding test results, and already passed the preliminary interviews with flying colors, but I still wasn't comfortable. I don't know, it must have kicked off something in me. I just couldn't let her into our world. It's a dirty part of the world, Nick." No kidding. Wish someone would have been looking out for me way back when.

"Anyway, Nick. I'm just an old man with memories here. And, hell, I'm going to miss my tee off. I followed her through the rest of the application process. I watched her go through a few months of interviews as she finished her degree. I got everything there was to get on her. Then it was nothing but me between her and this crazy dream of being a field agent.

She was out to save the world, or something. Finally we got to the last interview in the process. It took pretty much the whole day up there in San Francisco. We'd set up the orals in some hotel: unfamiliar, strange ground. We tried to keep them uncertain on what was coming. I turned a few other interviewers loose on her in the morning, still trying to shake her up, then I had at her for the rest of the day. There was no way I was letting her into our world, but it had to be her decision. There was no way I could justify cutting her loose based on her previous interviews and exams. She just kept coming back at me. She was telling me what she could do for her country, and how important the work was that we did. She was the most naïve creature I ever met. It must have been about six or seven that evening. We had run through the same scenario for the tenth time, when she finally got it. I will never forget that face when she realized what a female field agent may be called to do for her country. When she left that room wet with tears I hated myself, and have never been more proud in my life. Life as a field agent would have destroyed her, and I'm the guy who prevented that. I think of it as a feather in my cap. That's for sure. Maybe I'll get some credit on the other side. There are times I feel like a failure, Nick, but not that time. I've got to go. First tee's ready and waiting."

"One more thing, Fred, please.'

"Shoot."

"Know what she did after graduation? Seems like she dropped off the radar for about ten years, and that makes me a little concerned."

"After graduation? Not sure that I do. Off the radar, you say? Ten years? What's up here, Nick?"

"I'm trying my damnedest to keep her out of trouble, Fred. And you're right. She's still naïve, and this is a dirty world."

"Trouble! You've got my number. I may be old, but I've still got tentacles if you catch my drift. You call me any time if you think I can help. Ten years, you say?"

With that we were done and I felt a relaxation in me that I hadn't felt in … maybe forever. Now it was time to get to the station and see what kind of fires I had started with that FBI inquiry and how I could put them out.

33

Euphoric was how I felt. Chains were falling away and clarity was surfacing. I was beginning to understand the bigger picture and it was making sense. Something in me felt like celebrating. Even though I knew it was premature, I did not attempt to stifle the feeling. It would direct me to the self-assurance I needed to face the last of this macabre story. Breathing in the fresh spring air, I appreciated the mountain trail that led me upwards. Even seeing the snow-capped mountains in the near distance spoke the metaphorical language of power and presence that I now was seeking to remember. If Leticia had once been so powerful, and I was Leticia, doesn't that mean I, at one time, also owned that personal power? Not to mention the power that we all have innate access to. How to remember it, to re-possess it?

My mind began to reflect on my friend's email to me earlier today. She was asking me if I thought she and I were both caught in a snare of sorts, the kind that limits our personal expression, that essentially robs us of our power. She had gone on to ask what would create such a sabotaging hook. My reaction now, in this place of expansiveness and calm, was simply one word—*fear*. Seeing it through her eyes, I could see where she might find *her* fear. But translating that to *my* life, I was less certain. What fear prevents me from meeting Raymond on equal terms?

Continuing to walk up the side of the mountain, I could only feel the beating of my heart in my ears. No answer. Did I want an answer? I was feeling so euphoric. It was as if some miraculous Hail Mary was going to grace this last scene without any effort on my part. As soon as I recognized that familiar idealistic viewpoint, I knew I had better look again. Going quiet within, I asked in earnest, *what fear prevents me from owning my own power?* There in my inner landscape I was met with various figures from what appeared to be many different lives. Each one had a story to tell.

One woman in medieval dress explained how she had watched her mentor and teacher tortured and brutally killed for the power he owned. Another showed me details of the misuse of power, of the ugly and self-serving, righteous deeds done in the name of power. Still another pushed his way to the front of my inner crowd of karmic players to recount how everything was taken from him—his home, his family, his reputation—and how he was stripped of his political power. Sad stories indeed. Others tried to convince me that to be powerful was to be mean and unkind. To be powerful was to step on others less fortunate, or to take advantage in order to gain that power.

I looked at the lineup of ancient beliefs I held about power. Everything from power is bad. Power is corrupt. Power uses others. Power can be lost. Power brings great pain with it.

No wonder I was not effortlessly embracing this thing we call power. And yet, what was this power I felt I needed so badly? Pondering that question, I was guided to bring in what we know as *force* for contrast. What is power compared to force? Could we say force is coercion, brutish display of will, pushy testosterone? Wouldn't most of these stories be about force, not? What is power, authentic real power? I could feel the answer as a welling up from a reservoir of deep wisdom, a confidence of self, a trust of belonging to something bigger than just your own simple mind and self.

Who might show up as a role model for this? Someone who owns their own deep innate power and shines it? Of course, all good peaceniks remind us of Gandhi. But who is someone I know, someone I can say about them, "that is real power I can emulate?" I stopped under a tree to take a drink of water. Looking out over the valley towards town, my seeking took me to the image of Nick. His energy stood firm before me. I assessed it now. Yes, strong, confident, self-assured, wise, caring, calm, and considerate. Walking through each encounter I had had with him, was there a moment he did not possess these qualities? Indisputably, no.

There. I had written someone into my story at just the magic moment. This may be no Hail Mary, but it certainly was a mighty gift in the form of a powerful role model. Observing Nick's strong and rugged facial features in my mind's eye, I felt a strength of conviction, of purpose that fueled what needed to be done. If Nick could overcome whatever his clouded past plagued him with, if he could find kindness in his heart for Merkle, a cold-blooded murderer, if he could still possess an assurance of knowing who he was throughout it all, so could I. I imagined his face merging into my face. I witnessed his energy overlaid onto mine, our greater minds offering a sense of unity, merging for a deeper purpose. The wellspring of power and wisdom began to flow through me. Overcome by the inspiration of this heartfelt moment, I sat down on a boulder, which overlooks the town to the south and the mountains to the north. Next to this mammoth boulder at the top of the ridge is a tall and majestic Engelmann Spruce. I lay back on the boulder, looking up into the giant tree. The karmic figures began to whirl and whine, telling their stories and swirling around in the cosmic soup of a million stories of a million lives and a million heartaches.

My mind drifted off to human history, to genocides, centuries-long hatreds, rivalries, back to the Middle Ages and the Inquisition, the Crusades, the Holocaust, civil wars. How many karmic stories had I relived through my clients that took us back to times when humans were tortured and killed for being the wrong color, the wrong religion, the wrong race, having the wrong beliefs? I could feel that the energy that I saw fueling those Eyes back in November had to have been old, ancient, tailored, focused and honed to manifest with such intense blackness and harm. This energy had manipulated human expression for eons.

It all made so much sense now, at every level. The man in the truck, the Eyes, was Merkle inhabited by Raymond. And the vendetta that Nick described certainly fit the bill for a perfect energy match. Yet why had he chosen *this* old deserted logging road to dump Rebecca's body? And where was Raymond now? Was he still with the guy who had my gun? But where? Why? Some questions could not be answered just now. Perhaps a simple deed needed to be done and an essentially empty vessel could be occupied by anyone powerful enough to inhabit it. Could it be that simple? If so, what hope was there of ever stopping an energy force as dark as this from doing whatever it wished? Nothing.

If we all contain powerful creation energy, who is to say we have to express ourselves as only *good*? Any way we experience ourselves is our unique and personal expression of creation, right? Yet, it comes back to this question; What was my purpose for being involved? I knew as quickly as I had formed the question in my mind. *To transform this energy.* To help it dissipate. To help it take on a new form.

Is this what Raymond was asking for? To be transformed? That did not feel like an energy match. He felt threatening, not asking.

34

"Well, well, it's my Air Force pal."

"Hello, Chief."

"Every time I see you, I think it's the last time. I've been meaning to get back to you to thank you for hooking us up with the Feds. Little guys like us don't have the resources you big boys do, do we?" He tried to make some conspiratorial wink. I wasn't sure who I wanted to smack in the head, him or me. I'm the one who opened this can.

"Seems our little lady is way deeper in this than we thought. Care to see the next entries in this file that's destined to become a Sandpoint legend?" I just kept getting sicker in the stomach.

"What have you got?"

"I'll get you a cup while you settle in. Be right back." He left me for about half an hour, no coffee, but some seriously bad reading material.

I'm sitting in this small police station in this out of the way berg with some very bad evidence. Evidence that would have stayed where it belonged if it weren't for me. Two days before the general's daughter, Samantha, was killed in Maryland, Laura purchased an air ticket for one Jose Garcia Hernandez from Spokane to San Diego. No further trail on him from San Diego. However, his record shows two separate periods of incarceration for violent crime. Why would she do that? Also, her record shows incarceration in Acajutla, El Salvador. That's the one Higgs told me this morning that made me almost lose my breakfast. Acajutla is about 150 miles from where I thought Merkle was killed. But she was there ten years earlier. What was she doing in El Salvador?

Then nothing else of interest in the file. Nothing else you couldn't pick off the internet, anyway. So there's one serious piece of interest that happened a long time ago, and another that was way too recent, and way too wrong. Why didn't she tell me anything about that yesterday? Doesn't say anything about what she did to get arrested or how long she was in, or anything else. This is one piece of crap intelligence here. She didn't say anything about this Hernandez guy, either.

"Chief Longfellow, this is a bunch of crap." I said to him when he finally came back in with a lukewarm cup of coffee for me. I could tell I wasn't in friendly territory anymore. It was starting to feel like the Chief was seeing the checkered flag and he was going to make a go for it, nonsense or not.

"Not how we see it around here, son. This señor Garcia Hernandez is a known drug and weapons runner and she is part of funding his operation." I have spent the best part of my life keeping expressions off my face that would betray the true disdain or disgust I felt for the person I was forced to listen to. That's just what you sign up for if you're going to survive anywhere in the military. There is always someone above you. I knew I wouldn't get anywhere with him, so it was time for a flanking maneuver. I've also spent a significant part of my life developing flanking maneuvers when the position you need to take down is too strong to face head on.

"Chief, I just stopped in to say I'm out of here. This is your baby now." I stood up reached to shake hands and accomplished exactly what I wanted to do, short of slapping this bastard up side his head. I could tell he was caught way off guard. Only thing he could do was shake hands and thank me for my help.

I left the station and got back to work.

What I had to do next had to be done in person. Too many unanswered questions. Too many pieces not fitting together. And most of all, why was I one of those pieces on this chess board? I've been moved around my whole damn life. Sometimes a pawn, that just comes with the uniform—get used to it. Sometimes a rook. Maybe lots of times a rook. I've had a meaningful amount of power over the years. A rook is like a bull. Straight across the board. Taking down anything in his way. But a rook can't turn, can't go anywhere but straight ahead. Predictable. Kind of like the bishop, but at least the bishop goes at an angle. Maybe a little harder to predict. Maybe not. Depends on the opponent. Never been the King, that's for damn sure. Take a guy like me out of the picture and the game still goes on. Double sure as hell I've never been the queen. Behind the scenes with all the power. No way is that my part in this crazy game. Feels like the knight this time. Tricky little bastard. You think he's going here, but he goes the other way. Maybe that's it. Maybe I'm being played like a knight this time. Huh, what the hell. Time to talk to the King.

Left the car at the Spokane airport with an extra drop fee. I figured I wouldn't be around long enough to get the ream job on my expense report. Not this time, anyway. No commercial flights heading east for a couple hours, so I grabbed a taxi over to Fairchild AFB. Figured I'd grab something military. Fairchild is mostly air-to-air refueling, but you never know what they've got sitting around on the ramp. Losing my patience fast so I headed straight to the base commander. Didn't know him personally, but if you're going to pull strings, start at the top.

"Colonel Boswell?"

"Colonel Drake. What can I do for you?" He was pretty amiable, probably thinking I'd stopped in just for a hello.

"Colonel, thanks for seeing me and sorry for barging in here unannounced."

"That's not a problem."

"I need to get to the Pentagon, ASAP. Nothing out of Spokane for a few hours and this just can't wait." He looked at me like I was joking. It's really not a big deal to hitch a ride, so what's this guy doing in *my* office? I could read his mind on that one. He paused a second then took a look at the orders I passed to him. Simply told me to grab a bite in the mess hall and he'd send someone over to collect me ASAP. Walking out of that base commander's office got me to thinking. What if? What if the colonel, who wasn't a colonel back then wouldn't have grabbed me right out of flight school? Would I have had a regular career as a regular officer? Maybe that would have been *my* desk. Maybe I'd have had an office on some base somewhere. God, what a thought! Got a plate and a tray and headed for the food. Do I thank the old man, or kill him?

I was in the air within the hour, but in the back of a KC-135 air tanker on a training mission, and I do mean an old one. This is one far cry from that Citation X Craig Walker gave me.

For the next few uncomfortable hours all I could think about was that evening at Laura's. What she told me made sense on some levels, but was crazy as hell on others. Every time my butt started to fall asleep I did think of her again.

Anyway, I needed to talk to the general himself. I needed the unfiltered story on why the hell I'm the guy running around putting out fires. I am no investigator. No investigative experience. Wasn't even in uniform a few weeks ago. So why am I sitting in this ancient bird heading to the Pentagon, anyway? Just keeps getting worse. Talk about one boring job. Flying a couple hundred thousand pounds of fuel in an airplane that's almost as old as I am. If this bird feels a bad as I do, we're going down way before we get to Virginia.

I'm in and out of uncomfortable sleep when I pick up a change in pitch as the pilot starts to throttle back. Wow, can't believe I've been sleeping that long already. Would have swore that I just dropped off. No windows in this bird so I just sit back and feel how he's going to put her down. Smooth as butter as I hear the wheels just barely chirp on touchdown. Stopped at the ramp and doors open to ... what the hell? I've sure been to this sorry place before. Nothing in me feels anything like surprise after the initial shock, though. Standing about a hundred feet out is the old turd himself. Why the hell would anyone live in Minot, North Dakota? I walk on over and he just turns around towards a car expecting me to follow him like some duckling.

We don't say a thing as he drives off base and to his house. Once there he tries to act as sociable as he knows how. At least he's nice enough to offer me a beer. I mean he just shoves one towards me. I guess that's an offer.

"Where the damn hell were you going, Drake?" Nice to see you, too.

"I'm beyond a little tired of this whole thing. I figure it's just time to ask the big man why I'm in the middle of it all. This morning I was in the Sandpoint police station. You remember that Longfellow jerkoff, don't you? He shoves this pile of crap at me and the next thing I know Laura Wexler is number one on the international terrorist hit list. You remember her, right? It's bullshit, the whole thing is bullshit and you know it."

"Becky is dead, Nick, Samantha too. I don't smell any bullshit here." I guess I didn't expect that, but I did deserve it. Made me feel like crap. He was always an expert at that.

"It's not about that and you know it. Why me? That's all. You know I'm not up to this mission. Why'd you call me? Why not OSI?" This was one for the special investigations boys. "Someone who knows what they're doing. I'm in this too deep. I have no idea why. And now this setup for Wexler. She doesn't have anything to do with anything as far as I can tell."

"You took down Merkle, Nick. I guess that means you were up to the mission. We only had rumors that he was still alive. Just loose ends and rumors. You were on this, what two days? And you found him and took him down. Why can't you ever accept how good you are? You were always my best. I always used you when I needed my 'A' team, Nick. What's your personal problem with that?" I felt like saying it had been a hell of a lot more than two days, but felt like crap with what he was saying. I just sat there, beer in hand in his simple house in Minot, North Dakota.

"Time to step up, Drake. You've hit so many out of the park I can't count 'em. You've never failed me or your country. I know you think I gave you those birds on your shoulders back in '04 to apologize for hanging you out to dry in Africa. I knew South America was your thing, and I knew then you were out of your comfort zone. But that's just the way things went. You know that." What I felt about that bullshit promotion was not what I was prepared to tell him. It was out of order and just like this mission, made no sense. Just placation, no more.

"No apologies there, and none here. Now you listen to me, Colonel. We had some things going on back in '97 that you were not privileged to know about. Get used to it. You know that's how it was, how it is, and how it always will be." I definitely knew that and accept it, too. "General DeWitt headed an operation that I seconded and sergeant Hans Merkle was picked because of *none of your damn business*. Things went bad then and that mission has disappeared from history and will stay out of history. You follow me here, Nick?" I did.

"First thing. The only thing. He and I both lost someone we loved. We've both paid for our sins here, and we both have to live with that. Becky's not coming back and Samantha isn't either." This man could compartmentalize his emotions. Always could. I just wouldn't want to be around in the night when it was just him and a bottle of JD.

"This was a civilian investigation and is still going on both out in Idaho and Maryland. Those deaths were not military and we cannot tread on that territory. But I wasn't going to let who ever touched Becky walk this earth another minute. I thought about ten seconds before I brought you in, Nick. It was a list of one. I'm not sorry how I did it. When Samantha was killed, I spent time with Jack and the only conclusion we came to was that this was connected. We're old you know, but we're not stupid. We tracked back our common sins and that mission Merkle was brought in on was only one of many. I think we all got lucky, or maybe, what I really think, is that we both got fortunate that it was you I brought in. Not an investigator. I really do get tired of your whining, you know." This was not the best day of my life, sitting here.

"You are forbidden to continue on to see General DeWitt. Is that clear?" He didn't wait for an answer. "You are to return to your home and are authorized leave. Take some time, Drake. You'll get orders and be back in saddle sooner than you think. You are ..."

"Colonel." I stopped him. "I'm not going to argue with you. And I'm not going to fight you on this." I remembered what Laura told me about laying down the sword. "But I'm not going home. Mostly, I'm not going to hang Laura Wexler out to dry for you or the general or anyone else. We make this right. Right now." I could see the wheels turning in that head of his. "I know you can do this for me. For her." He didn't move for what seemed like ten minutes, but was probably only 30 seconds.

"Get back on out to the flight line. I'll get on it. But know this. This is because I owe you. Owe you big. But you owe me, too. We're in this together. Always have been." He stood up and it was clear I was dismissed. Any normal person would have put out his hand to shake, but he was reaching for that phone of his as I walked out the door. Never could tell how many people were on the other end of that phone, but it always seemed like anyone he needed. At least I didn't bother to look back when I took his car keys on the way out. I'm sure he could find a ride later.

35

For the past few days all I had done was prepare myself energetically. I don't like to dawdle, especially knowing there could be others in this macabre play, and for them it wouldn't seem like a choice, yet I had to ready myself or it would be an exercise in futility. I had one shot at this. You don't come up to a bully and say, never mind my last three failures, I really am going to kick your ass this time. Or maybe you do, I tried to let myself think I had options.

Besides keeping an open heart and an image of self-assurance, I was looking for anything in my own system that might sabotage my strength. I was working overtime to release or update old programming, whichever was required. I found old fears associated with the consequences of shining too brightly and images of myself as a peacemaker, but never the cardinal character. My inner strength was definitely being attended to as I found ways to step beyond the limitations of those beliefs. But I still had not found anything karmic that might be about the life of Raymond and Leticia. Did I need to? Or is that how I was going to confront him? No sooner had I thought this than a shiver of goose bumps activated my left arm, my personal truth validator. This left me feeling unprepared. What would I find? And why open it when I knew Raymond would be there too, which he would be if I opened a karmic bubble with his name on it?

Wasn't there a way I could have previous knowledge? What was I afraid of? I knew my open heart would protect me. Yet even this thought made me realize I had given some power away in this story. Yes, that was obvious or I would not have needed to do so much work around it. I decided to reclaim whatever authority I had given away—at least that I was aware of. I called to my mind every teacher, partner, friend, student, or boss that I may have inadvertently given power to or deferred to and just reclaimed what was mine.

Sitting with this surge of power and strength, I felt full of my own destiny. I wondered about my deceased husband. Had I left power with him? Had I allowed a certain amount of victim-hood to remain on his account? Of course I had. And nothing saps your power faster than playing the victim card. You are either a co-creator or a victim, you cannot be both. I felt a pang of sadness in having to give up this treasured vestige of him, yet I knew this was key. Sitting quietly with him, readying myself, I heard the phone go to my answering machine. I guess I had never turned the ringer back on from earlier, not wanting to be interrupted during my inner work.

Open to a distraction, I listened as I did not really want to give up this piece of him stored in my heart. Even though it was not honoring, it kept him still in my story. Oddly it was someone from the police station saying officially I was not allowed to leave the county without notifying them, or something like that. I think my ears were in as much shock as my mind and they refused to listen. What did this mean? *What do you mean, what does this mean?* Only one thing. I am a suspect. Oh my god. Where do I put that? What did they discover and didn't Nick tell them I was innocent? Could he? What if I really was the one who did it without my knowing? Was I being framed because of all this higher-up stuff? Don't get ahead of yourself. You have one task right now and do not let yourself be distracted. I needed to stay focused. I knew this was easier said than done, yet I did not want to drain my reserves of energy thinking about what ifs right now.

I attended to my old story, well, to my stubbornness about holding onto the victim part of it anyway. I knew this was a necessary piece of my power puzzle.

Where do I begin? I called in the image of my husband, before he took his own life. I expected to see him sad and tragic, as he had been in his final days. Instead, I saw him glowing. How could this be? I allowed myself to sense and feel him in his newness, wherever and however that was. What I felt was truly gladness and joy. Could this be? Shocked, but delighted, I listened. Without words he conveyed his transition to understanding and a different story, to a state of knowing that he had always held the key to his own joy. He radiated and as we connected I realized I had kept him trapped in my mind as suicidal and morose. That's how I last knew him to be.

Opening my heart to his *now* story, even though it did not include me, I allowed him to transform before my mind's eye. I could feel him correct my last thought. I was still in his story and he in mine. He indicated he was here to assist me on the non-physical plane. *With Raymond?* I felt his response was yes, with Raymond and with any other need. I recalled Rory and my experience assisting him pass into the spirit realm. Was my husband there with Rory? Were they both there to assist me, did they know each other, had they helped each other heal? I wondered. He smiled at it all, I knew he knew. I felt so snug, so loved, so complete. No victims here, only a being of great resolve and compassion, strength and caring, and peace. That's what he had always wanted, there it was—peace. I felt the same peace course through my system, connecting us together in a place or time not here, not there. I felt a sense of freedom, for us both that I had not felt in many long years. It felt so wonderful. I welled up with love for him and the knowing that he was exactly where he should be.

All my sadness drained as the victim card was swept away with one instant of knowing. No longer did I hold him in a story that felt he had no choices. We smiled at each other, filled with the present moment and our continued love for each other, even though it would take a new shape now. I could see him being a part of my energy healing work, no longer my physical partner. I felt my heart open in a way it had not in a long time. He could feel that heart expand and I could feel him nod. Tears of joy filled my eyes. A welling up of intense warmth and light overcame my entire being. I knew that this awareness would forever shift my sadness and remorse, guilt and pain about him. And it would erase my nightmares and loosen the grip of his torture in my mind forever.

Just then, in my state of expanded love and acceptance, I heard Hilde run out the lower doggy door to bark a warning that someone was coming up the driveway. Part of me hoped it was Nick, but as I got up to look out the window, I saw it was a police car. That didn't take long; they were making sure I had not left the country. I put my shoes on to go down and greet them. I saw it was two uniformed officers, yet neither was Strickland or Longfellow. Perhaps they just had some questions. As I walked down the long stairs on the outside of the house, they introduced themselves and asked me to join them in the squad car. What for, I asked? "Taking me downtown." That sounded so Hawaii Five O. "Book 'em, Danno." Was I being booked? One officer suggested I gather a jacket and we got in the car. I let Hilde know I would be right back, I expected I would at least. Would they drive me all the way back up here? I guess they would have to. I suggested I drive my own truck, but the driver said that was not necessary. He sounded pretty formal.

I tried to make small talk, but neither one answered. I then noticed there were no door handles in the back seat. I suddenly felt very claustrophobic. *Don't go into what ifs, Laura. Just take one step at a time, keep that heart open. Breathe.* It was kind of stinky back there. I didn't really feel like breathing and as I began to settle into the back seat, the energy left behind by others began to surface in my awareness. Fear, panic, confusion, chaos, remorse, anger, I tried to stifle my association with it. But then thought if I had to sit in it for the half hour drive into town, I may as well clear it out, which felt better, but I was still left with my *own* confusion and inner panic.

I was taken to the desk of Officer Strickland, or was it Investigator Strickland? Without much ado, he formally acknowledged that he had some questions he needed clearing up in the case of the recent murders. He advised me on my right to council and then started asking me questions about my credit card being used to purchase an airline ticket for someone named Jose Garcia Hernandez. What was he talking about and what did this have to do with anything and why would I need a lawyer? I pleaded ignorance because I thought he was crazy. Why would I buy an airline ticket for someone I didn't even know? Sure he had the wrong person and certainly the wrong credit card, he then proceeded to show me a receipt with my name on it, not signed, but clearly my credit card. Someone must have stolen it to use it. Have you lost your credit cards? I looked in my wallet and they were all there. So someone stole my card and then replaced it? Oh dear. What was this about? What did this have to do with the murders?

Strickland said there was some reason to believe I was in cahoots with a group of South Americans that had spear-headed some sort of vengeance murders. I remember Nick saying something about this guy Merkle having just come from Central America. Then Strickland was asking about my time in a South American prison. Wow, what didn't he know? I tried to explain my innocence. It was during the time my husband and I were sailing around the world and we were oblivious to some local regulation that landed us in jail for a night until the mix-up got straightened out and it was Central America anyway. He just kept jotting down notes, never even giving me an appreciative nod or uh-huh to let me know he understood. It seemed that everything I was saying was incriminating me even more.

Then he asked me about my association with the CIA and I felt sick. This was feeling like some sort of cover-up or frame job. Some of my distant family members still joke about me being in the CIA, because they knew I had interviewed with them, what, about 20 years ago. They thought I hadn't been able to let anyone know the position I had taken, like it was top-secret. I let them believe it. It added some color to our normal Midwestern family. I never considered myself actually working *for* the CIA. It didn't help that I disappeared around the world for the next 10 years either. Did my aunt from Tennessee tell them this? How did they find her? Same last name, I guess. I am going through all this in my mind when he interrupts my thinking to repeat the question he thought I was ignoring.

After several more questions and about an hour and a half, I was escorted to a cell. What? What is this about? Don't we live in a country where we are innocent until proven guilty? He said I was being detained because they had reason to believe I was cohorting with terrorists. Oh god, the ever-loving terrorist clause, of course, how could I forget about Der Faterland and its quest for power? Anyone could be detained after the Patriot Act if they were suspected of being a terrorist. It felt like everything I had ever resisted was being stockpiled for this one day. I assumed this would all be cleared up in the morning and asked if they would let me call my neighbor to go up and feed Hilde. I could hear her in my head saying I reneged on my promise that I was coming back shortly. All I needed right now was guilt from my dog.

Still trying to understand what was going on, I sat quietly on the bed in my little jail cell. This made the back seat of the police car smell like lilacs. I noticed I was breathing shallow, and knew I should clean the energy up before I could shift my rotten attitude. I could clean the energy, yet almost as soon as I did, it felt like it began seeping through the walls, from the ceiling, the cement floor, back into the space filling the room again. I tried patching the walls and ceilings with a barricade of protective energy, but it seemed that would not hold it off very long. This place was steeped in negative energy and I was only able to hold it back so long. Finally, I gave in to it. I stopped resisting and opened up to embrace whatever it was.

I could hear Raymond, his distant echoey laughter, making himself known. Was I going to have to confront him *here* of all places? That suddenly made me want to shore up against it all. Retreat to my heart castle and pull up the drawbridge. But I knew I could not. This would leave me most vulnerable, as illogical as that seemed. I knew this with total certainty. I decided I wouldn't make a move. I would stay in my own place of comfort: my open heart. I could manage that. Sitting with the energy of all those who came before me in this cell, I sifted through it, shedding love in places where there was only angst and fear. When I came upon a wave of anger, I allowed it to vent in my heart, to dissipate for being heard and acknowledged. Quietly, intently, I focused only on keeping my heart open to whatever happened, to whatever I felt, to whatever passed through me. I sensed a sweetness and innocence, I cuddled it. I felt the presence of deep darkness, evil and remorse. I thanked it for taking the burden of that role from others in society so that we didn't have to play it. I knew any of us were capable of playing that part, yet these others had stepped forward to claim it, and its requisite karma.

Somewhere in the middle of that, I must have fallen asleep because I was being awakened by the sound of keys jingling. I thought I was in a movie, but reminded myself that this was not movie, this was my *present* life. Not a past time bubble, but the one I was currently occupying. This brought me to alert status quickly. I sat up rubbing the sleep from my tired eyes, still unable to see who stood at the door.

36

Not a bad trip back, all and all, same KC-135, but the second crew. You've got to love the Air Force. Just another training mission. What, maybe $15K an hour? God bless the taxman. At least on the way back we refueled a couple F-16s. Now that's a sight. I'd never been on this end of the hose before.

I'd been on a phone patch most of the trip back from Minot getting the back story of Laura's file. The more I learned, the more the whole thing felt like some kind of old television comedy hour. I couldn't wait to shove this one down Longfellow's throat. No way that was a bridge I wouldn't burn. Didn't matter by now. What I had to do next was so far outside legal I wouldn't want to ever be caught as much as jaywalking in his town.

Seems that the Feds hadn't shared the whole story with Longfellow in the first place. No reason not to, but as always there had to be an agenda somewhere somehow. That air ticket for that Hernandez guy was purchased with Laura's credit card, but not from her computer. Seems there was some Rosa Flores person who bought it. Seems she's some local caterer in town. Could be a connection there. Feds have got a man in town now following on that. Doesn't seem like rocket science to me. Got to wonder who the hell Longfellow's got working investigation.

And the El Salvador connection. That's even better. One night for not clearing customs correctly. What'd they do, get off the boat before the port captain came out? Kids. You're in a foreign port, you jump to and follow the rules. Naïve kids, that's all they were. One night in jail in Acajutla. Who would have fed that one to Longfellow? And why? And why is he sitting there with this file that must have been spoon fed to him like baby food?

Nice drive back to Sandpoint from Spokane. Nothing I can do tonight so I stop for dinner in a little burrito place. Still can't put anything together, and am still trying to ignore that the chief may have her pistol connected to a dead man. He didn't say anything about that connection so maybe it was never registered. She didn't say how long she'd owned it or where she bought it. It's been so many years since I've needed a civilian weapon I don't know what they're doing nowadays as far as gun tracking. Got to check up on that one. I'll ask her in the morning. Sure would be a gift from Santa if that gun wasn't traceable back to her. Either the colonel totally blew me off on that one or he's still in the dark himself.

Another hour and I'm back to my hotel. What's it been, one whole day? Seems like a month. Nothing beats a hot shower after a day like this one. Red light's flashing on the phone. Who knows I'm here? I've got a cell phone. Listened to the message, and man do I get one shot of adrenaline through the heart. Son of a bitch arrested her! What the hell is that man doing? And that little shit Fed left a message here? What's that about? Covering his ass, but not really wanting me to get it? He could have called me on my cell. What's the agenda here? I'm running about a million scenarios in my head as I'm out the door. I actually get the guy on the phone before I get back out to my car.

"Slow down, Colonel Drake."

"Yea, right, I'll slow the hell down. What's going on? Why is Wexler in jail? What the hell are you doing out here, anyway? Why'd you call my hotel? Haven't you …"

"Sir. Sir. I tried your cell number since 2:30 today. I've been trying to reach you everywhere. Took some work even finding out you were registered at the hotel."

"I'm not showing any messages." Time to prioritize. I'll figure this out later. "Give me what you've got. Forget the phone."

"As you know, sir, I'm tasked from the Seattle office," I didn't know where the hell he was from, "to investigate the connection of one Rosa Flores and one Jose Garcia Hernandez, a person known to have international drug connections." Yea, yea, to the point here. Why is she in jail? "This Flores is Hernandez's aunt. She also has a catering business in town and is known to cook for special events. Ms. Wexler owns a retreat center in the mountains near town here." I'm sitting in my car with the engine running and about to climb through the phone and choke this guy to death. Where do they grow these FBI guys? Get to the point! "I found charges to the same credit card in three stores in town, all for food supplies and all preceding and during a women's retreat I found posted in the calendar section on Ms.Wexler's web page. I did interview two of the three checkers who processed those purchases and one of them personally knew this Rosa Flores. We also were able to ascertain that the airline ticket purchased with the same credit card was purchased from a computer in this Rosa Flores's home." I really did not need a full after-ops briefing on this, but this guy was on a roll and what he needed was a pat on the head and a gentle kick in the butt. I kept listening. "I am working on the hypothesis that Ms. Wexler gave Flores her credit card for food purchases related to the women's retreat and that Flores used that credit card to purchase the airline ticket for Hernandez. At this point I believe Ms. Wexler was unaware of these purchases." Here he paused and was either waiting for his doggy treat or a pat on the head. I couldn't tell which. Good investigation work, I'll give him that. But let's take some action here.

"That's one hell of a piece of good work, Martin. How long have you been on site here?"

"37 hours, sir."

"One hell of a good job. Meet me at the jail. Let's get her out, OK?"

"Oh," he paused, "I'm not authorized to take any further action, sir." And he sure as hell was not in my chain of command. I've dealt with guys like this before. The harder you push, the more they don't move. And I sure didn't have anything on Longfellow or Strickland. And, it was getting close to midnight.

"Stand by for me. Will you do that, Martin? What's your first name, anyway?"

"Charles, sir."

"How long you've been a field agent, Charles?"

"I've been with the Bureau two years, Colonel." I noticed he didn't say he'd been a field agent two years. Hell, this could be the first time they let him off the leash. This certainly wasn't the biggest case they've ever dealt with. Kid gloves here, Drake.

"That's excellent work, Charles. I need you to stand fast and be at your phone. I have no idea why you couldn't reach me today, but you can bet I'll be all over it as soon as I can. Must have been something on my end. Right now I'm going to find you some authorization so you can get this woman out of jail. We both know she doesn't belong there."

"I'm just in my hotel now, sir. My phone is on, but there really is nobody I can reach for authorization at this hour."

"I'll get back to you." And I hung up and was back on the line in a second.

"Richards." After one ring. We always used to joke that he never slept ... or ate, or took a crap.

"I was just briefed by some Fed on the ground here. Longfellow's arrested Wexler. He doesn't have anything even approaching an accurate file on her. He's out of line on this one and we ... I, helped him. I need her out and I need you on it, now."

"What about that handgun? What's on that?" I didn't need that question. The only thing that could dirty up the whole thing.

"No confirmation, but I'm going with no connection back to her. Been years since they made that pistol. I'm not picking up any registration trace-back." Of course I had no idea about any of that. He didn't say a word. "This Fed out here is just a kid with no balls to take action. I need him to get a call," He still paused long enough to run the moves through that head of his.

"Wait one." And I was on hold. One thing I've accepted in this life is that I'll never know how he does what he does.

After about twenty minutes he's back on the line. He could have called me back, but he doesn't wait for you, you wait for him. Always been that way.

"Give it a few minutes then hook up with your boy and get her out." That's what I wanted to hear. I could feel the tension drain out of my muscles. "And Drake?"

"Yea."

"This has got to end at a complete dead end, you know." Now that's the understatement of the century.

"That is the mission as I understand it." And I was off the line.

"Chief Longfellow. Thanks for coming back in at this hour." He didn't seem as put out as I would have thought. Not considering I was standing here with some Fed probably not much older than his own grandkids.

"That's not a problem, Nick. And this is?"

"Charles Martin, Sir. FBI. I'm in from the Seattle office." Longfellow's face told me he hadn't expected that. No turf wars between him and the Air Force. No reason for that FBI. That was a whole other ballgame. Probably nothing but turf wars. Time to see if this kid was up for the big leagues. Longfellow didn't say a word.

"Sir, I was tasked with the investigation of one Rosa Flores ..." Time for me to zone out for a few minutes and take a mental rest. I'd heard this story before, and it wasn't a short one. By the time it was over, I could tell Longfellow was going to throw in the towel. My respect for the man just shot up a few points. Martin told me he could call in a FAX from on high taking jurisdiction. I was prepared for a bare-knuckle fight on that one. I knew it wouldn't be pretty, but come hell or high water I'd still walk out with Laura tonight. Kid went in and presented his case not stepping on any toes, showed finesse. Nothing the chief could do but step aside. I think he knew it was all a pile of crap anyway. He just wanted to close this case and she just looked too good to be true. International drug running and the South American connection. Maybe he had had enough time to go back over the case and realize it didn't hold water.

He looked right at me, not Martin. "We did a little looking around ourselves, Nick. Not just sitting on our hands here." I could feel what was coming. "Had Rosa Flores in just a couple hours ago. Got the whole story. Woman must have apologized about a million times for using that credit card. All she was concerned about was that good-for-nothing nephew of hers. Good intentions gone wrong. That's all." I was back to my famous poker face. Been in this spot before. "What'd you think, I was going to hang Laura Wexler?" He must practice that little one-eyed blink thing he does. Makes you want to smack him in the face. Then why the hell is she still in jail?

"Doesn't surprise me in the least, Chief. I just got back from Washington, myself, today." I was on the way to Washington, at least. "So I hadn't heard anything about any of this until a few hours ago when I met agent Martin, here." Kid was still smiling proud about his investigations even though it seemed to me the Chief trumped him. "I'm not questioning anyone's professionalism here. I am wondering why Laura is still in your jail though."

"You do have a thing for her, don't you, Nick?"

"I do feel a degree of protection for her, yes."

"Yea, protection, that's all." He just wouldn't lay it down.

"And," I paused, "why is she still in jail?" If I choked him to death right here and now, I'd be in the cell next to her.

"Take a look over here, Nick." We all went to the duty sergeant's desk where there were monitors observing the cells. "She's been sleeping like a baby. I figured to let her sleep, then send her home in the morning." God! I couldn't believe it. Man thinks he's running the Hilton here.

"Chief. I understand. I really do. Good motivation. But I'd like to take her home. Right now. If that's OK with you." He looked at me long enough to say that it may be OK with him, and maybe not.

"Sure. Of course, Nick. She's all yours. Sergeant, take these men back with you and release Ms. Wexler."

When that cell opened and woke her and she looked up at me I don't think I have ever felt anything like that before. Then the sergeant told her she was free to go. She came over with tears in her eyes and gave me the hug of my life. We all walked out of the police station together. I thanked agent Martin still smiling his job well done. I drove Laura home and she never let go of my hand. Sometimes you get a good day and you know that you have a purpose in this crazy life. Sometimes it's all worth it.

37

Looking out over the bare beginning of a blossoming spring, bundled in a blanket on my deck, I pondered the last few days. Now that it was over, I felt the shock of having been detained, *not detained, why was I using their polite word?* I had been thrown in the pokey. Odd how things were working out, although not really from an energetic standpoint. Just as I had found the inner strength and capability to confront the past that contained Raymond and his darkened energy, yes, almost instantly, I was removed from my safe haven and placed in a container of fear and anger. Those were his emotions. That is where he thrives, not me. I had gone to his home court.

As I let my mind wander, sipping tea on autopilot, I could feel the eyes again. I gently followed the thread, expecting to see them in one of the memories of his possessions. Instead I was taken to the last image I had of Strickland at the station. Strickland? Yes, there they were, the same darkened, threatening and deeply evil eyes. Why had I never noticed them before, the similarity, if that is what it was. My internal voice offered, *they weren't like that before.* What did this mean? Why did I have this habit of asking myself questions I already knew the answer to? Point in case. I recalled the moment again. I turned one last time to respond to something Strickland said just as he put me in the cell. What was it? Then I caught them. The eyes had grown very dark and ominous. Yet, the sensations I had when that cell door closed were so overwhelming, I'm sure I let it go as swiftly as I had acknowledged it. What did he ask me, or say?

Strickland had not been possessed, I believed that. Why, I am not sure, other than there are so many more qualities that become very pronounced as soon as someone is fully compromised by something that powerful and dark. Was Raymond making himself known, just for that moment? Was it his way of destabilizing me? I remembered now. When I said something about not understanding what any of this was about, he replied something like, *this is bigger than either of us*. And it was Raymond's voice. How did I know that? Was I remembering it from the scene I witnessed with Leticia in their home in another time or did he actually say that yesterday through Strickland?

Not wanting to fixate on this one event, something in me shuddered at my dismissal. I fell away from that thought and returned to my tea and the view. *Stay present. Breathe.* Yet what if Raymond was … perhaps I was just projecting my own fears onto this incident and really it was nothing more than that.

I left my tea and blanket to head down to an area below the deck where a small sapling was bent totally over from the winter's snow and trying to upright itself. I knew a certain amount of time and sun would rectify the situation, but I welcomed the distraction and wanted something I could do that might somehow help right now. An hour later, after following a trail of bent trees and uprighting them, I returned to the house. There I found a message from a woman at the police station saying I had left some form blank that I needed to finish. Her voice sounded harsh and impatient. Will it never end? It feels like I am being singled out and made the receptacle of negativity. Just as I thought that, I could feel the hair on my neck stand up, not because I was pretending to be a victim, but because I suspect there was some truth to it. And I suspected I also knew who was behind the poison arrows.

Down in my studio, I decided to look for clues. Years ago while teaching at a university, some of my art students suggested we look at *my* work the same way I looked at theirs. They asked me to bring in three of my most recent paintings for them to analyze. We agreed that an artist's work is often telling of their inner state of mind and perhaps even of issues they are working out, unbeknownst to the artist himself. So I did, and my students saw something that seemed so obvious to them, but that I hadn't picked up on. Each painting had the light source around a bend. A river flowing around a bend with the light setting beyond the viewer's vantage point, a canyon with the sun out beyond the viewer's sight and so on. They suggested I was working on something that had not yet manifested itself, that hope was *just around the bend*. They were absolutely correct.

I thought I might gain some clarity about what went on these last few months from the paintings I had done over the winter. I got them all out. Some were already framed, some were acrylic boxes and some were just sheets of watercolor paper. I placed them all along the back wall of my workbench. I rearranged them. Not sure why, but there seemed to be something intuitive about how they needed to be. I stared at them, trying to see what underlying message could be gleaned. Nothing came. I decided to describe the pieces to myself to see if there was a theme.

They were definitely darker than most. The colors were richer, but definitely darker and more opaque. That could just be from winter's light. I went on: a somewhat abstract river scene with something on fire at the confluence of two rivers. A scene of a mountain meadow filled with colorful flowers and a path, something in the sky behind it that might pass for a sunset, or something on fire. So far the language of metaphor was saying: paths leading to something hot/on fire/dangerous.

I picked up another piece: an acrylic on board of a wild red sunset reflected in water with turbulent clouds. I saw the clouds insinuating very high mountain tops. Oh, look another winding path with something fiery at the end: an acrylic on canvas of a marshy, Alaskan-looking tundra area cut by a serpentine river leading to a range of rugged mountains. This one looked strong and powerful with the massive mountain tops and churning clouds, yet the foreground was precarious and spongy. The dark clouds again, I kept that theme in the background and continued through the pieces.

Perhaps the message had to do with dark clouds, but that wasn't much of a message, since I knew that consciously. Yet think winter, where was my consciousness then? Could I have said I knew I was being oppressed by a dark cloud? No, not consciously, only later, looking back.

What about the path, the river, the water leading somewhere? Had I painted any people or faces this winter? I looked at my line-up and there were none. Yet as I recalled, I seem to remember a piece that was quite disturbing to someone in one of my groups and so I had hidden it away under some shelves. I got it out, there it was. A long slender wooden box painted vertically in crimsons, maroons, dark flesh. It was very dark, not only in color but in content, especially for me. There was a central figure— nude, twisted, falling down with a look of absolute terror on his face. He was trying to catch himself from falling, yet there was evidence of other bodies also falling behind him, around him, pieces of other bodies also reaching out. It reminded me now of Dante's *Inferno* and Rodin's *Gates of Hell*. Did it resemble the crumpled figure in the trunk I had witnessed?

Could I look at things in a different way to remove the terror? Is the fear of falling into hell what created the terror? Yet when I turned it on its side, viewed from a different perspective, was it simply a lounging stretch? Standing with this piece in my hand, I could feel something shift. I also knew from these paintings, I had not taken a man's life. It would have shown up here. This character was not me falling into hell. I suspect I was picking up something all winter and needed a path. I needed to follow a trail ... an energy trail ... to what? The power and grandness of the mountains, the strength of the churning clouds, the majesty of the red sunset or the warmth of the fiery confluence? Or all of them?

Speak to me. I summoned my paintings to reveal what I was missing. Backing up to the couch, I perched on the arm, getting a wider view of them. As I did, I began to see them all as *one*, not as separate pieces. Each one a part of the other, they offered a clandestine message, but only in this order. I remembered intuitively placing them one by one along the wall. It began as a whisper, but then the message grew louder. I walked back and placed the long falling piece at the very right, only not vertical, as I had painted it, but horizontal, draining it of the terror. That was the key. I stepped back again and viewed them from the other side of the room.

It was a *waterfall*. All of the paintings together produced a beautiful, wide, cascading waterfall. Each piece added its own color and images. The images of boulders and shadows outlined the water flowing forcefully over mountain rocks. A waterfall? What was the significance of a strong and turbulent waterfall? Think dams, hydroelectricity, nature's power. What does this have to do with anything? I could feel something more literal trying to come through, but as one of my friends says about me, I speak *metaphor* when sometimes I need to speak *literal*.

Was there a waterfall near here? Of course there was, just up Reindeer Creek road, near Reindeer Lake, about five miles from here, not far from where that woman was found last November. I could see it in my mind's eye. It was the exact same look, horizontal, raging this time of year, logs strewn across it. There was no doubt, as I regarded these paintings in this order, from this distance, in this light, it was *that* waterfall. As I made that awareness, my left arm shuddered with goose bumps. Yes, I got it. My truth validator had gone off.

Filled with purpose, I ran up to the house. I knew I had something to do. Finally the moment of action had arrived! But first I wanted to call

Nick and tell him what I had uncovered. Really, I think I just wanted to tell someone I was going up there in case I never came back. Since the lake is usually frozen until about the 4th of July, no one goes hiking up that trail, so if something happened to me, I would be nice and decayed by then.

Nick said he wanted to come with me, to wait for him. Funny how he trusted my instinct and knew there was something important about this waterfall. Was there something buried there, was there a bigger clue to Raymond? Was there a treasure, what Raymond had wanted back? I knew there was something. I could feel it, but I also knew I did not know what it was. And I was glad Nick was coming with me. But what if this was the place I had to face Raymond, could Nick be there? I thought it would be safer if he could, my only ally right now.

That reminded me, I had forgotten to call the police station to tell them I would come the next day to fill in their beloved blanks. Since I had to wait for Nick, I thought I might as well call now. Strickland answered the phone. I was surprised to hear his voice. I was also seeing his eyes in my mind too. I introduced myself and mentioned why I had called. He seemed surprised and said he thought everything was in order, but put me on hold to check. When he came back, it was as if he were another person, his voice had changed and he seemed rather gruff. He said some things were not as they should be and again repeated that *this is bigger than either of us*, just as Raymond had said to Leticia all that time ago. What was he talking about?

38

Woke to one more beautiful Sandpoint morning. Still tired from running half way around the country yesterday, and didn't get back to the hotel until either late yesterday or early today, not sure which. It's getting hard to keep up.

Once again time to regroup and plan the next move. Looks like this is going to be a high caffeine-fueled morning.

Start with what you know. I learned that one a long time ago. Sometimes it's more than you think. Here we go again. At least Laura is safe and out of it now. I'll never know what was up the chief's butt. He couldn't have truly believed she was in cahoots with international drug runners. I still don't know how or why she has anything to do with this whole deal, anyway. One passing glance at a guy in a pickup truck who may, or may not have even been Merkle. Should I follow up on that truck? Why? Seems like it should have shown up somewhere if it was involved. No, won't be anything there. Then how did Merkle know how to find her? It was him, no doubt. Every thing she described made sense. Sense? None of it made any sense, but that doesn't mean it's not exactly like she described it. At least she's safe. That's all that matters. Shut down the endless loop of nonessential crap in the head and get back to work. I finish off another cup and realize all I'm doing is thinking about her, and not the mission.

The mission. That's an evolving entity. What is it now? I was tasked with the killer of Becky and Samantha. Done. Mission over. Time to go home. I'm still completely in the dark about this other guy. Who was that, and why would I care? A Colt .357 is not the rarest of handguns to be found in rural areas like this, I guess. There's no law of the universe that says the gun she lost is the same one they've got tied to the murder. She was pretty clear that she hadn't had the gun out of its case for years. Why the hell would a woman like that have a big-assed Python anyway? Can't hardly lift the damn thing, and probably take her hand off with the recoil. Colt Python, humph, what the hell?

I spend the next little while going round and round and finally decide I can relieve myself from duty. Colonel tried to cut me loose back in Minot, yesterday. Actually ordered me to head home. If something went haywire with his men, it's his problem. Feels good. All around, feels good. Time to head home.

I get about twenty feet from checking out at the desk when I see her number light up on my phone. Feel myself light up a little bit, too. At least I'll get to say goodbye. Wouldn't have left town without that.

39

If there is one thing I have come to know as truth it is that what *you* think someone *else* is thinking is *not* what they're thinking. I tried to apply this right now. I was making the assumption that Nick was going to show up all excited about my ridiculous idea of a waterfall because all my winter paintings lined up to point to that. How insane, now that I think about it. Yet there are things you know instinctively, but can't explain why. I've made a career of it, so this one thing I trusted. But why would I expect Nick to? I knew he had a kind of inherent protectiveness and figured he would probably try to talk me out of this and go up himself to see if it was safe first. That was not going to happen. Whatever was there, I had to discover it. I knew I had to deal with this dark energy and even though no one seemed to feel there was any threat anymore, I knew better. I knew it was a matter of time, and the way things were going, not that much, before it would make itself known again. Little did I know that only moments later it would.

Hilde ran out to Nick's car to greet him. She already knew he was welcome, not that she had ever been much of a watchdog, but she usually barked her welcomes. Today was just an animated tail wagging welcome. Obviously, they had some history together now.

Nick had already started up the stairs to the deck when he saw me in my jacket heading down. I was ready to just get in my truck and head up to the waterfall. He said he wanted to talk to me first. Here it comes, I thought, his thinking better of this, and me waiting here. But that is not what he said. He genuinely wanted to know everything I had encountered and discovered since we last spoke. I showed him my line-up of winter paintings and the waterfall they all created together. It seemed like he was trying to be as prepared as he could for something as non sequitur as this. I filled him in on the details I had left out on the phone, but mostly it was just that I felt convicted that I needed to go there for whatever reason I did not know. I couldn't tell if he was stalling or trying to ascertain if I had gone totally out of my mind.

"Listen, it gets dark up here early. I need to get going while there is still good light. Are you coming or not?" I finally had enough talk.

This is when I saw something shift in his demeanor and I could feel an icy wind run through my heart. His voice changed, he became accusing and threatening. I did not want to look into his eyes, yet I knew I had to. Was this his normal behavior or did someone else suddenly take the helm? Indeed, the eyes were the now familiar blackened evil, penetrating and cold. They looked unyielding and severe, like all mercy had been stripped from them. I knew what had just happened, but he did not. How could he? And for me to try to explain it to him in his present condition would only inflame the possessor. Wanting out of the situation as quickly as possible, I shifted my tack. I knew that to defend was to invite attack, so I became as agreeable as possible. Inherently I knew that I was not in danger if I did not provoke him, yet I really did not know this person at all or what he was capable of. Who was one moment ago my most protective ally was now a demonic threat, an enemy within my own home.

Hilde looked up from her bed in the corner of the room to show me she felt it too. Her ears were pressed back against her head in the docile position and she began to move, slowly getting up from her reclining position to head down the inside stairs through her doggy door. I looked once more and she was already gone. Usually I followed suit. She had a good instinct for these kinds of situations, as if entertaining persons who were possessed was my norm!

Taking my lead from Hilde, I walked Nick to the door assuring him he was right. It was not a wise idea to go to the waterfall, or even think about it. We would find something more substantial and logical tomorrow. He followed me out the door and down the outside stairs. I sadly watched him drive away still filled with darkness. He did not turn to wave or even say goodbye. Now was not the time to be melancholy or sensitive, I knew what was happening. To pretend it was a personal slight was immature and egoic. He was on his own. I should help him. No, he can find his way back out. Nick must have faced worse than this before. I could not address Raymond through Nick. I had to encounter him on a different turf. Neutral turf obviously, since it was now apparent that he wouldn't meet me on my terms.

40

Driving back out of this nut-case's mountains, back to town and wondering why I had to be involved with this in the first place. Everything seemed fine when she called this morning. Clues, she said. Clues about what? I still didn't have a bead on that damn Python or the dead guy packaged with it, and was at a standstill when she called. Driving her back from the jail was nice, I guess. Seemed so then, not so sure right now. Damn valley. Nothing but a bunch of trees. Can't see a thing. I'm sure ready to get back to my desert.

I can't believe she's going to go up to some waterfall. Probably going to get eaten by a bear or something. I came up here to take care of whatever she was talking about. I could have gone up with her, I guess. Hell with that, anyway.

Everything feels off. Just off. Not clear on what or why. She just went on and on about a waterfall. Showed me a bunch of paintings. Nice stuff all and all, I guess. I sure didn't see any waterfall, though. So what was the deal? What just happened in the last two hours? What changed? Feels like the death spiral. At least what I imagine a death spiral to feel like. You're in the clouds. Zero visibility. All you have are your instruments. As soon as you start trusting your senses instead of the instruments you begin that slow, wing-down attitude. That begins a slow, imperceptible spiral. But everything in you feels like you're straight and level. You look right at the attitude indicator, tilting to one side, but you don't trust it, don't believe what you see. Then you start distrusting the other instruments. Maybe they're all wrong as well. Your mind shuts down, so you keep trusting your feelings over the instruments. One hundred percent of the time the next, and last thing you'll ever see is mother earth filling your windshield, welcoming you back home. Never been in one, but this sure as hell feels like I'm halfway down that spiral.

Got to try to get back on instruments. What's wrong here? OK, there I was, one step away from leaving all this behind me and going home, when she called. That much is clear. Happy to get her call, OK with that. Drove back up to the house and there's that dog again. What a piece of work it is! I cannot believe Hans Merkle checked out because of that dog. Guy's got to be the laughing stock of hell by now. Maybe I'll ask him about it when we meet again.

She looked glad to see me and I think I was to see her. You know, right now I can't remember what the hell she was talking about. I mean I'm drawing a blank here. What was she talking about? Damn dog kept running around in circles. Doesn't that drive her crazy? I remember that first mission when Merkle got attached to the unit. That guy was good at what he did. That's for sure. Can't believe he bought it 'cause of that dog. We were the craziest nonsense unit in the service. No doubt about that one. We were the pinnacle of bureaucratic thought. Who's idea was something like that, anyway? Guys from every branch of the service except the girl scouts. And who would have thought to put someone like me at the top of it, anyway? All I remember about my sorry life was that I was just some kid heading to the Air Force Academy because he wanted to fly the cool stuff. Next thing I know the old man snatches me away and I'm his little bitchboy for the next twenty years. What was that all about? What was my entire career about, anyway? Did we win? Were we winning? That was always the unofficial question. Me, running this mixed-bag unit: interdiction, elimination, discovery, coverage. What were we doing then, and why the hell did I take back these birds anyway? I look in the rear view mirror and sure as hell don't see a full-bird colonel looking back.

Where's my mind? Where are the instruments I can trust?

What's she going to do, anyway? Some bear's probably going to eat her. Going up in the mountains alone. Oh, no, not alone. She's got Lassie right there with her. Right under her feet. She's safe. That's for sure. Stupid dog.

Why didn't the colonel ever move up? That man should have a couple of stars by now. Why's he still in the loop? Man should be out to pasture down on some golf course in Florida by now. Just him, a cigar, and a pair of checkered pants. Now that's a picture. That's for sure. I remember when I first met him. What did he think of me? Why me? Man, we sure did some shit together though. Got into some hairy places and back out again. No doubt about that. I should have left her in jail anyway. Didn't do anything for her at all. Drove her home at least.

What ever happened to the unit? I wonder what Castle's up to these days. Did he get out, or go to Afghanistan? What happened to him? Guy was one crazy mutha, that's for sure. Not so sure I was glad to have him in the unit. Yea, I was. A good man. Got the job done, but not so great at following orders. Wonder if he ever got out. Crazy Marine. Why's a guy join the Marines, anyway? Crazy Marine sure didn't like taking orders from Air Force. That's for sure. Haven't thought of that guy in a long time. Haven't thought of any of them in a …

"Whaat the!…" Holy mother! What the hell was that? Moose. Was that a moose? Goddamn. My heart's pumping about a million beats a minute. Biggest monster I've ever seen just about T-boned me. I swerve just in time to miss him and he goes down on his knees right in front of the car behind me. Now that's what I need. To get taken out by some monster moose. Heart's up to about a million beats per. Whoa! Looks like he's back up and back in the woods. I pull off to the side of the road, and me and this guy from the car behind me are poking around in the trees trying to see if the big guy is hurt. No sign.

"Whoa, dude. He almost got you."

"No shit. All I saw was this black mass about a foot away from my side window."

"I can't believe you didn't spin out when you swerved. I mean, you really started to go sideways. I thought you were going to roll for sure. Good driving, man."

"Hey, thanks for not hitting me. And not him either. How close did he get to you, anyway?"

"Right on him. That's how close. Think he's OK?"

"I don't see anything. I think he's OK. Took a knee back there, but I don't think he's hurt. I didn't feel him hit me. He must have just got scared and slipped. Man, it's going to take a minute for me to come back down. That was a close one. That's for sure."

"That's for sure. Hey, good job, man. That's some serious racecar driving back there. Good job."

"Thanks." And we both got back in our cars.

What a shot in the arm. I'm still shaking and wondering where the hell I am. Looks like a few miles back to Sandpoint. Wow. How'd I get back down here from her house. Don't even remember the road out of her mountains. God, this place is beautiful!

Soon as I get a signal I'm on the phone to the colonel.

41

I gathered my jacket back up and rushed to my truck, loaded the dog in, turned it over and headed down the hill. This time, instead of turning down to go into town, I turned left to go up the mountain. This was my hiking road, the same direction to the waterfall and also the location of that first woman's body. I could feel a sense of dread coupled with the knowing I had no choice. A feeling of something coming to fruition that had been a long time waiting filled my senses. I was on red alert. The fear was gone with Nick, but heightened focus replaced it. I knew from Raymond's insistence through Nick's vocal chords that I drop the idea of the waterfall, that it actually *was* where I needed to go even if it was a trap. I was going there expecting one. No, I did not have a back-up plan other than to bring something to conclusion once and for all. And I think my conviction was worth something. There was no hesitation or delay, no waffling, only the focused arrow of great clarity.

Driving up the rough road to the turnoff, I had time to think. Was Nick actually disconnected? Would he be OK by himself? I suppose I was asking as much to validate my decision to come up alone as to assure myself that this was not his true nature. Was I already defending him in my mind? Perhaps, but I walked through the indicators of being temporarily disconnected from one's highest source. This was not a full-on possession by another being, but rather the presence of dark entities in his personal energy space. It would cloud and distort his world. In fact, now that I thought about it, I am sure I used this term because it feels easier to connect something, to plug it back in, than to try and empty someone of a possessor.

The eyes are the easiest indicator. When beautiful blues suddenly go dark gray and cold, something has shut the light off inside. Indicator number one is easy. Believing it is something else altogether. Attacking or insulting, fear-based reasoning, digging into someone's deepest wounds, using their vulnerabilities are sure indicators that someone else is at the helm. They look for an opening in your energy system and usually get it if you engage and try to defend and attack back.

I knew Nick would have no memory of this encounter and I was glad of it. I hated thinking he would carry a feeling of being unkind to me. He was so much bigger than that. But what still bothered me was that he would probably have no memory of the waterfall, or where I told him it was, and that meant I was on my own. I was OK with that. For what I had to do, I was on my own. In fact, now that I thought about it, what was I going to do? What was it that Raymond wanted from me? What if I gave it to him unintentionally? What then? I could see there would be no stopping him if he kept jumping into everyone in my path. This thought gave me comfort. I used to think that when I become compromised by the biggest, baddest, darkest entities, I should feel honored. That meant I was deemed a worthy opponent. But right now what I was feeling wasn't honor.

I only hoped that Nick would find a way to jolt himself out of this negative place. If he couldn't find a way himself, and I trusted his innate intuition, I would help plug him back in later when I returned from the waterfall. If I returned from the waterfall.

42

"I'm drawing a blank out here. Wexler's out and back home. Longfellow seems OK with the Mexican kid and the air ticket. Fed did a good job and he should be back home by now. I can't tell you anything about the weapon. Let's just see if it fades away. I can't tell what Longfellow's going to do with the investigation. Seems like the kind of a guy who would like it to be solved, but would be just as happy if it just died. One way or the other." I'm going on like a school girl. Must have been that moose. Man that shook me up. Another inch and he would have taken me out. Merkle by a dog and me by a moose. Now that's some kind of karma.

"Listen, Drake."

"Yea, sure."

"You remember Trindel and Adams?" I did, vaguely. "Couple of B-grade off the books guys, right?"

"That's about right. They're the ones I put on it. Should have been a no-brainer. Should have handled it easily." Shouldn't have been there in the first place. Not on this one. From what I remembered of them, they shouldn't have been on this one. Too important.

"What do mean by, *should have been a no-brainer?*" I asked, but I already knew where this was going. "This was a no-brainer. All they had to do was clean up the car and take it back to Hertz."

"Didn't happen. One's dead." I listened to that and felt some kind of completion. At least he validated Laura's psychic vision. That in itself would have burned his butt.

"Who's the dead one?"

"Trindel."

"You got someone on Adams yet? That's above my skill level you know."

"Not really, no. Not above you, Nick. Anyway, we're looking at the end zone here. Adams just got in touch." You've got to be bagging me. Guy takes out his partner, screws up the mission, and then calls home. Why didn't I just delete that first email and stay out of crazy-town? "Sounded like he's hanging from a thread. I didn't get much from him. Wherever he is, cell coverage is intermittent at best. Far as I could tell he says Trindel was an accident. Says he freaked and bolted. Says he took care of your rental car, but then freaked. He's still up there."

"Up where?"

"Sandpoint. He's still up there. Says he dumped the car and took up into the mountains."

"The mountains? What the hell? You've seen this area. It's mountains everywhere. Where in the mountains?" I didn't have any place in my head to put the idea of this fool heading up into these mountains, or why he would want to do that in the first place.

"No idea. Neither does he."

"You think I'm some kind of Jeremiah Johnson or what? I can't find a man in the mountains. End zone. You been drinking, colonel? I can't even see the field, let alone the end zone."

"Think I don't know that, Nick? I need you to sit tight and stay ready. I put John Castle on it. Remember Castle?" John Castle. Damn. I haven't thought of that guy in years, but somehow hearing his name sounded strangely familiar. One crazy Marine. Now that's a picture. John Castle up here in the woods.

"Sure I do, but you just can't track a man somewhere *up in the mountains*. Not even Castle. Especially not Castle. Man like that, you've got to put him on a strong scent from the git-go."

"We got a fix from the cell phone, Nick. Adams is along some river called Reindeer Creek. That's a few miles north of town. We're not sure exactly where, but the signal was clear enough to get Castle on it. Adams should stay near water so it shouldn't be long." Reindeer Creek? I'm starting to jack back up on the adrenaline.

"ETA?"

"End zone, Nick. I said we're looking at the end zone." I couldn't believe it. Reindeer Creek! That's Laura's river. I don't need John Castle anywhere near her. I hung up and almost took out a fully loaded log truck on the U-turn.

43

When I turned off the main road onto the narrower road to the lake, I noticed there had been a huge logging operation since the last time I had been up here. Where there had been a dark forest of tall cedars and white pines, it was now open and stripped. It looked ragged and violent, yet I knew within a few years, it would be a different story. At this moment though, the raw, raped look did not help my vulnerability. I forged deeper up the mountain road to the Reindeer Lake trailhead where the waterfall was. As I drove that last rough mile, it had not occurred to me that the road would not be open. I went as far as I could in four-wheel drive before I was stopped by the snow. Of course, at this elevation, I knew that. I just had not stopped to think about it. I started to back up, but noticed some tracks in the snow. I got out of the truck to have a better look. Definitely tracks, men's shoes. I placed my foot near it. It was only a size larger than mine.

Why I didn't choose to go back and get the police or someone I could trust? I don't know. Honestly, I don't think I am invincible. What was I thinking then? I remember reading about a woman who decided she could jump a gap in the San Francisco Bay Bridge with her car during an earthquake. I always wondered what she was thinking in those last fatal moments before she plunged to her death. The report said that the road ripped apart right in front of her and the hole spanned quite a few feet. Was she thinking, "I've waited in this much traffic and come this far, I'm not about to stop now?" Was she thinking of the last action movie she had seen, and thought she could gun it and fly through the air and make the other side? Did she just think, "Screw it, I'm sick of this commute anyway?"

Yet here I was, not much brighter by those standards. I have always had the Sherlock Holmes' syndrome, which I thought was what made me so good at my job, but I should have had better sense. I was unarmed, and my dog was the first to flee in a moment of conflict. Amazingly, I wasn't afraid.

I knew I was on home turf. I knew this land better than anyone around here. If someone was up here, they would be out of their league. I looked again at the shoe tracks. They were clearly not hiking boots, this again reassured me that I should go on. I pulled the truck off the side of the road as much as possible, into some bushes, and got out.

Hilde was sniffing and running, she loved the smell of adventure. I followed the tracks. They were headed down the road to the trailhead and the waterfall. I knew the water would really be running hard because the snow was melting higher in the mountains. I should be able to hear it pretty soon. Still with about a quarter mile to go, the tracks stopped. Where did they go? I looked around. It was as if they just disappeared. I looked up to see if there was a tree limb above them. There was, but no one was in it. Did the tracks lead off into the forest? Nothing that I could see. It was possible that the snow had begun to melt in areas of the road that got more sunlight than other areas and that was how I lost the tracks. They wouldn't have made marks on the soil if they were made on snow. Did that mean the tracks were days or hours old? I didn't know.

I decided to head on. I was almost there. I usually drove to the trailhead, so this part of the road was not as familiar as up ahead would be. *Stay present*, I thought. *Make no assumptions. Let yourself follow whatever energy trail you encounter.* It felt like I had a purpose now, so I let myself get on task.

Rounding the last bend before the trailhead and the waterfall, I could hear it roaring already. I tried to recall my fond memories of swimming, soaking my tired feet and of painting here. The trail was covered in deep snow and the water certainly didn't look very inviting. Yet I knew where I was and I knew I had a purpose here.

There was an old wooden bridge across the raging creek that had blown out years ago in a spring washout and only one arm of it was left still dangling across the water. To begin the trail, you had to manage across that single, twisted and splintered beam. But to get to the waterfall, you simply needed to follow a little trail to the left of the bridge through the brush on *this* side of the creek. Hilde and I stood perfectly still at this point. We both were listening, senses on full alert, for what we did not know, just that we instinctively knew we needed to.

I stepped forward first, Hilde in tow, and headed through the spring-softened snow following the trail towards the waterfall. Then I thought, if this is a trap, should I be taking the obvious route to it? I decided to cross the river and come back on the waterfall from the other side of the river. This would afford me a view of the waterfall from the middle of the bridge too. The only thing was, it would also put me smack in the middle of a precarious balance beam in full view out in the open. I hesitated, but Hilde was never afraid of scaling the jagged wooden beam of the bridge, and she took right off across it. Just then, I heard a noise off in the brush near the waterfall. It was clearly something being disturbed. It could have been an animal alarmed by the appearance of the dog, but I suspected it was what I had come here for. Or rather who. My resolve seemed to wane a bit at this point. Those unasked questions that would have been more appropriate to ask of myself before this now came surfacing with a vengeance.

I heard a boulder move, either from someone stepping on an unsteady one, or it could have been from the water. *Follow your instincts, Laura. This is what you have been trained for. Focus with clarity of purpose.* Then I saw Hilde wag her tail and head off in the direction of the waterfall. This meant only one thing: a person was there. She never wagged her tail at four-legged creatures.

44

Racing back towards Laura's and can't get any signal. That's great. Was she going to go looking for this waterfall right away? I just couldn't remember. Too strange. I remember her calling me and going out there today, and how glad I was to see her. I think she was just as happy to see me. Was a little strange about how all her paintings made up a picture of a waterfall and how she thought there was some meaning in that. God, I wish she would have let me take her up there. She shouldn't go by herself. Man, I sure hope she hasn't gone up there yet. Could she really know that Adams is up there? Is that who she thinks is at that waterfall? How could that be? She didn't paint all those pictures last night. How long has Adams been there? Is Castle really boots on the ground already? How is that possible? Why did the colonel bring him in without me knowing?

I keep looking at my cell phone and there keeps being no signal. I figure I'll see if there's a phone at the gas station before turning off onto her road. Then I get to thinking I don't have any idea what waterfall she's talking about. Maybe it wasn't on the Reindeer River anyway. Maybe we're talking about two totally different things. Maybe it's a coincidence that Adams is on some river and she gets this psychic message to go to a waterfall. Yea, maybe Santa Claus is coming to town, too. I have no idea how she knows this stuff. But she's been right-on more than once already. That I know.

Right before the gas station, my phone rings that I've got a message. Where'd that come from. I look down and it's showing nine messages. What the? ... Damn kid. First eight are from that FBI kid. I guess he wasn't BSing me. Last one's from Goddard. Goddard? CIA? What the hell's he want? I click on that one and all I get before I'm back out of reception is, "call me. Found something strange on Wexler." Now what is that, and why am I getting all this now. Strange on Wexler? What could that be?

Still no more signal, so I pull into the gas station and, of course, she doesn't answer the phone. Ask the girl at the counter about any waterfalls in the area and she looks back at me like I'm asking about the far side of the moon.

"Any maps of the area, then?"

"Just that one on the wall over there." She points to a large road map, and that sure as hell doesn't help.

"Waterfalls?" Some shabby looking local guy standing way too close to me, asks. "Heard you asking Dot over there about waterfalls in the area."

"I sure am. Do you know this area well?"

"Spend a lot of time all around here. Lots of hunting. We got deer, elk, moose…" I'm not interested in hunting.

"Friend of mine told me about a waterfall I need to see up on a river called Reindeer Creek. I really enjoy hiking up to waterfalls, and I've got some spare time while I'm here."

"Where you from?" He starts some small talk I have no time for.

"Just here for another day and I really would like to find this one."

"Well, Reindeer Creek is no river. And I don't think I'd go out of my way. I can direct you to Jeru Creek falls. Way nicer."

"If I don't see Reindeer Falls, my friend is going to get his feelings hurt. You know?"

"Yea, guess so." He seems a little defeated. Maybe he wanted the scoop on sharing *his* waterfall. "Just go on up about five miles, cross over the bridge and turn to the right. Go up about six more miles past an area that was logged all to hell. Totally clear cut. Terrible logging job, that one was. You'll see a sharp left turn after about half a mile of clear cut. Gets pretty rough. Go to the end. You can't get lost on that road. Dead ends at the trail head. Two falls up there. First one right near where you'll park and another a little farther up. Don't look like you're set for hikin'."

"I've got my boots in the car. Can a car make it up that road?"

"Wouldn't take *my* car. Need a truck."

"It's just a rental. Think I can make it?"

"Maybe. Just go slow and don't hit any rocks. Was in half OK shape last season. You better turn back around if it's still too muddy, though. Snow's mostly gone down lower, so we do get mud. Haven't been up that far yet this year, so may still be plenty of snow on the ground. You get stuck in a car and you've got yourself one hell of a walk back down."

"Hey thanks. You've really helped me out."

45

I decided to go under the bridge, to the water there. I knew I couldn't cross right where I was, the water was too strong, but I could see what was up by the waterfall without being seen myself. The underbrush all around the water's edge would hide me. I listened for a shot. Out in these parts, if someone suspects a dog to be a wolf or coyote, they might take it out. I only hoped Hilde would not come looking for me, waging her tail, giving up my location. Whoever was over there, she was not afraid of, that was all I could assess. Yet what if they had already poisoned her? I tried to stay focused on the task at hand, *see without being seen first*. I caught a glimpse of Hilde's rear end swinging back and forth, white-tipped tail still waging. Someone was petting her or engaging her, assuming she had not found a treasure of dog treats. I moved in a little closer, trying to stay dry, not knowing if I was stepping on a rock under the snow or a space between them with water underneath. I tested the next step—solid. I leaned to be able to see the rest of the picture. I needed to see up the waterfall better, to get a wider view of the area. As I leaned more forward, the rock I was standing on slipped out from under me and my boot splashed into the water.

I jumped back onto the water's edge and if I thought I might have gotten away without being detected, that illusion was destroyed. I fell backwards into some brush that caught me before I went down, yet it caused a ruckus of sounds and swaying brush. Hilde came running over, and so did someone else.

Steadying myself, I could see clearly now that a man was headed in my direction. He did not look evil or criminal, only a bit tattered and frayed. My first thought was that maybe he lived up here, but I already knew that no one did. He certainly looked ragged enough to be North Idaho, but his clothes were not flannel, denim or duck. He was wearing a dirty and torn black leather jacket. This, in one swift moment, gave him away as being a non-local.

Deciding to play innocent, I called out a hello! He responded with a query to see if I was OK. What was this guy doing here? He seemed so familiar. Did I know him from somewhere? I saw the relief in his eyes that it was me, not sure who he might have been expecting, but I was not it. "Do you have a fire up here?" I asked. That would have made sense. Looking at him now, closer, I know I knew him. Let your mind go to the energy. Where have you encountered this energy before? I came up blank. OK where have you encountered this face? Then an image surfaced.

Just then he took my hand to help me through the tangled brush. His hands were soft and smooth, another indication he was not from around here. "What are you doing up here?" I asked. He didn't have a vehicle, a tent or a fire. How had he managed so far? "Do you live near here?" He did not answer, but instead asked what I was doing here. I muttered something about checking out the trail to the lake, but I think he knew I was a little off the path for that to really be true. On second thought, he had that deer-in-the-headlights sort of a look, so he might not have thought anything of the kind.

Where had the image gone that was just in my mind before he took my hand? There it was again. *It was the man with the gun held to my head.* It seemed like a lifetime ago now, but this was definitely him. I had burned that face into my skull pondering it so many times. I remember him lifting my own gun and pointing it in my face. How could I forget something like that? He was my *energetic* murderer! There he was at the waterfall. What do I do now? I tensed up, naturally, not prepared for this. He sensed my constricting and responded in kind. He pulled back as if in protection.

I had expected to find Raymond or some clue to him, but instead found this cast off shell of a used Raymond vessel. What good was that? Was it dangerous anymore? No, there was no more darkness in the eyes, only fear and paranoia, or panic, or both. I decided to take the lead and connect, to see where this was going. I put out my hand to introduce myself, saying I live about five miles down the mountain. My dog and I are looking for roots and certain rare plants. He seemed to be placated. He did not give me his full name, only Ron.

"Ron, how long have you been hiding up here?" WHY did I say that? *Let's get right to the point, Laura.*

He looked shocked and relieved at the same time. He started blubbering and I could tell he had been out in the elements too long, and was not thinking straight. I tried to find us a place to sit down.

Just as I bent to sit on a rock so I could ring out my wet sock, I was knocked off balance and heard a deafening explosion. As I fell forward I thought I saw him fly backwards with his arms splayed out to his sides. Then, nothing but blackness and unconsciousness. Yet for me, this was only the beginning.

46

I flew back up her road about 100 miles an hour, and stopped at the house, just in case. I could tell she was gone because that dog wasn't running around in circles. Checked out the whole place anyway. No Laura. Seemed like a long ride continuing up that mountain. Road did keep getting rougher, but if I slowed enough I could make it around the rocks without bottoming out. Broke out of the trees after about three miles. No kidding about the clear cut forest. Looked like the aftermath of an air strike. Snow wasn't gone and the mud was getting worse after I turned up that last road. Guy certainly did know his mountains. There were fresh tire tracks and I had to believe they were from Laura's truck. Mountain woman with a truck. Man, I loved that woman!

I'm out of the car before it gets stuck, and hoping that it's not too much farther. I'm no mountain man, and my cardio strength is nothing to brag about. At least I'm still walking a golf course. No cart. That's got to mean something.

Little farther on and I start to see what looks like a second track in the mud. Looks like one vehicle followed up another, just staying in the same ruts. This is not what I need. This isn't even possible. I'm moving faster and breathing heavier and thinking that this really is not possible except that everything that has happened since the start of this has not been possible. Breathing still harder and wondering what I'm going to do if I find Adams and Castle and Laura all in the same place. As far as I remember John Castle could snap me in half if he wanted to. Adams, I have no idea.

One of the tracks veers off the road, but I can't see the vehicle. Other one goes straight on. Standing there for a second not knowing which one to follow. Back and forth, straight ahead or off the road? I close my eyes for a minute and feel Laura on the left side of my face. It's like she's just touching my cheek with the back of her hand. I take off to the left.

A couple hundred yards ahead I see her green pickup. I'm moving, but aware. No people around and I'm hoping I don't have another couple miles up the trail to the second waterfall. Guy said it gets pretty steep. And this is no golf course. That's for sure.

Come around the last clump of bushes. I can already hear a waterfall, but no voices. Come around that last clump and freeze for all of a second that seems like an hour. There's John Castle standing there looking bigger than ever. Some skinny guy is laying in his own blood over by the river and I see Laura falling into the water in slow motion. Castle's arm is just coming back toward himself. He must have just hit her in the back of the head. I was watching it all happen in slow motion and couldn't do anything about it. Castle started to reach for his sidearm, still in slow motion.

"Castle!" I yelled in a voice that didn't seem like my own. That must be what they mean by the primordial scream.

"Colonel Drake." He said as he turned back towards me. His hand stopped short of his weapon.

"Stand fast, sergeant." There was no please or question in my voice. No choice given. There was no more question as to what would happen if I found John Castle here. He didn't move and I ran towards Laura.

47

I found myself falling into Alice's world again, swirling around and around, like before. Only this time I landed on my head. It was aching and I rubbed it as I lay on the ground. I knew I was on familiar ground; familiar feeling, familiar smells. I had been here before. As I looked around, I recognized the upper waterfall a couple miles farther up the trail from where I had fallen. It was smaller in width, yet the water flowed more turbulently down the mountain creek cascading off a steep and dangerous ledge. Unlike the other waterfall, this one fell down below the trail. The lower one descended into view from above. This waterfall was strewn with logs and shaped in a way I wasn't familiar with, yet when I got up and bent over to look below, to where the water fell, it was the same as I remembered. It was rushing and turbulent, a drop off with huge boulders at the bottom. Definitely not somewhere a human body would want to fall.

I turned around to look up the trail and there he was. *Raymond.* He stood in his confident elegance and personal power, deeply centered and patient. In fact, it seemed that he had been waiting for this moment for a very long time and he had no intention of rushing it. He looked just as I remembered him from the scene with Leticia, except this time he was staring directly at me. I knew I was not just energetically present, but then where was I? What exactly was happening? I didn't recall climbing the mile or so to this waterfall. How did I get here? That question didn't seem to be important, like in a dream where only the nonsensical makes sense. Yet as I stood there I could feel the pain in my head begin to throb.

I could feel the connection between us. It didn't feel demonic as I had anticipated, only ancient and entangled. Not knowing where to begin, I could feel a lifetime of questions begin to burble to the surface of my mind.

Hello, Laura is what came out of his mouth. Not Leticia, but Laura. I knew he knew me in this now. How else could we have become so entangled?

"Did you plan for me to see you that day in November in that man Merkle?" I asked.

"Did you *plan* to see *me*?" he parried.

I knew what he meant. Our karma wasn't something *we planned*, it was a whirlpool we fell into. And we weren't going to be done with it until the whirling spit us out.

"What is our unfinished business?" I asked as I wanted to get to the point. Strangely, I did not feel intimidated or small as I had expected. This man was an equal. Yet I did not have all the information. I could not put all the pieces together. As I said that, as if he were reading my mind, we were swept down the river, into the waterfall, and falling with it onto the boulders below. I screamed, but no sound came out. I could feel water in my mouth and eyes. I tried to grasp at something along the sides, but it was flowing too fast. Rushing water poured over me in gushes that made it impossible for me to breathe. I panicked and tried to pull my head towards air, but as I did so, I must have hit a rock. I felt another pang of pain. I heard Hilde bark and growl. Where was she? I couldn't see her. Landing on a rock, feeling broken and sore, I tried to hold onto something so I would not be swept on past these rocks onto more boulders in the river. I could feel the swift and raging spring waters try to claim my body to send me downstream to the lake like it did everything in its path. Gagging and clinging, I managed to hold fast and get a foot jammed between two rocks until I could push off and grab for a large boulder near the edge. Leaning into the new boulder, I let go of my hold and was pushed violently under water again. My one foot was still wedged between two rocks and holding me in place. If I let go, I would be dragged down the raging river, if I didn't, I might just drown.

48

"That Adams?" I asked as I looked past him.

"Yes, sir. I just got here. Just about to finish up here."

"I said stand fast. No, don't just stand there, grab her damn foot. She's going to drown. Get that damn branch off her foot. Now!" He did as he was told. And as he lifted the branch I took her into my arms and pulled her out of the water. Wasn't in the water more than 30 seconds so I knew she wasn't going to drown. I looked up at Castle and said, "John. I cannot believe you struck this woman. What the hell is wrong with you, Marine?"

By the look in his face I could tell he was shamed and couldn't answer that question. From what I had seen Merkle go through, and what I had just gone through today on the way out of Laura's house, I knew the man was not in control of himself.

49

I managed to lift my head in a moment when the river waned from its surging. Quickly, I blocked all pain from my senses and leapt in an adrenaline surge to the water's edge. It was only now that I realized the water was freezing. Shivering, I looked for Hilde. Nowhere in sight, I no longer heard her either. But I did see Raymond standing on the opposite side of the waterfall and the boulders and the rushing waters, composed and dry. How could that be? Clearly he knew something I did not. It was as if he were magic and I was flesh and blood.

I needed to warm myself before I figured anything out. It was early spring, but here in the mountains it was still winter. There was snow everywhere and the water was simply the snow melt of just barely moments ago. Breathing deeply, I rubbed my hands together and started jogging in place. Bringing blood to the extremities, I could feel life pulsing through me again. Yet what I would do for some dry clothing. How had Raymond gotten down the falls without getting wet, or even disheveled?

As I pondered that in my mind, Raymond suddenly appeared next to me, on *my* side of the river. How was that possible? It wasn't as if he flew, he simply manifested there. I didn't see how. He could see I was shocked, but still the wheels turned seeking an explanation. Where was I? Was this another experience I was encountering in my mind while my body was safe and warm in my room? If so, why was I feeling so cold and sore? Yet as I recalled, I certainly felt the energetic impact of the gunman. *The Gunman*, he was by the other waterfall. Why had I left him to come up here? What was he doing there? And why was Raymond here? Think. How did I get here? I must be dreaming. Then wake up now. I willed myself to awaken.

Raymond was coming closer to me and he had assumed the Eyes I had recalled so often this winter. I recognized I was sleeping, which is usually all it takes to wake up from a bad dream. Wake up! Wake up! Nothing was shifting.

I noticed Raymond wasn't really walking over the boulders, it was more like he was floating over them. There I was clinging on for dear life, and he was floating over them. What the hell was going on? He looked more and more threatening as he neared. My resolve and equanimity were slipping as quickly as the warmth from my body.

Then from behind Raymond I could see a glow. It was someone else. *For crying out loud, how many people could possibly be up here on this remote mountain trail at this time of year?* The glow began to warm me, even from where I was standing. I knew that energy signature. But how could this be? It was my husband. He died seven years ago, yet there he was as big as life, also floating like Raymond. So everyone knows something I do not. Was there something invisible they were walking on? He smiled at me. I could feel an immense love well up in me, warming my soul and filling me with a deep presence and a knowing. That knowing was that *I was dead*. I was in *his* world now. I was so joyful, I leapt towards him. As I did, and just in the nick of time too, I floated into the air. Raymond was just reaching out to grab my arm.

I was in the spirit world, no longer bound by the limitations of the physical. If I believed I were still in my body, I would still be bound by the laws of gravity and whatever else I believed impossible. Why did my head still throb? Maybe I still believed it should. My whole body ached and I could feel the shiver of cold still course through me. I reached out for the man I had missed for so long now. But he was gone.

Weren't we supposed to be together now? I had always hoped he would be there to greet me when I passed over. Maybe I was in some kind of transitional place.

50

Once Castle freed her foot from the rocks I lifted her out of the water and held her in my lap. She was barely breathing, but I could feel the slightest tremble of a shiver so I knew she was still alive. I took off my jacket and wrapped it around her trying to warm her body. There was nothing else I could do so I waited, hoping that wherever she was, she was safe.

I knew that there was something else going on that none of us knew anything about. Everything in my life was about weapons and combat. I've known a lot of enemies, but I could see every one of them. I had no idea what I was fighting here. I just held her and looked up at this tower of a Marine. The very best we have. And I knew that neither him, nor I, nor all the weapon systems in our arsenal stood the slightest chance against this.

51

Just then Raymond bellowed at me. All sense of floating and fairyland vanished with that demonic moan.

I could see he wasn't finished with me, dead or not. I guess I was in Raymond's world now. But I was no stranger to the energetic world. Now that I knew that was where we were, I thought myself into dry clothes. They were dry.

Strangely, the clothes I thought onto myself were the very ones Leticia had worn the evening I had energetically spied on them. I suddenly felt that I *was* Leticia. I knew something. What Raymond wanted had suddenly become clear to me. Reading my mind, he made a swift attempt to knock me sideways. I flew in the direction of the river again. I thought myself up instantly, missing the raging waters by inches. I flew up to a ledge above the falls. There Raymond was waiting for me. I formed a force field of love around me. I knew that if he were resonating with darkness, love would be to him like kryptonite was to Superman. Indeed it was. He squared off against me.

"I know what you want, Raymond," I heard myself say, not in my own voice. Yet it was not clear to me at this point what that was. I could feel his darkening powers pushing against mine. I knew he would not give up before he got what he wanted. But I knew *one* thing. Love is more powerful than anything in this universe. *Stay in that place of love, extend your love to him, remember the love for your husband, feel Hilde's love, let the feeling of absolute love be your being right now.*

Suddenly Raymond pulled a dagger out of his black coat. I knew it was to threaten me, but I was in the energetic realm. No dagger could harm me. He saw I countered it with this thought. He took the dagger and swung it up around his head and slashed down into the earth with it and as he did so, the earth caved in where his dagger had pierced. And again I was falling, tumbling into the darkness, grasping out into the void, falling. The uncomfortable feeling of being unequivocally out of control permeated my being. Then I landed. My body already was aching and sore, cold and numb in places, so I wasn't able to assess what damage had been done this time.

Instantly I found myself in a group of women, all dressed in dark clothes, not from this era. In fact, on closer examination, I was in a coven of witches. And I was dressed as they were. Raymond was there, the warlock, no doubt. How many lives had we been together? From across the group, he held up ten fingers in my direction in answer to that. I looked to see what these women were engaged in as my left arm truth validator went off. I wondered what we were doing here, yet I knew it was part of Raymond's plan to undo me or at least to bring me back to the place where he had power over me. I was not sure. I looked to see if he had read this last mental thought, but if he did, it didn't show.

The women were involved in something intense. I knew I was a part of it. I felt the familiarity of each person, knew the intricacies of each relationship, the vulnerabilities and the strengths. Raymond was our teacher and I was the star pupil. To this I got a piercing look. *But I was.* And perhaps that is what began our war? Had I challenged him, gone beyond him, chosen a different route?

I made my way to the center of the circle of women, to see what they were intent upon. There I saw a mangled deer, still breathing, but bleeding and hurt, lying crumpled and weak on the ground. The women did not seem concerned about the deer's pain, but about something else. *I knew what it was.* I had forgotten this lesson. Of course, I had forgotten this lesson. It was our coup de grace, Raymond and I. We were seeking life after death. We had taken injured animals and were locating their energy source and trying to capture it, to use it, to animate something else with it. Perhaps it wasn't life after death as you think of it, but it was *reanimation*. No one had succeeded until I discovered the key. Was this the day I had done that? Was this where he was taking me? To my culpability? To my part in this macabre story? He only stared at me with those intense and threatening eyes. Had I not already been accustomed to those eyes through all our stories together, they certainly would have undone me.

Did he want *me* to do it again? Had he forgotten? Yet, and I pointed this question in my mind to Raymond, hadn't you already done that with

Merkle? And then Ron and then Nick just today? And who else? I could feel his distaste for my suggestion. He glared at me. Obviously, it was a technicality I was not familiar with. Those, he indicated, were simply cases of spirit possession. He could split part of his being off and inhabit others. That was very different from reanimation. That was baby's play. What *I* knew was what he sought.

Was this the nature of our relationship? I was not afraid of him. Was he as potent as I thought? Or was he bluffing? To this he stabbed me behind the eyes with his thoughts. I could see he was a powerful man, yet he was unable to harm me. He clearly wanted something from me that he had not yet gotten. If he had, I assume he would no longer have use for me. It was difficult to operate from a place of divine love here in the coven. The main energy was learning, intensity, witchcraft—what was that energy? It felt like greed, desire, usury, egoism, playing god. I did not want to engage in the reanimation project, yet everyone was looking at me, waiting for me to do something. I had done this before. I could not. I would not. I remembered how. But I no longer felt it was in my integrity… yet, I could feel myself being influenced, coerced.

I looked up at Raymond, "Why did you inhabit Merkle? Why did you influence him to viciously murder those women? Why did you force the gunman to kill his own friend? What did you want from all that? Why don't you incarnate into your *own* vessel and do your own work? Coward!" I screamed. All the unasked questions now came fully to the surface. Why? Why? What do you want? What is this about? Then I realized he had *never known*. He faked that we discovered it together, but *he* had never found the key.

I could feel the coercion pressing harder on me, bearing down on my being, weighing on my mind, as if only I could do this one thing: *follow the energy trail of this deer*. I began to engage with the deer. I felt the life slipping, the panic, the fear, the inherent desire for life sustaining her. I followed that to its core. There I located the source of life, her creation energy, her god-self, as I would call it now. I began to breathe it in. Just then, something in me felt the abhorrence of it. I hesitated. The bearing down continued. I breathed again, this time with powerful confidence. I began sucking the life from the dying deer and watched as her body became limp.

52

They say time is relative. If I live to a hundred I'll never know how long I held her there by that river. Maybe a minute, five minutes? A lifetime? Thoughts and fears came and went. The shivers slowed, then stopped. Castle didn't move or seem to even breathe. The dog was hiding in the bushes and we waited. The breaths slowed and became more and more faint until there were none left. There was no movement in her body, and all I could feel was peace. Peace in her, and in me. I was ready to die that day up on her deck, but here I was by this river letting her die in my arms.

The tears came and blotted out my world. She was all I had left and that was disappearing in my arms. All I could do was lay my cheek against her face and whisper, "Laura, Laura."

53

Just then, from where I do not know, I heard Nick's powerful voice scream out my name, "LAURA! LAURA!!" It jolted me from my focus and I let the breath out. The life returned to the deer, she kicked and tried to get up. The color returned to her pallid skin. The life force that I was taking was being returned to its source. It was not mine to take. It was not anyone's to take. Not now, not ever. I could feel the blood coming back to my face, to my body and being. I was not Leticia, or a witch. I was a con-sciousness beyond both those, beyond Raymond and his greedy desires. *I had to choose, was I staying here or choosing life?* Could I still choose the life I had created for myself? Was it too late? As if he felt me slipping from his grasp, his eyes began to grow red and piercing. He focused them on me as if they were laser beams. I could feel their passion, but also their pain. He was so close.

"Leticia, Leticia! Stay with me here, we were powerful together. We *are* unstoppable, Leticia! Our love is unstoppable! Don't you see how powerful we can be again? You know this is your world. Look how natural you are here, look how you thrive, look how you take control, look how you dominate! You OWE this to us, to all of us, we have worked so hard. You owe this to ME! You know you do." He was animated and crying, angry and pleading at the same time, his fists clenching and releasing as I had remembered so well. So close to his Holy Grail, he was desperate. Was it me or the power I was capable of that he wanted? I was not sure. Yet I did feel the pull to reunite with him. It felt so natural, so effortless, so … unstoppable. He was right, unstoppable.

I let my mind return to the roles we had played in each other's lives, each one with the theme of challenged love, lust, control, power, manipu-lation and ultimately dishonesty. I could feel the ending in my bones. The invitation he was offering had already soured in my mouth. I did not like the person I was with him. Allowing the desire for more than was mine jaded my thinking. Where was my integrity? It was there, it was just a different version of integrity. I could feel the rationalizations, the inner justification, yet behind it all was self-serving ego, pompous delusion and grandiosity.

Again I could hear him pleading, begging to come to him, to love him again. Yet he did not know love, he only knew possession, and that is not love. Love is freedom, allowing, accepting.

Reading his mind now, whatever shielded him before was either no longer present or I had just unlocked it. I could feel the experimentation of Merkle and perhaps dozens of others before him. The hope that Merkle was powerful enough to break into what he desired, the psychopathic nature that would give him the ability to create and watch all the phases of dying to try and discern the key to life. I could see his desperation once he located me in this lifetime. His attempting to unnerve me, to gain my attention, to distract me, possess me even, to access what he so desperately wanted. Still, I was not afraid. I knew what they wanted was mine and it required something none of them had. And I would not give it up. Avoiding the thoughts that were key, I had enough mind control to lock that knowledge away from prying minds forever. Wrapping the memory in a blanket of love, I could feel the ones I had loved as well as the ones whose lives I had sucked away join me in my commitment. A promise to them all, I was honored that they would want to assist me in protecting this unique gift.

I was struck by the knowing that I needed to assist Raymond. I needed to unlock our karmic bond to allow both of us the freedom we deserved. How was I going to do this? He did not appear to want any help, only that his will be done. But this bond was mine, too. I had every right to break it with or without his permission. I began to soften towards him, knowing now what I did about him. He was looking for something that all mortals desire; eternal life. Yet he already had it. After all, whether he was in a human vessel or not, he was alive. I allowed my mind to focus on his, to send thoughts of this nature to him. I shared the truth as I knew it with him. We are Beings of Light and only chose form to create experiences to understand more clearly that this is what we are. So often, this is not what happens and we get trapped in the ego's interpretation of ourselves.

I then began to radiate the truth in the form of love—simple bright, radiant, passionate, warm love to him. It filled him with this truth to the exclusion of his darkness. I showed him, not the past, but the future, his brilliance used to assist others, used to warm his own soul. I showed him the resplendent sun that shown from within, beaming out in all directions. He allowed himself to be filled with this knowledge, with resistance at first, but the bright warmth felt so welcoming and familiar, he could no longer fight against it.

I showed him a picture of the two of us, as one brilliant being of One-ness and love, connecting with all those whose lives we had stolen, those who participated in our story. We invited them into our sphere of light to redeem ourselves and them at the same time. I knew what he wanted was our exclusionary love, but what I could offer was *inclusionary* love. I opened my heart to him, I invited him in. I invited *all* of them in, the witches and the deceased, the betrayers and the betrayed. Then I took a locket from around my neck that must have been Leticia's. Opening it, we both saw it contained an ancient picture of him on one side and me on the other. I removed it from around my neck and offered it to this radiant flame that had become our combined energy. It was so bright and warm, it softened and then melted the gold locket. I could see he was weeping, as much from joy as from grief.

Then I watched as he pulled a pocket watch from his pant's pocket. As he opened it, I could see the same two photos were inserted into the inside of the lid. He looked at them with melancholy and powerful memo-ries, then tenderly laid his watch in the brilliant fire as well. It began to melt and merge with my locket, forming a third entity. We watched as the gold swirled and reformed, melted and moved. It began to form wings, like a soaring bird. We could see there was a destiny in there sending us a message. What a beautiful metaphor, a singular entity flying high, sailing through life, powerful and capable, yet symbolizing freedom!

I could feel myself being pulled from this place, from the experience with Raymond, with the on-looking women. The dream was coming to an end. I was waking up, but with the love of Raymond, not the fear, coming with me in my heart.

But if I was dead, what was happening?

54

I sat there, defeated. Another life without meaning ahead. More of the same life without meaning.

Looking up to Castle for something, anything. Support? Understanding? I got nothing in return but a blank look.

From nowhere, I began to feel a welling up of love inside me, against me. I turned to see what I felt and it was that dog. She had laid her head against my lap and was looking up at me with eyes filled with the deepest feeling of love I've ever felt. We looked at each other for some time and then I understood. Deep in me I suddenly knew what she was telling me.

"LAURA!" I shouted as loud as I could in a voice that wasn't mine.

Then as innocently as a baby waking up, she opened her eyes and looked into mine. A smile and a deep breath were my presents from a god I've never had time to believe in. She looked at me and in that moment I knew everything was going to be all right.

If you enjoyed *The Untidy Witness*

Be sure to watch for

The Untimely Coincidence

Second in the paranormal mystery adventures of

Laura Wexler & Nick Drake

Due for release in 2015

About the Authors

Julie Hutslar and Ed Hunt live in the mountains of the Northwest with their faithful Blue Heeler, Moki. They find adventure in hiking, ocean sailing, motorcycling, and flying a classic aerobatic airplane together.

"*Relationships: Gifts of the Spirit* shows us that we ultimately must accept responsibility for our own lives and the relationships we are in."
John Gray, Ph.D.
Author of Men Are from Mars, Women Are from Venus

"*Every now and then a book comes along that is written on a fairly common subject, but is a book that looks so very much deeper. It 'lifts the lid' so to speak. Julie Hutslar's book, Relationships: Gifts of the Spirit is just such a book. If there is one reality common to everyone, it is relationships. The book looks at relationships from a more holistic viewpoint, taking time to explore the deeper levels of cause, rather than skip along playing with effect. A story so beautifully illustrates a point, and this book is full of meaningful stories that engender exactly what the author is communicating. This book helps* remove blame in relationships, and offers the opportunity to relate to life and relationships from the framework of a greater reality. "Self-empowering" is a most overused term, yet this book gives many practical, useful, and applicable ways to constructively "self-empower" a person for the long term. I highly recommend it. This is an engaging, and very interesting book that has the rare ability, if used, to "soul-empower."
Michael Roads
Author of Talking with Nature/Journey into Nature, Journey into Oneness

"*This book teaches us how to find direction and depth in a chaotic and seemingly shallow world. Ms. Hutslar shows us how to develop the strength to follow what we have learned.*"
Luciane Berg, Ph.D.,
Professor of Pyschology

Once in a while there is a voice of clarity which resounds above the chaos and points the way; no lecturing, no guilt, simply a kind and gentle arrow towards our highest potential. Now, not later; no ifs, no buts, just an invitation to step into a world created by love and out of the illusion of discomfort and unhappiness.

Julie Hutslar, in The Mask, the Mirror, and the Illusion, speaks clearly and openly, has a gift of communication and translation, and constantly questions accepted reality and authority. Questions to her own higher wisdom prove to be pathways to self-awareness which she shares through stories, analogies and examples. What you take away is a clear focus on living in your greatest potential.

You are walked hand in hand through the maze of insane thinking we've all come to accept as normal, and offered practical suggestions for seeing through this mind-created illusion to unveil the truth of who you really are. It isn't about changing and becoming something else. It's about remembering who you have always been.

When life just isn't fulfilling in ways you know it could be, when you have a gut feeling that your experiences could be richer, and when you are certain your relationships could be more loving and honoring, where do you look? This is when you are ready to hear the voice of your own highest self and witness the light that shines from within that will guide you. Julie simply assists you in opening your sleepy eyes and finding that you have always had the way imprinted upon your heart.

"Julie has a most helpful ability to clearly bring many of the "shadows" in our mind to the light of truth. These are the hidden misperceptions that control our thinking and our lives in ways we do not see. Her insights go straight to the heart of the issues with a rare clarity. You will come away from this reading with an appreciation for her ability to hold steady to the truth."
Tom & Linda Carpenter, Dialogue on Awakening